The
Monster
In My Room

The
Monster
In My Room

Rosa Nicole Booker

First hardcover edition April 2020

Book jacket design by Ronald Antonio

ISBN 978-1-7328667-0-6 (hardcover)

www.rosiecoleybee.com

For Baba Ganoush.

*I could not have done this without your love, support, and
encouragement to face my darkest fears.*

This Was A Good Year

Olivia smirked at her own thought bubble, *"Why does he always have to be right?"* She regularly complained to Lawrence about the nightmare that would constantly wake her up in the middle of the night, drenched in sweat. He gave as many supportive words as he could, but after almost a year of having the same nightmare, Lawrence suggested she find a professional to talk to about the nightmare. After thorough research she found, Dr. Luke, a seasoned therapist who toted a background in child-trauma and dream analysis. It took several sessions to reveal that the nightmares commenced with the news that Olivia was pregnant with her third baby. She became pregnant with a baby boy which was very exciting for her daughters who were five and seven years old, but a bit of a surprise for Lawrence and her who weren't planning on a third.

Dr. Luke gave Olivia homework. Her homework was to go home and start writing a poem, a story, or a list of all the things that could be causing anxiety, worry, or stress. Dr. Luke couldn't squeeze much out of Olivia after the first four sessions, so this writing activity was an effort to get to the depths and root of Olivia's nightmare. Between trying to commit to a career path and working on her mental health, she was exhausted. She tried writing all the ways her therapist suggested. After filling her wastebasket with balled up notebook pages it dawned on her to start at the beginning.

Thinking she might have a lot of memories to unload, she ditched the notebook paper and created a new document on her laptop. After typing a few pages about her first memories of childhood, she discovered that writing her authentic truths seemed to flow easily for her. This made her think about the book club she belonged to. The group was fun, but none of the books she read with that group gave her the rush she felt of putting her own ideas into story. She imagined herself only writing a few pages to complete her therapy homework but after writing for a few days, the story took off and her fingers didn't slow down. It got to a point where she finally felt comfortable telling Lawrence that therapy was making a difference.

Olivia gazed across the room for a while before she spoke, "So Babe, okay, I know I can't make up my mind about what I *really* want to do yet, but did I tell you I have always wanted to be a writer?" Lawrence's brow began to levitate as was natural for him any time his woman used that upward inflection at the end of her sentences. There always seemed to be some new idea with her. Yesterday she was going to apply to law school to help families settle their disputes outside of court. On Monday, her dream was to open up a restaurant where the customer was intended to make up the prices, depending on how her food moved them. Last month, Olivia's master plan involved opening an all-inclusive studio. The studio would allow customers to get their weave tightened, brush up on dance skills, take family photos, and learn about a Shakespearean man giving a monologue to a skull.

Olivia possessed the skill and acumen to have chosen any of those options and excelled in them. A dark chocolate woman, easily mistaken for a poised middle-schooler due to her stature and weight, was sitting swallowed in the sofa chair. At barely five feet tall, on a good day, she often sported her long curly hair in a high puff to give the illusion of more height. Her facial features were angled and dainty. A lot of things about her were small, but her loving heart was her largest attribute.

Lawrence took a deep breath and then replied, "I am sure you would be an awesome author, Livia." There was absolutely nothing wrong with what Lawrence said or how he stated it. But Livia had so much self-doubt in her mind, that she truly believed Lawrence always hid his honesty in the cuff of his sleeve.

"Baby. Oh, forget it. I am going in the bedroom to lay down with Salem since you haven't taken the initiative to put him to bed." Olivia left the computer screen and scooped her dozing baby boy up from the carpet where he was surrounded by a moat of toys. With his binky gripped tightly in his lips, he burrowed his whole face into her neck, digging his little infant toes into her ribs, while trying to find his spot. They would be down the hall for the night. Yawning, she mumbled to Lawrence while walking away, "Goodnight Baby. Love you. Save my work...log me off...please."

Lawrence courteously attended her command. As he reached for the save button on the document, his honesty began to slip out of the cuff of his sleeve. He confessed his true thoughts, *"What is she thinking? Becoming a writer? Ooh, if I did not love that woman...."*

His doubt urged him to take a peek at what she was writing. Seeing that she even named the first chapter *Ode to Poppa,* he began to read:

Chapter 1
Ode to Poppa

I ENTERED INTO this world as the fourth part of a family. I was the completion, if you will. A married mother and father along with their four-year-old son, were made whole when I joined the family. Or so I thought.

Momma told me my dad, Bradley Stone, was away at the time I was born so he was not part of the welcoming committee. He finally met me when I was four months old. On the day we met, he had just returned from an overseas work trip. Momma never told me why, but her and my dad just couldn't get along. Their relationship seemed to have suffered from the long separation, so Bradley moved out after a couple years of being back and he'd get us kids on the weekends. But by the time I was nearing adolescence, he took a job overseas again. I had no idea the second time he moved out of the country would leave close to a 20-year gap before I'd see him next.

My dad, Bradley, was absent from more than just our lives. My mom, Stevie, was left to become both parents in one. Stevie was humble though. She knew she could not go this alone and relied on a close friend named Hyde. Stevie and Hyde were partners in nursing school. He was the baby brother she had always hoped for. He was also single with two kids. His main focus was to be the best father he could be to his children. We were made for television – a very "Brady" kind of bunch. The only difference with our family was that Momma and Hyde were lacking their third child. It worked out. Momma took the day shift and Hyde took the night shift parenting all of us kids during the week. They both worked at Rainier View Hospital. We had few hours when they were both home at the same time. There was an early dinner schedule, but that was what kept our family tight – that was the one thing that Momma made sure never changed. Her goal was to fight for some form of stability in our lives.

✳✳✳

Lawrence's sneaky reading of Olivia's childhood story was cut short. Livia had to say it for the second time. This time she was a bit louder, but not enough to wake Salem, who was asleep in the crook of her arm. Her voice barely stretched to the end of the hall that led to the living room, "Guac?" Lawrence came to the end of the hall to answer back, "What?"

"Guac, why do you always say, '*WHAT?*' That is so rude."

"Why do you always yell from the other room, Livia?"

"Baby. Baby? Are you coming to bed? Salem is knocked out. Can you put him in his crib?"

He walked into their room and carefully lifted Salem out of her arms. "Yes, I can do that," he agreed.

"Can you check on the girls too? That stupid nightmare woke me up again and then I thought I heard giggling."

Lawrence taxied down the other hall where the kids' rooms were. He heard no giggling. He carefully lowered Salem into his crib. The house was quiet. By the sound of it, Livia was already asleep again. He was okay with that because he wanted to get back to reading her story. Lawrence had never really heard Livia tell her story in this way. He slowly passed the hall to the master suite, trying not to make the floors creak. Looking at the screen, he picked up where he left off:

After finishing their family dinner, Momma was off to the hospital once the table was cleared. The rest of us huddled up on the couch with Hyde and watched our TV programs. Every night we fell asleep together on the sofa. I was always the first to fall asleep on Hyde's arm. Both of Hyde's kids were in middle school. My brother Kelpie was in elementary school and I was in pre-school. Hyde's son, Madison, was older than all of us kids. Half asleep, Madison helped his sister Lindsay to her bedroom. The commotion notified Hyde it was time to transition, he lopped me over his shoulder without as much as a blink from me, grabbed Kelpie's hand to get him up, and walked us upstairs to our room.

It was Hyde's house, so my brother and I shared a small room upstairs that used to be the playroom. Hyde went back down to the family room and pulled his bed out of the sofa. Momma got his room. There was no way he could make a woman sleep on the couch, even if it was a pull-out. He wanted to enjoy an adult program with the kids way off in dream land but was too exhausted to take ninety seconds to please himself. Hyde hadn't realized that the Sand Man had lured him into the arms of a tall-dark-and-handsome, until Madison nudged him awake. "Where's the remote, dad? I can't sleep with the TV going," he asked in a loud whisper. Under the blanket Hyde could feel a sticky remote adhering to his thigh hairs. He told Madison to turn it off at the source and sent him back to bed.

Madison was not the only one who could not sleep that night. Kelpie found himself frequently sneaking to the top of the stairs, late nights, to catch a glimpse of Hyde's adult programs. There were occasions when I would be spying over Kelpie's shoulder. One time I asked why there were naked people on the screen and Kelpie snapped at me, "They're just playing! Go back to sleep Ollie, or I'm gonna tell Momma you were out of bed!"

This night was different because Hyde was too pooped to get it to the right channel. Kelpie decided to come back to the room where I was fast asleep. Thinking about Hyde's TV programs he'd snuck to see on previous nights, he watched me from our bedroom doorway. He squeezed his eyes shut attempting to erase his thoughts. Nothing. He opened his eyes and there I was. My legs and arms where hanging every which way. The glow from the streetlight, pouring through the window curtain, was the only way my dark, cocoa complexion could be seen in the night.

The bed looked large with my tiny body in it. It was the most adorable toddler bed with pink, teddy bear sheets. Teddy bears were my favorite. I had all sorts of teddy bears. I was only four at the time. Kelpie stood there wondering what it would be like to copy the actions of the people in Hyde's TV program. Kelpie had dark skin too, but not at all like mine. Kelpie was eight going on nine, and he was a husky boy. He couldn't even fit in my bed by himself, but he wanted to get in it with me. Kelpie could not hold back his curiosity. His pajama bottoms were on the bedroom floor. He stood in the middle of the room holding his *"thing."* I felt my slumber slipping away as I scrunched my nose, smelling some*thing*, and then slightly opened my eyes, "Kelpie?" I was confused by the display I thought I must have been imagining. Kelpie's sweaty, bottomless body was crouched and hovering over my bed. He had partially pulled back my pink, teddy bear blanket. My sprawled body began to retract into a ball, like a turtle finding safety in her shell, but I had no shell. Tears welled up in my eyes with fear. The image in front of me became so blurry with tears, I could barely see.

"Shh! Ollie, don't say anything, I am just gonna lay down with you." Kelpie quieted my voice by placing his hand over my face, "So don't move." All Kelpie could see under his hand were tears pouring out from both sides. Hyde woke up.

$$***$$

Lawrence's reading was interrupted again, this time by his own doing. Lawrence hadn't *noticed that his tears were not silent. He sniffled while reading* about Olivia's dark past. *"Guac?"* Livia called out from the bedroom, squinting to see the clock, "What time is it? I thought you were coming to bed," she grumbled. Olivia called Lawrence, Guac, for as long as he could remember. It was a pet name she gave him after their first intimate experience during her freshman year in college.

$$***$$

It all started when she noticed him on campus with the basketball team. Lawrence had a rich caramel skin tone that looked soft as butter. He was tall and thick. His voice was so deep that even his whisper seemed to cause more friction than Olivia's old-school washing machine. He wore his sandy brown hair cut short, and a pair of grey-green eyes flecked with purple, rested perfectly under his brows. But her favorite part was the stubble he left on his chin. Just imagining one slight graze against his lips would give her butterflies. What made him even more attractive to her was that she had always seen him in a suit. He was magazine cover material. He was quite a few steps above the ball cap, white tee, basketball shorts, sneaker wearing guy she was used to.

Their first night was in Olivia's dorm room. Her roommate, Gene, was hardly ever around. Gene was quite the party animal. After Olivia finished cheering at an exciting home game, she decided to skip the after-party. She had a huge paper due Monday that she hadn't even started on. She got all the way to the dorm's courtyard before she remembered her gym bag and keys were still on the floor in the locker room. She left her gym bag there in a rush to give her boyfriend, Cole, a congratulatory kiss for scoring the game-winning shot, and to let him know she would have to skip the team celebration that evening.

Livia started to make a mad dash back to the gym before they locked it, but she was suddenly stopped in front of two bright Lexus headlights. Lawrence's voice rumbled from the driver's side window, "Allow me to apologize, Miss." Livia waited for her heart to begin again. "Oh! – Hi! – Lawrence. – I mean Coach Livingston." Each word he spoke was long, low, and powerful, like the hum of an old country engine. "OH-livia. Right? You can call me Lawrence if you want to. Olivia, if you're needing the gym, it is closed. They locked it behind me."

"My keys and gym bag are still in there!" she whined.

"Well, I am sorry, but the custodian won't be back until morning, and I actually forgot my keys today too. Otherwise I'd let you in myself," he said apologetically. "I could give you a lift home..."

He agreed to drop her off at her dorm but questioned how she'd get in without the key. Maybe her roommate was home. Maybe someone from the RA's office would be there. Livia and Gene were tired of getting charged by the resident advisor for spare keys. Most of the students complained about having to live in the outdated dormitory, but its unique courtyard style allowed Gene and Livia to leave the bathroom window cracked for desperate times. This was one of those times. Once through the window, Livia made her way to the front door of her dorm room. Her intentions were to go outside, run back through the courtyard, and wave off Coach Livingston from the sidewalk so he'd know she made it in safely.

But when she opened her front door, she was shocked to see Coach standing there in her doorway. She quickly ushered him inside to make sure he wasn't spotted by anyone in the courtyard. Livia had always been short as a kid and well into her teenage years. But Coach Livingston was at least six feet tall and highly recognizable as the basketball coach. She wasn't sure why he came inside her dorm until he begged to use the bathroom.

Completely flushed with anticipation, Livia pointed him to the bathroom. She could hardly compose herself. She had the absolute finest man on earth in her dorm room — technically in her bathroom. Livia could not stand still while waiting for him to come out of the bathroom. She let her hair down out of her juvenile-cheertastic ponytails. She threw her ribbons on the floor and spotted Gene's bright green panties lying there. As she knelt down to get them and also pick up other random crap off the floor, she became close and personal with some size 12 Ferragamo shoes. Lawrence's strong hands reached down in assistance. Livia tossed the panties under the bed and grabbed onto his hands. His hands were as soft as his lips looked.

Lawrence had loosened his tie. "Do you mind if I have some coffee before I go," Lawrence stated as more of a comment than a question. Livia began to let go of his hands. She was really feeling the moment. This was one night she wouldn't be worried if Gene did not come home. But she figured Coach must have a long ride back to his place. Turning away and opening the mini fridge to select a cold coffee drink, she realized all she had were energy drinks. She then felt Lawrence cradle her arm. "I meant you," his voice revved in her ear.

Her very next thought was of how his tongue felt inside her mouth. It was like a silky pillow. Then as he lifted her, feeling light as a feather, her feet were no longer on the floor; she became aware of a tug at her skirt. Not everything about this man was soft! She felt his pressure rise and he lifted her legs around his waist. He backed her against the wall as they continued kissing, he pulled on some protection and gently became one with her all in one fell swoop. Her breath was taken away. She wrapped her arms around his neck, tighter than his tie, and they were so close she could almost taste his cologne.

Their lips met and their tongues danced. Lawrence's physique was solid and thick but not too bulky. She could feel his body in a way that Cole's skinny, rock hard, protein shake, muscles had never felt against her dainty frame. Lawrence held her, snug in *his arms as they lay squished on her college dorm bed. Livia had never experienced this amount of passion and attention to detail as she had with Lawrence. This passion was lasting, and Livia actually felt a genuine connection.*

"Don't you just love guacamole, Lawrence?" The random question rolled off of Livia's tongue as if reciting poetry. "It's thick and smooth, hot and spicy, packed full of flavor and I could just eat it by the spoonful." Lawrence was beginning to rethink his act of impulse with this teeny, teenage, halftime dancer. "You-Are-My-Goo-Wok," she told Lawrence. He gave a playful smile in response, as he hugged her tightly and planted a kiss on her lips.

Lawrence was half dressed before Livia even noticed he'd gotten out of bed. She was not fully asleep, but still replaying each kiss and caress in her mind, lost in her thoughts. He didn't want to leave her. His bed at home was about three times larger. Lawrence really wanted her, to take his "coffee to go." Livia needed a passing grade on her paper but could not pass up an invitation to breakfast in a California king bed, on the coast, overlooking the ocean. She agreed to go with him – sneaking out before sunrise. She packed up her books, left a note for Gene, and took a ride to Coach Livingston's beach house.

That memory about how they met made it even harder for Lawrence to fall asleep. Nevertheless, that was the day he fell in love. That was close to ten years ago. Now he was getting in bed with a more mature, but still teeny, now 30-year-old Olivia, mother of three. Lawrence rested there with the image of teeny, teenage, halftime dancer and wondered if he had come on too strong that night in her dorm room.

All the times she tried to catch his eye during games and the numerous occasions she accidentally bumped into him on the basketball court, he had blatantly ignored her. He was trying to be professional and responsible back then. And now, it was hard for Lawrence not to think of himself as a villain, as well, after reading about the four-year-old Ollie. It didn't matter that in real life Livia regarded him as her superhero. Lawrence wasn't sure if that night with the *missing keys* was intentional on Olivia's part. He didn't have any plans to ask her about her intentions either. But it was undeniable they were both harboring secret chemistry, that was building between the two of them, for more than a few months prior to that night.

To be fair, Livia had shared her past with him before, but they had not discussed the full detail of the horrific memories she held inside. Every now and then she would give her interpretation of what the other people in her family were thinking and doing while she was being abused. Lawrence was always amazed by her interpretations. He wished he could wipe away her memories as easily as her tears. The way Olivia wrote out her story, how she imagined Kelpie standing in the doorway, and how Stevie missed the signs of abuse, truly broke his spirit. Lawrence could only imagine how difficult it was for Livia to write about her past. He wanted to be able to comfort her, but he couldn't reveal that he had snuck out to read her therapy homework.

For Olivia, talking about her childhood was like telling the story of *Jack and Jill.* The memories played in her head during waking moments and haunted her thoughts while she slept at night. But like some theories behind *Jack and Jill*, she felt her childhood to be a much more sinister story beneath the surface.

After the small portion of the story that he read, Lawrence had to know what was next. He couldn't help but think why on earth Kelpie could get away with his actions. Lawrence wiped his face off, crawled into bed and embraced Livia like it was their first night together. Livia remembered that touch. "Guac. I love you, Baby," she whispered, almost in her sleep.

"Good night, OH-livia," Lawrence whispered back.

Saturday morning was supposed to be a kid-free day for Livia and Lawrence. Livia's birthday was that previous Tuesday, but Lawrence had a truck load of projects to do over at The Academy and stayed in the office late into the night. Livia vehemently implored everyone not to make a big deal of her birthday this year. After having her third child and still struggling to find a career path, Livia just did not have the energy to be excited about another year passing by where she didn't feel like she'd accomplished much.

When she stopped to think about it though, Livia could have used a day to herself. Lawrence's mom, Grandma Sugar, backed out of babysitting duties early that morning. There was no way Grandma Sugar could miss out on a close-out sale. Claire, Maya, and Salem where the main benefactors of Grandma Sugar's shopping trips. Her shopping trips were all about the kids. She just preferred shopping without the interruption of snack breaks, potty breaks, or necessity for naps.

"Wake up, girls," Lawrence yelled to Claire and Maya, "It's family day! We're gonna to serve Nahn Nahn, breakfast in bed.

Pancakes! Remember Nahn Nahn just had a birthday?" Nahn Nahn was a term of endearment they used for Livia. Salem started it because he couldn't say "Ma Ma." The words, "Da Da," came easily to him, but he had a hard time pronouncing the letter "m."

"Ooh, Daddy Pop, I love pan-a-cakes! How many do I get?" Claire, their oldest daughter, slid into the dining room with her purple, fuzzy, princess slippers, pulling up her oversized pajamas and hopped up on a stool at the breakfast nook. She was seven years old. She had a couple baby teeth missing but sported a colossal grin all the time. Claire adapted her mother's looks with her father's grey-green eyes flecked with purple, and a head full of sandy hair. She was a fifty-fifty mix of both mom and dad.

"You mean, how many *may* you have?" He corrected her. Lawrence was always correcting the girls and Livia out of embarrassment they might sound improper in public one day. "Help your sister up," he instructed Claire. Lawrence could not see Maya, but she was never too far behind her big sister. Maya, almost six, had one hand tugging on Claire's pajama shirt. Ever since she was a baby, it soothed her to have some sort of fabric between her fingers. Her head rested on the small of Claire's back, the pinky and ring finger of her left hand in her mouth, eyes still closed, Maya's butt swayed back and forth as she hummed her favorite song. Claire reached back without looking and coaxed Maya onto the stool beside her. The beads in Maya's hair hit her back as she plopped down in her seat.

Maya was a carbon copy of her father; his complexion with the same eyes and hair as her sister. It was too early to know for sure, but Claire seemed to take after her mother's height and Maya after Daddy Pop. They were often mistaken for twins, which is why Livia tried to keep their hairstyles different. Claire got to sport her curly tresses in its natural state on weekends, but her hair was usually styled in ponytails with bobbles or two French braids with barrettes during the school week. When it was time for a trim, Livia would let her sport a blowout for a day or two. Maya wore small cornrow braids in a new pattern each week with ten to fifteen beads strung on the ends of each braid.

Lawrence served the girls pancakes, fresh strawberries, blueberries, and bananas while he got Livia's plate ready. He prepared banana pancakes, poached eggs, and a hot cup of chai tea. These were her favorites. He carefully carried her tray to surprise her in bed. Claire and Maya sipped their orange juice and came down from their places to assist him. Claire grabbed the newspaper and hand-made birthday cards, while Maya struggled with creamer for the tea. Lawrence carefully passed Olivia the tray as Claire and Maya climbed in bed with their mommy.

"Aw! This is the best birthday surprise, guys! Where is Salem?"

"He is still knocked out sleep." Lawrence had just finished his sentence when they all heard Salem calling.

"Nahn Nahn, Nahn Nahn, Nahn..." Salem was awake, standing against the wooden bars of his crib, calling for Livia. Salem was a chunky, little, *Milk Dud*. Round and brown with dark, curly hair like Olivia's.

"I'll get him, Liv. Enjoy your breakfast." Lawrence tended to Salem and his morning ritual of singing songs to him during diapering and dressing, while his three ladies laid in bed, giggling and enjoying the best breakfast in town. Daddy Pop washed Salem up and put him in a fresh diaper and outfit with an "I heart Mommy" shirt. Salem was ready for the day. Lawrence came back into the master bedroom holding Salem and traded Mommy Salem for her breakfast tray.

"Livia, my gift to you is peace and quiet."

Lawrence planned to take the kids out to the park to burn off some energy and then to the library to explore what new and exciting educational books were on the shelves. He also remembered reading a flyer Livia showed him about Nikki Grimes, an author who would be there doing a reading and signing copies of her children's books.

Once Lawrence was long gone with the kids, Livia was unable to go back to sleep. She couldn't manage to get the sleep her body deserved. It was probably because as soon as she began to fall asleep the nightmare would start. Livia couldn't sleep without Lawrence close by. She remembered where she had left off in her book. It was a hard place to stop. She knew she had to write this story but had not calculated how heavily it would weigh on her heart. Livia believed she'd passed the most difficult and emotional portion of her story, but she had to finish it. She knew she could do it. She had to do it. But it had to be piece by piece.

The house was in pristine condition as she ambled through each room. For once she had the house to herself. And now, not knowing what to do with it, she decided to run a bath. She enjoyed the steamy bubbles in her jetted tub and fantasized of her Guac. She knew her romantic, afternoon getaways with Lawrence were simply a mere memory now that they had three kids. She loved the way he'd draw a bath, add fresh rose petals, and light lavender candles. She thought about how he'd bring her a glass of champagne and rub her shoulders while she relaxed and listened to Miles Davis's *Kind of Blue*.

Livia towel dried her still youthful skin, nearly traceless of the children she once carried, and oiled her entire body. She pulled on one of Lawrence's old, holey t-shirts from his college coaching days, a pair of black, boy-shorts, and some ugly, but comfy, house boots. Taking advantage of a quiet house, she began to write some more:

✳ ✳ ✳

Hyde sat up in his bed. It was nearing 4:00am. He liked to have breakfast ready for Stevie when she came home in the morning. The coffee pot was on a timer and had begun brewing. The menu was usually light, since he would be repeating the same task for us kids before shuttling everyone to school by 8:00am. After putting the toast in the oven, he unlocked the front door so Stevie wouldn't need to fumble with her keys. He set the table with a steaming hot mocha, two slices of buttered toast, and a bowl of oatmeal with a banana on the side. Then got back in bed.

Just as Hyde could pull the blanket up to shield his eyes from the kitchen light, Stevie walked in. Standing at the foot of the pullout bed to see if he was in asleep, she whispered and patted him on the ankle, "Morning, Hyde." She went in the kitchen to enjoy her morning ritual of breakfast and reading the paper. Once her place was cleared, she headed up to her room to fold laundry and watch a morning show. She attempted to be stealth, but even as a 4-year-old, I had bionic ears. As soon as Stevie had settled on a TV channel, I was there at her door. "Mom-mahhh," I cried. I shuffled my little feet across the rug and pulled myself up into Momma's lap. She let out a sudden gasp, "Olivia, Baby, you are wet." Immediately I looked up at my mom's face with huge crocodile tears and wailed, "Kelpie was on top of me!"

Stevie put me down and grabbed for my hand, "Shh. Everyone is still asleep. Let's get you in the tub. It will be time to get ready for school in a little while, anyway."

Eventually all had risen and joined in the dining room for breakfast. Kelpie sat across from me at the table. His stare beamed through my skin and he spooned food into his mouth without taking his stare off of me.

I let out a huge outburst, "STOP LOOKING AT ME!" The tears flowed down my cheeks onto my shirt, my nose running as I began to hyperventilate. In a flash, Hyde was kneeling at my seat.

"Honey, it is okay for people to look at you. We are all just enjoying breakfast like any other day. Shh, shh, shh. It's okay, Ollie. Sweetie, just finish your cheesy eggs."

Stevie came rushing down the stairs in her bathrobe. Hyde filled her in on what the commotion was all about. Smoothing down my hair, she kissed me on the top of my head and wished everyone a good day at school. On her route back to the bathroom she mumbled, "My little cry baby." Hyde and Lindsay cleared the dishes while Madison helped usher Kelpie and me out the door. Once each one of us were in the car, there was complete silence. No one wanted to speak out of turn or look in the wrong direction. That only intensified my insecurity. The whole trip to school, I rode with my eyes shut tightly and my hands muffling my ears.

The classroom was no prized getaway. In addition to random nights of Kelpie climbing in my bed, there was one little boy in my class that always wanted to sit at my table. During coloring one day, he asked me to look under the desk. I thought perhaps he had snuck candy into class or kept a bug he had found on the playground. When I focused correctly, I realized he had unzipped his trousers and had his penis out. I could not understand why he would share such a sight with me, but I quickly raised my hand to alert the teacher. As if on autopilot she warned, "Jonathan! Please keep your clothing on in the classroom."

That was all the teacher did! No punishment for him. No justice for me. Just like with Kelpie. Momma never punished Kelpie for what he did to me. I began to wonder if his and Jonathan's inappropriate behavior towards me was actually inappropriate at all. No one seemed to address it with any sense of urgency or concern.

Later in that year I was on the playground, and Jonathan was at it again. I got a huge rush from zooming down the slide. As soon as I jumped off the bottom edge, I could hear my name being whispered from underneath. I ducked under to see what the beckoning was for. Jonathan grabbed me close and gave me a huge kiss in the mouth! My first reaction was to push him down and find my way to the toy cars in order to drive far away.

Maybe if I had driven far enough, I would have found Bradley Stone. Only a father could save his baby girl from such torture.

Chapter 2
Aren't There ANY Good Ones?

I DISCOVERED AT a very early age that most adults don't indulge in investigating the troubles of a toddler. My only option was to live with the constant torment of being abused. I cannot begin to imagine the words I used to explain what was happening to me at that time. All I know is that they could not have been descriptive enough, because there is no way any adult would consciously allow these incidences to regularly occur. So, after several failed attempts to out Kelpie and Jonathan, I kept my pain to myself.

Right before my kindergarten year, Stevie and Hyde decided to part ways. Hyde was my bodyguard. Without him around, there would be no one to protect me from Kelpie. Hyde only intended for the co-living to be temporary. He politely asked for his space and privacy back after almost a year of us living with him. Just as well, any man that attempted a serious relationship with my mother could not accept her living situation and would break things off shortly after their first visit to the "Hyde and Stevie" abode. So, Momma got a day shift approved from her boss and found a sweet, cozy, modest apartment nearby. And by sweet, cozy and modest, I mean small, tiny, and crowded. It had only two bedrooms, which meant I got stuck rooming with my brother again.

With Momma on her own, that put a lot of responsibility on Kelpie to be in charge while she was working. On a typical day, Momma would wake us up, kiss us goodbye, and bus to work. Kelpie would make us breakfast and walk us to school once we'd eaten and dressed. Later in the afternoon, students grade 1-6 were dismissed from school. Kelpie would walk to pick me up from the sitter before walking us home since I was in half-day kindergarten.

Momma may not have done anything about Kelpie's abusive actions, but the one thing she *did* hear me out about, were my babysitter horror stories. The first sitter was just your average slacker. She lived in a studio unit in a complex down the road and stayed home during the day with her son, a couple years my junior. My first day there, the door was already ajar when I arrived. I walked in.

***

Olivia had been writing her story so intently that Claire and Maya startled her. When Livia heard the girls at the front door, she hurried to save the file to her desktop and scurried to the foyer to greet everyone, "Hi guys! Did you have lots and lots of fun?!" Salem reached his arms towards her, and the girls each commandeered a hip. The four of them did a zombie walk towards the couch in the sitting room and toppled onto the sofa. Lawrence balanced himself over the pile, his pride and joy, to lay a sweet kiss on Livia's lips. "Whew. It sure will be nice to come home and relax after worship service tomorrow," he said.

"Oh, Honey, that *would* be nice. But it might have slipped your mind about our dinner guests tomorrow."

"Aw shit." Lawrence complained.

"OOOOH. Daddy Pop said a bad word!" the girls sang in unison. "Sorry girls. What I meant was – Yay. Fun. Yippie," his enthusiasm was fading rapidly. He trailed off his choice words with a low chuckle and joined the pile in exhaustion.

BOOKER

A Sinner Dinner

awrence drove the family home after a great worship service Sunday morning. Livia always enjoyed the lake route to their home overlooking the water. It was magical to watch the sun glisten on the tiny waves. You could see the entire city along that drive. The drive also gave her a chance to reminisce on the days she used to sleepover at his beach front condo in Cali, during her college years. She loved waking up there, opening up the curtains to marvel at the ocean. It sounds so cliché, but she missed the long walks on the beach they used to take. Ever since they moved up north, Lawrence had tried to find the perfect view of the water for her to get that same sensation. Unfortunately, as beautiful as the lake was, it could never compete with the passion the ocean carried.

Lawrence took their turn up the hill, a bit more than a short walk from the lake. They had a great view. "Liv, Honey, were you daydreaming again?" He let out a loud chuckle. "Huh? What?" Livia said, trying to snap out of it. A large part of her daydream was to keep her thoughts off of the dreaded dinner guests. Livia frequently did things and agreed to things she was not always totally on board with. She was kindhearted, but sometimes, too kindhearted. God bless her though. Even though she was running from The Lord, she wholeheartedly believed in doing to others as you would have done unto you, like the Bible teaches.

It consistently agitated Lawrence to witness her practicing "good works," but not ever join the church they attended regularly.

"Babe, the kids and I have been waiting like thirty seconds for you to hit the garage door opener…"

"I know, I know. Sorry guys. I was just taking in this gorgeous day. Oh! Shootie pootie! Girls, Nahn Nahn forgot we needed to stop and pick up dessert on the way home."

"Livia, we just pulled up. It was a great service, but now Daddy Pop is gonna shoot a poot if we have to go out again. Just have Kelpie and the new girl bring something. It's enough that we're having them over for dinner."

She thought about asking Kelpie for a minute and then shrugged her shoulders. That would have been the easiest solution, but she didn't want to spring it on him at the last minute. Livia decided to just whip up a quick batch of her famous macadamia nut, butter cream, cookies instead. Although it wasn't a very quick recipe, everything about her cookies were made from scratch down to the fresh vanilla beans.

Everything had to be perfect. Livia always wanted to impress people, even the ones that couldn't care less about *and* the ones that were hardly worth the time. Lawrence rounded up the children and put on their lounge clothes. He slipped into something comfortable himself and took Salem in the back for a nap that was much needed by the both of them. The girls had activities-a-plenty to keep them occupied in their "princess quarters." Livia tied her apron around her church dress, not to have to change. Sher put her prepped dinner on the stove and in the oven to warm everything up. Once the cookie batch was also prepped, it was put in the fridge to set before baking. Livia realized she still had about an hour to kill before her brother and his girlfriend arrived.

With the rest of the house busy on a separate agenda, this seemed like an opportune time to start writing another few pages or so. She snuggled cross-legged into her computer chair, accompanied by a mug of chai tea, and got ready to write about the babysitter...

✱✱✱

Pam was just sitting on the couch smoking a cigarette. The entire room was hazy as she watched some program on television; a talk show I would guess. Her frizzy-haired son sat in the middle of the rug playing with his fire truck.

"Hi Pam? I'm Ollie. Remember, I'm 'posed to start coming here now?"

"Yes, Ollie. I am Pam. Do you remember **that**!? Go on and get in there until Kelpie come and pick yo little bad ass up." She ordered.

Inside my head I was questioning her living conditions. The "there" she was referring to was her son's crib.

I supposed she expected me to take a nap in there like I was some toddler. Heck, her son wasn't even napping. Why did I have to? She looked like she meant business though, so I climbed in, shoes, backpack, and all. I just made myself go to sleep best I could. I did not care for this Pam character or her little bad ass son. And I'm not just saying that because she said it to me. I mean he was really bad. He came right up to his crib and started clanking his fire truck against the rails, chanting, "Girls are ugly! Girls are stinky! My bed! My bed! My bed!" He didn't stop for a minute.

Do you think Pam said anything to him about his mouth? You are right – not a damn thing. "Oh, heck no!" I thought. Even as a kid I knew she was trippin'. Then she begged him over to her with a juice box. That was good enough because he had just begun to reach in and grab at one of my braids. "Leave that heffah alone, Dooney Doon. Can't chu see she sleepin'?" She was totally off. I didn't choose to be sleeping or even want to be in his crib for that matter. This was the one time I couldn't wait to see Kelpie. But even *he* wasn't due for at least another hour or two. I was pretending to be asleep while she chatted on the phone to whomever. She told the caller, *"Don't have time to be lookin after no heffahs!"* At that moment, I could hear Kelpie coming up to the door from where the crib was positioned.

I jumped up out of that crib so fast! "My brother is here!" I yelled. I zoomed out the door before she could say anything; as if she cared. I am halfway surprised she didn't set me out on the porch when the time welded down. I started in right away, telling Kelpie all about it. At some parts he laughed, like at the little boy's name and that the lady called me a "heffah." And at other parts, like the part about her smoking cigarettes and me having to lay in a crib, he actually gasped.

"Well, Ollie, I know it is bad, but you know like I have told you about *other* things, you cannot tell mom. She works hard and she is paying a lot of money for you to stay with Pam. And I am responsible for you after that. We don't want to make Mom mad."

I couldn't understand why he'd want me to keep the endangerment of my safety a secret. He always wanted to control everything. And, mostly, he did. But by the middle of that week, he witnessed her raising her hand at me for knocking down Dooney Doon on my way out the door. Dooney Doon, sporting an ugly Shawn Kemp haircut, had poured milk in my backpack and I was trying to get revenge. Kelpie pleaded with Momma to stop sending me to Pam's. Momma agreed, but do you know that *heffah*, Pam, still got paid!?

Being that my mom didn't have many resources and needed somewhere for me to go, she took a suggestion from my school information board. The new lady was another stay-at-home-mother, but she was quite a bit more together than Pam. She had a son two years younger than me too. I was thinking, "Not again! Doesn't anyone have girl children?" Well it didn't matter because that lady was charging more than my mom could afford. I came up with an idea myself. My best friend Kamryn was in my class and also walked home after school.

After careful convincing on my part, mom set up arrangements for me to go over to Kamryn's for the rest of the week. That didn't last though. Kamryn thought it would be a great idea to hold me down while her big brother laid on top of me and kissed me. I didn't tell Momma what happened, just that Kamryn and I weren't friends anymore. I don't even remember speaking with Kamryn outside of the classroom after that. That same weekend happened to be my Grandma Mary's 60th birthday bash. She was my dad's mom, but we were very close to her. It was refreshing to be able to end such a crazy week with a fun party like that. I also was able to visit with my Auntie Tess. She hardly ever attended family get-togethers.

"Hi Tess! I didn't expect to see you here," Momma blurted out. "I mean, how have you been? It's been so long since I've seen you last."

"Oh – Hi, Stevie. I been around. I'm good. How my lil' niece and nephew doin'?"

"Good, good. They are in school. Ollie is in her first year of kindergarten. She is only half-day though, so it's a bitch trying to find childcare I can afford for her."

"You should let me keep her," Tess offered.

"You'd do that for me, Tess?" My mom wanted to confirm it was a real offer.

"Yeah, I mean, my afternoons are free. And I wouldn't charge you to keep my lil' niece. She could get to know her cousin a lil' better too. The way they sittin' here playin' now... Don't they look like sisters?"

"That is the hugest favor, Tess. Thank you! We just live down the block from the school and you can watch her at my place while the girls play. She gets dismissed a little after twelve and Kelpie usually gets home shortly after three. Well, anyway, I can call you tomorrow with all the details. Thank you!"

After my mom and Auntie Tess finished talking, I was excited about getting to play with my cousin more often. The rest of the party was great. I was playing with all my cousins but especially with Auntie Tess's daughter because all the other cousins were boys. That Monday I was so excited to finally have a girl to play with and have my auntie watch me instead of some crazy, mean lady, or have what happened at Kamryn's house happen again. I know what you're thinking, this is starting to sound good, but don't you remember me telling you that these were horror stories? All I can say is I am glad I am still alive, and so is my Auntie Tess for that matter. It would be at least a decade after it actually happened, before Momma would tell me her side of the story.

The first Monday with this arrangement, Kelpie was instructed to go straight home so that Auntie Tess could leave if she needed to. My brother actually did what he was told. He got home to our apartment and ran up the stairs yelling, "Hi, Auntie Tess!" But when he got to the landing, the door was cracked open with my teddy bear keychain hanging from the lock. "Auntie Tess?" Kelpie sang. But there was no one there. He even called my name, but there was no answer. Kelpie ran through the entire apartment looking for us. He went outside and called my name for at least five minutes. That's what Momma would do when it was time for us to come in.

After exhausting all efforts, Kelpie knew he had to call the hospital. "Hi Ma'am. Can you page Nurse Stevonia Thomas? Hurry! Please, Please, Please!? This is her son, Kelpie Stone."

"Hi Kelpie. This is Judy. Didn't your mom have a talk with you about calling her at work? If Ollie is bothering you, your mom will take care of her when she gets home. Okay?"

"No, Judy! This is an emergency! My sister is missing! Page my mom, now!"

***

Livia had gotten so carried away with writing about the babysitters she lost track of time and was interrupted by the doorbell. She quickly minimized her computer screen as Kelpie pushed the door open and waited in the foyer. "Hello! Sis? L.L.!?"

"Hi Kelpie! I'm in here!" Livia called from her office, hurrying to greet them at the door. "Sorry to barge in, Sis. The door was unlocked." Kelpie apologized as she came into view.

Livia gestured with her hand, "Come on in. Dinner is ready. Everyone was just kind of relaxing, that's all."

"Well Sis, this is my new bookkeeper, Sandra."

"I'm Stone's *fiancé*!" Sandra corrected.

"Oh, *Stone*. What happened to your old *bookkeeper*?" Livia asked with a raised brow.

"You know I don't have an old bookkeeper, Ollie. I was doing all the work until the business got booming, right?" Kelpie spoke through his teeth, winking behind Sandra's back, hoping to make a smooth recovery. He'd had three fiancés or "bookkeepers" in the past year, and four if you counted the exotic dancer.

"Well, I guess that is right, *Stone*. Your business is *booming*. Hi, Sandra. Welcome to the family I suppose. And please, call me Livia. Both of you. No one calls me Ollie anymore."

Hearing the commotion from the back room, Lawrence came to chime in, "Hey guys! Sorry I didn't come right away. Welcome to our home, Sandra; I think is what I heard. Nice to meet you. I am Lawrence, Olivia's better half."

"Hi Lawrence. Do you have three names too, or is it just Ms. Ollie-Livia-Olivia?" Sandra retorted.

Lawrence shifted focus, "Okay...Hey Kelpie. Where are the twins?"

Kelpie begrudgingly answered, "Their mama be beefin' so I ain't even go by there to see my boys. Tia talkin' 'bout, 'she don't want Kelan and Kelvan around a woman she don't know.' So, that's on her. She bet not ask me to come get them when she get booed up."

This evening was obviously off to a bad start. Lawrence gave Livia "the eye" while he took Sandra and Kelpie's jackets. Once they sat down, the actual dinner was pretty silent. Lawrence tried to break the ice with talk of music, but Kelpie was so passionate about his utter dislike of one of Lawrence and Livia's favorite artists that Lawrence decided to let that subject alone. Sandra picked at her food. Not because it was bad. Livia was a great cook. Sandra was just very insecure with her appearance. When it came down to dessert though, Sandra was like the Cookie Monster come to life. Shortly after gobbling up her fifth macadamia nut, buttercream cookie, she excused herself to use the restroom. Everyone tried to ignore what she was doing in there. However, it was obvious that she was forcing herself to upchuck.

"Hey Brutha-in-law, L.L. Cool Bruh, when you gon' let me trick your ride? You know it's on the house. We have been crazy jammed at the shop, but I can always make time for you, Bruh."

"Kelpie, I choose to keep my life *trick* free, if you get what I'm saying. Appreciate the offer though. I appreciate the offer."

Livia escorted the girls to their room to play while Kelpie continued telling Lawrence about his latest remodels. Salem was content sitting in his play-yard set up in the middle of the living room, tapping away on his learning laptop. Sandra was still in the restroom. Livia almost knocked on the door to check on her but decided to stay out of Sandra's business. Instead, she headed back to clear the dining room table. Lawrence broke his conversation with Kelpie to help Livia.

"Hey, Honey. Let me get the dishes for you," Lawrence insisted.

It was not unusual for him to pitch in with housekeeping, but he was yearning for a tap out from Kelpie's shoptalk. "Oh no, Lawrence, you guys are having a great time. I've got this one. I am going to let the dishwasher do all the work today anyhow," Livia assured him.

Sandra finally collected herself and the loo was finished collecting the contents of her stomach. She tried to find her way back to the dining room, but rather found herself in front of Livia's computer screen hitting maximize after poking around Livia's office for a few minutes. She had zoomed through three pages before she heard someone coming. Hurriedly she minimized the screen and quietly pushed in the chair. Sandra turned around slowly and was relieved the coast was clear. Except when she looked down near her waist, there were four long-lashed eyes peeking back at her. "Whatcha doin'?" Claire and Maya said in a sing song voice.

"Oh, there you are! Sorry I'm late, girls," Sandra thought fast to reply. "Aren't you two hosting a tea party somewhere nearby?" Sandra attempted to save her behind by pretending to have been looking for the girls' room. The girls fell for it and pointed her in the direction of their room. Just then, Livia came to check on them. All of them. She came up behind as they were about to enter the room. "Claire Simone Livingston! What has Mommy told you about inviting strangers into your room!?"

"What about me, Mommy?" asked Maya.

"You too, Maya Jane!"

Sandra interjected, "Excuse me, Olli...via, sorry, but I am not a stranger. I will be their aunt in two weeks so...."

Livia could not believe the gall of Kelpie to plan on marrying someone he barely knew and not have mentioned their engagement before the dinner party.

"I am really not concerned with who you may think you are, but I am concerned about my children. Thank you for your input. If you are still with my brother in two weeks, which I strongly doubt, then you come *talk* to me about *my* children before you go barging in their room!" Livia grabbed the girls by their hands and marched down the hall. "Kelpie! It is time for you and your company to go." Livia firmly stated. Lawrence immediately stood up in agreement with Livia without having the slightest clue as to what happened in the hallway.

"It's **fiancé**, Olivia! Stone, now I see why it took two whole months for you to bring me around your family. Let's go please – since we've been asked to leave."

Kelpie and Sandra promptly exited the house, down the steps, got in their *"tricked ride"* and peeled out of the driveway. Lawrence and Livia poured a glass of wine for themselves and toasted to making it through dinner. Then they gathered the kids in the downstairs family room to watch a movie. Sunday nights were family movie nights. And just like most Sunday nights, all three kids were fast asleep by the time the movie was over. Livia laid out their clothing for school the next day, while Lawrence carried them to bed. After they were all down, Livia was able to fill Lawrence in on the whole hallway fiasco.

"Honey, please, tell me again why you persist on inviting him over here?! It never ever goes well," pleaded Lawrence.

"Because, Guac, he is my brother. My only blood sibling. And no matter how much hurt he's caused me; I still love and care about him. Honestly though, I just really wanted to see the twins today. I should try reaching out to Tia myself, since she has full custody anyway. If Kelpie had told us the twins weren't coming—"

Lawrence butted in, "Well, Olivia, I have a lot of loved ones who'll never even know my number. It is so hard to understand you sometimes, but very easy to admire you. Come over here." Lawrence pulled her close, picked her up, carried her down the hallway that led to their room to *tuck* her in for the night.

At about 5:00am that next morning, Lawrence blinked his eyes a few times and squinted at Livia climbing back into bed with Salem in her arms. Salem was totally fine in his own room and own bed, but Livia ran to grab him anytime he let out even the tiniest peep. No sooner than she lay down with him, Salem was snoozing. Lawrence let out a puff and a grunt as he scooted over to the edge of the bed. "Guac? You sleep?"

"Mmm-Hmm," Lawrence aggressively hummed. "Well it sounds like you are up, Guac. Baby, I was thinking about starting a home staging company." Lawrence rustled the blankets a little to distract from his deep sigh. She continued, "I mean, whenever we have guests over our place, they are inquiring about who our interior designer is and how we must have spent a fortune on someone. And how many of their homes have I ended up doing after they realized I was the designer they were inquiring about? Huh?"

Lawrence took a moment to respond, "Nobody, Liv, nobody…," Livia smacked her lips and rustled the sheets. "Uh-uh- I mean a lot, Babe. So many! All, Liv, all of them."

"Never mind, Lawrence." Livia got up out of bed and snuggled Salem against her body to go put him back in his own room.

Lawrence popped his head up and snapped his eyes open, "Baby! Where you going? Don't just get up and leave. I'm sorry. I am listening to you! It's just that it is like five o'clock in the morning, and you are talking serious business. You are an **awesome** designer and you know I know you would rock at putting stages in people's homes."

"Staging homes, Lawrence," Livia snapped.

"You know that's what I meant, Baby. And what about the book?"

"Mmm-hmm. I am just going to put Salem back into his crib." Livia's voice could be heard down the hall as she disappeared from the doorway.

BOOKER

Love Hurts Sometimes

J ust an hour after putting Salem in his room, everyone in the house was milling about and proceeding to get out of the house on time for school and work. Livia and Lawrence had few words to exchange which was the norm at the instance of an unresolved discussion. Olivia was still holding a grudge over Lawrence's lack of interest in her home staging company idea. Everyone in the house continued to carry out their morning tasks as routinely as possible keeping the noise to a low hum out of respect for Salem's sleep schedule.

Livia put the finishing touches on the girls' lunches and proceeded to stow them in their backpacks. Maya, at tortoise speed, smacked on the last few bites of her cereal which always turned into mush by the time she finished. Claire carefully pulled her hoodie over her head and stared in the mirror until she'd smoothed her hair down around her face and had every strand in its correct place. Livia, as usual, helped Maya complete her morning regimen and once Daddy Pop was ready, they all lined up to give Nahn Nahn a great big kiss goodbye.

Halfway through the smooches, Livia picked up the phone without saying hello. If her ringer went on too long, the ringtone would stir Salem. Livia glanced at the name on the phone then locked the door behind everyone.

The caller could hear her grin through the receiver louder than her excited whisper, "Hi Sabrina!!" Livia was free to take the call since she had been writing earlier that morning, only taking a break to get the family out the door. She had stopped writing right in the middle of a babysitter story:

It took Nurse Judy a moment to react to Kelpie's demand on the other end of the phone. She was startled by what it meant if he was telling the truth. "What if Ollie *is* missing?" she thought. There was a code when my mom was being paged for a real emergency with us – it was STEVONIA. Momma despised being called on by her full name, but when she heard it, she knew one of us was in danger. After hearing the page, Stevie came running to the nurse's station. Momma talked to Kelpie on the phone and made sure that he was stable and safely locked inside our apartment before she dashed out of the hospital. She desperately wished that my father, Bradley, was around. No one was sure if he was currently in this country. He frequently accepted jobs overseas while periodically coming back into town to manage the property he was granted in his grandfather's will. Stevie tried calling Bradley, but he didn't pick up his phone.

Calling the police was out of the question. Stevie didn't want to be scrutinized for leaving Ollie in the care of Tess, given Tess's track record. One of the hospital receptionists and trusted colleague of Stevie's, agreed to drive Stevie home to get Kelpie and also drive her around to look for me. Stevie was quiet on the ride home, trying not to panic. She knew there was always a slight chance Tess could relapse. She just didn't expect Tess to relapse while taking care of Ollie.

As soon as Momma got home, she hugged Kelpie to assure him everything would be ok. She sat him down and calmly asked him to tell her exactly what had happened. Kelpie was a storm of tears, sniffles, and sobs. "And...and...and I called for them, but...but...but...only thing left was Ol...Ollie's, Ollie's KEYS!!!" Kelpie broke down, clenching the teddy bear keychain in his hand. Stevie tried to soothe him as best she could before leaving him at his friend's house to go looking for Ollie. "When Momma comes back, Ollie will be with me. Okay?" She looked Kelpie square in the eyes and hugged him tightly before exiting. After they closed the door behind her, she whispered eerily to herself, "Tess is fuckin' with the wrong bitch."

At first, I was having the time of my life. Auntie Tess was taking us to so many parks. It was me and my cousin against the world. We played on swing after swing, after seesaw, after slide. It was great! Auntie Tess was not even on the playground telling us what to do all the time. Which was good, because after the second park she started talking funny and acting funny like she had taken too much cough medicine.

Auntie Tess had at least one friend of her own at each park. She told me that she was going to play with her friends while we girls played with one another. My auntie was a grownup. The only time I remember grownups having playtime was like on Hyde's TV program that Kelpie used to sneak and watch.

I had no idea that grownups could play in the daytime, outside, while *everyone* watched. My cousin let me know that it was alright. She told me that Auntie Tess takes her out all the time, but that it was better with me. If I wasn't around, my cousin would have to just sit and watch the grownups play. Sometimes Auntie Tess would even make my cousin be friendly and play with some of her guy friends too. But she never asked me to do anything like that.

The sun was going down, and I started to feel hungry. I started missing home. I wondered if Momma was home and what Kelpie was doing at home without me. Watching Auntie Tess play with her friends made me angry at Kelpie though. It looked like the same games Kelpie would always make me play, even if I said I didn't like it. My cousin told me that Auntie Tess usually wins the game because the guys will give her money like when you win a prize at the fair. "So how do you know when she don't win?" I asked. I really felt bad that I even asked. My cousin cried a little when she told me how she knew. On those nights, she told me, they didn't get to eat dinner and Auntie Tess's face would be black and blue.

Well on this particular night, Auntie Tess must have won really big because everything we ate for dinner was big. We had big fries, big burgers, and really big shakes. She even gave us each a dollar. She said it was for being on her team.

Even though it seemed like she won big that night, thoughts of her winnings began to fade once Momma busted through the restaurant doors. "Mutha –Fuckin' – Tess!" my mom screamed. I had never heard her talk like that. I knew it was going to be bad. I was so glad to see Momma, but sad for Auntie Tess. Against Stevonia Thomas, she was bound to come up black and blue. I wrapped my arm around my cousin and hugged her under the table with me until it was over. I didn't realize I had had such a vice grip until Momma snatched me out from under the table. I did not want to let go of my cousin. We needed each other.

"Honey, I know this is a crazy day for you. Momma is so sorry I let her watch you! I really thought it would be okay if she was just sitting at the house with you. Please believe me, I had no idea she would take you out like this. Baby, you don't have to tell Momma what happened today. I don't want you to have to relive what happened today.

"We are gonna go get Kelpie, then I'll get you guys ready for bed. It has been a long night, you have school tomorrow, and your brother really misses you! He cried his eyes out for you. I did too, Baby. I am glad you are safe now!"

I guess Kelpie really was afraid for me because that night he did not ask me to take off my pajamas and get into his bed like other nights. He just let me sleep.

***

Livia took a much-needed break from writing about babysitter horror stories and was glad to take a phone call from Sabrina. Sabrina was like a sister to Livia ever since their college days. They shared the same major, fashion sense, love for cooking, and twin facial expressions when it came to giving someone the "stink eye." Sabrina lived a short road-trip away from them and was Godmother to the kids.

Every month or so, she would make the two-hour drive to visit Olivia's family and stay in a condo she owned on the waterfront. Sabrina owned a restaurant in both cities called, "Plethora Platter." Her menu was flavored with international cuisine. The Northwest was fertile ground for Sabrina, and her restaurants became vastly popular after being open only three years.

"Hey, O. Stone! Sorry I didn't realize it was so early. Salem must still be sleeping?"

"When you gonna stop calling me that? Yes, he's asleep, but I can talk. Just let me get to the bedroom."

Livia skated down the hall in her house boots, stopping to glance into Salem's room. Still out. Salem slept until 8:00am most days so Olivia had maybe fifteen minutes or so to catch up with her friend.

"Okay. I'm good."

"Yeah girl. I know I have not called in a while. You know how it is sometimes. I just don't stop to breathe! But I wanted to give you the heads up early. I am not able to come get the kids next weekend."

"Okay. Girl, that is fine. I know the restaurants get crazy busy this time of year. The kids will understand."

"O. Not the restaurants," Sabrina said, now sounding stern.

"Okay, okay. So what? You and Troy got big plans? What is it this time? Paris?"

"Olivia. Listen. I am in the hospital right now... I'm being released soon but have to come back for surgery... That nigga tried to kill me!"

Livia's jaw almost dropped into her lap as she sat back on the bed. Sabrina had to give her the whole story. Livia more than lacked approval of Sabrina's relationship to Troy, but they were older now. Sabrina had to make life decisions for herself. Troy was always causing Sabrina to break dates with Livia and the kids. He was very possessive and controlled her every move. He usually chose things Sabrina liked to do; it was just that Sabrina wouldn't get a chance to use her own mind.

Troy had proposed to Sabrina after only knowing her for four months. She was excited about the idea and she genuinely loved him, so it did not seem odd to her. Plus, they set a wedding date for two years out. The problem was, it caused a huge rift between her and Livia.

Livia felt like she lost her best buddy but forced herself to cope with the idea since marriage meant Sabrina would have even less free time. Troy wanted to marry Sabrina and for her to birth some outrageous number of children. He told her she would have to give up managing the restaurants to be home more. Sabrina agreed, though Livia knew her heart was truly in being hands-on with her restaurants. Deep down, Livia just wanted Sabrina to have the same love and happiness she was experiencing with Lawrence and the kids. It just didn't seem like Troy was going to be the one to give it to her.

When they would get into tiffs about the restaurants, the wedding plans, or future children, Troy would plan lavish international trips so that she would eventually side with him. They had even been to the Tutankhamun Gallery in Cairo. Who would argue about something like wedding colors after a trip like that?

Troy was fine as long as he was in control. Sabrina had recently been offered a deal to open up three new locations over the next two years, with the understanding that she would relocate to each new city and get the restaurants started. She would need to prepare for Chicago, San Francisco, and Seattle. Originally, Sabrina enjoyed the small business of two modest locations. She had just never really known her taste for major success until it was served to her. Once she had decided to accept the deal, she had to postpone the wedding date and children were certainly a tentative subject. She told Troy about the new plan.

Troy was not, in the least, entertained by this idea. He came to terms that it was going to be a hard battle, but that didn't stop his ego from using his controlling tactics. Sabrina knew that his talk of Beijing and the Forbidden City was only a ploy. She was catching on. Not that she was totally in the dark before; she really had enjoyed all of the exotic getaways. But her mind was never more set in stone than it was the day she took the restaurant deal. She fancied the idea of becoming a national chain and possibly stretching her palate to other countries. That would bring the theme and mission of *Plethora Platter* into fruition.

"Oh my God, Bri. He tried to kill you?! I don't think I can take this over the phone. Let me make a few arrangements. I'm bringing Salem. I have to come see you."

It *Seams* Alright

The phone eventually went to voicemail. That was the fourth call she had to make. Livia had been working on a few formal gowns for some girls in the neighborhood and needed to reschedule fitting dates so she could go be with Sabrina. Creating gowns was a talent developed in high school when Olivia chose to show up at her first homecoming dance wearing an original piece. Back then her talent was instrumental in her independence. She used it to land a position at the fabric store, after school, and on weekends. With her own money, Livia was able to make more independent decisions.

She had the girls' fittings scheduled for this week, but she needed to cancel. She did not know what she could do to help Sabrina, but knew she needed to be with her friend. She couldn't imagine what it would feel like to lose Sabrina, her sister in spirit. Lawrence knew when his woman was hurting. He inherited Sabrina as a sister, too, and if it weren't for the academy, he would've gone along to make sure everything was alright.

Lawrence had no problem handling the girls while she'd be gone. They adored their Daddy Pop. And Lawrence had always been accommodating of Livia's periodic visits to Sabrina's. He understood their need for each other. Livia decided it'd be good to bring her laptop as she packed the last few items for her overnight trip to Sabrina's. Livia paused for thought, *"Maybe I'll write a bit now... just in case she needs every second of my attention when I get there,"* and then she began chapter three.

Chapter 3
Sleep Over Sleep Under

KELPIE HAD BACKED off of me that night I went missing, and for a long while after that day. He was really afraid for me that night with Auntie Tess. Momma had decided that if I was brave enough to handle a night of Auntie Tess's escapades, that I would probably be okay at home by myself until Kelpie got out of school. Before leaving for work, she would prepare a snack for me that I could eat after school. Most days I would stare out of the window. For a quasi-poor neighborhood, we had a really cool view. Months had gone by with me being on my own for those few unsupervised hours.

Of course, there were those days where I was being a typical six-year-old kid without supervision. I remember my brother coming home one day just in time to throw flour over the toaster before it charred to a crisp. I loved cinnamon toast. I just was not quite sure how to make it. But I was feeling mature and self-sufficient.

I slathered margarine on my bread and sprinkled lots of cinnamon and sugar. I put on way more than Momma would have. Then I stuck both slices in the toaster, lowered them down, and awaited my delicious treat. The next thing I realized there was a weird smell coming from the toaster and it had begun to smoke! All of a sudden there was a huge grey cloud. I didn't even hear Kelpie come in, but he saved the day.

One day I phoned my mom at work to alert her that I had to call 911. She was so scared for me and asked me a lot of questions. I was just concerned for the house on the other hill, about a mile away. There was smoke coming from their roof. But it was not just their roof. There were so many that were smoking!

All of these homes seemed to be on fire. My mom was calm once she found out that I was okay. Then she had to explain to me that I should only call 911 if *I* was in danger. She also let me know that those homes were not on fire, but that there was smoke coming through the chimney from the fires that were burning in their fireplaces. Oh! Well, how was I supposed to know?

I did not get in trouble for calling 911, but I did get in trouble for what I did to my dolls. I wanted someone to feel the pain I was feeling from what I had to endure from Kelpie some nights. I took Momma's scissors and cut off all of their doll hair as well as their arms and legs down to the wire. I hid them behind the couch so there would be no evidence.

That weekend, Kelpie asked Momma if we could move the couch away from the wall so that it could face the window. I even helped to push it, forgetting what I had hidden. The unfortunate reveal of dismembered dolls got me sent directly to the room and unable to watch TV for the rest of the weekend. "But, Momma! That's not fair! Kelpie never got punished for what *he* did!" I tried to plead my case.

Momma stood up for Kelpie instead of me. She stopped my plea, "Uh, no no. Kelpie does not have anything to do with this. All of his toys are still intact. Just go to the room! You are lucky I don't beat you."

✳✳✳

It was time for Livia and Salem to get on the road to Sabrina's in order to beat rush hour traffic. Claire and Maya were sad that they could not go. Lawrence gave Livia a tight hug and sent along a stuffed bunny for Sabrina.

Bunnies were her favorite and she owned many bunny - themed items. Livia tucked the bunny inside one of the bags and hit the road. Salem slept most of the way there. He woke up and was calling for his Daddy Pop by the time they pulled into Sabrina's driveway.

It was tough to look at Sabrina going through recovery. She had bandages all over her body. Sabrina hated hospitals and refused to stay there. She arranged to have a full-time nurse at her residence and the doctor would call to check on her periodically.

No sooner had Livia walked through the bedroom door did tears begin streaming down her face. Salem lightly patted Livia on the face, which made a quiet splashing noise with the wetness of her tears. He hugged her closely around the neck and patted her on the back. That just made Livia break down into sobs. Her knees gave way and she knelt down on the carpet.

Salem crawled over to Sabrina's bedside and pulled up on her blankets. "No. No. Salem, she can't pick you up, Baby." Livia rushed over to him. Livia was embarrassed to be crying in front of her friend. Sabrina hadn't been crying at all. Sabrina offered comfort, "It's okay, O. I'll be okay. I'm alive! These bandages will come off at some point and I'll be good as new."

Livia leaned over and kissed her on the face without saying anything in return. Sabrina had bandages all over her face. Her hands were wrapped up like lobster claws. She had a bandage wrapped around her neck as well. Sabrina was under the covers, but she had stitches and bandages down her side and back as well. "I have to get surgery on my hands in the morning. I figured you could drive me. I was originally going to have the shuttle come pick me up." Sabrina was speaking in everyday tone and jargon, as if her life had not been threatened at all.

Livia still could not speak. The nurse escorted Livia and Salem out of the bedroom so that he could help Sabrina eat her dinner. Her hands were not useless but had lost some feeling and made it difficult to handle food, especially with a fork or spoon. The nurse was also there to assist her in the bathroom and with bathing. Once settled in the spare bedroom, Livia received a call from Lawrence. He left a voicemail wanting to make sure they made it safely. Livia was still not talking and just replied with a text. The text read – *Not good baby. Me n Salem r safe. Call u 2morrow. Xoxo the girls 4 me. Pls pray! Luv u. Good nite.*

Livia settled Salem in the playpen with toys and took an opportunity to write. She searched the bag and got out her laptop:

✳✳✳

I sat in the middle of Kelpie's room wailing. I felt like Kelpie never got in trouble for the things he did to me, and no one ever heard me out. I served my restriction that weekend for cutting up my dolls. Maybe I should have cut Kelpie instead. Then, maybe, someone would ask me *why* I would do something so horrible to *him*. And *maybe* I would have the chance to tell them it was because of the nasty things he was doing to *me*. But I didn't have it in me to harm my brother. I actually loved him very much. I just hated what he was doing to me. And I was left to wonder if there was anyone who loved me enough to stand up for me.

Momma was relieved a couple years later when her cousin, Perry, moved back in town. It meant more help with babysitting. She sat us down on the couch one evening, to tell us she was going to an out-of-town training. It was paid training and a huge opportunity to expand her resume. That meant we had to stay with Perry. He lived with his wife, Reece, and her sons, Aaron and Tommy, from a previous marriage. Her boys were thirteen months apart, older than me, but younger than Kelpie. Momma liked that we were able to be with family. Plus, she and Hyde don't speak that often anymore, so he isn't a viable option. That, and Auntie Tess ruined things with dad's side of the family.

After a while, it became routine that we'd go to their house every other weekend. Perry and Reese loved having Kelpie over. He fit right in with their boys. Reece really liked Kelpie because he was old enough to watch us while her and Perry went out on dates. She and I did a lot of fun girly stuff too, from time to time. She was all the fun of having a mom, and none of the yelling or punishing. It was cool.

Perry planned a movie night for all of us. He says young black kids should be educated in important black films. He rented *School Daze* and *Do the Right Thing* by Spike Lee. I think Kelpie must have been taking away more of the sexual lessons out of the movies rather than the lessons of colorism and activism. I got tired of plugging my ears and closing my eyes during the strong language and sex scenes. I started complaining and talking through the whole flick. By the third outburst, Cousin Perry sent me downstairs to bed early. But I couldn't sleep. All I could hear was everyone else laughing and having a great time. I was just glad I didn't see *Jungle Fever* until I was quite a bit older and could understand better.

Finally, the movie was over, and Perry sent the boys downstairs to bed, too. Every time we spent the night, Reece would make up pallets in the basement for all of us to sleep on. I hated that it always had to be a slumber party. I prayed for the day I'd have my own room to myself. I imagined it with a huge lock on it so that I would be safe from the Boogie Monster.

The boys did not care whether I was asleep or not. They were loud coming down the stairs, talking about the movies. They liked seeing the boobie shots. Now you know they were peeking!

They seemed to be getting bored and I thought they were going to go to sleep. But I was way wrong. "Hey guys, you want to play a game?" Kelpie asked them. Aaron, the older one, and Tommy looked confused because all of the games were upstairs, and they'd get in trouble if Perry knew we were still up. "It's a game I made up, but you will get in trouble if anyone knows you played it, so you have to promise not to tell! Never mind. You guys would lose anyway. Go to bed."

Kelpie was using the same tactics he used on me. I was under my covers, trying not to move, and hoping they would want to play without me, being that I was almost asleep. Kelpie made Tommy put a chair up against the door to the stairs in case Reece or Perry came to check on us. He called the game, "Who Can Last the Longest." He pulled out his penis as he explained the game. The boys were always comparing their boy toys to see whose was bigger, but Aaron and Tommy thought this felt a little different.

"Eh, man, what if Ollie wakes up?" asked Aaron. "She knows how to play. She is part of it. You'll see," Kelpie explained. Kelpie grabbed a small bottle of baby oil from his sock and rubbed it on himself. Then he tossed it to the boys and told them to rub it in until they could get their penises as big as they would grow. My pillow was already drenched. I had been quietly crying because I knew what was next. Kelpie took off my covers and shook me until I looked up at him. "Please, Kelpie. I'm gonna tell." I begged.

"Ok, you can go ahead and tell. Go upstairs right now. You know you will get in trouble for being awake and you are already in trouble for ruining the movies, so go ahead and tell." Kelpie said with a shrug. I did not want to be in more trouble. I just wanted to be left alone. But I felt cornered, so I took off all of my clothes like Kelpie asked me to do.

"Okay guys. This is how you play. Come on Ollie, bend over, you know how this goes." He made me be on all fours, with my behind in the air. "Okay, Tommy, I will go first. You put your thing in that hole right there. Come closer, Aaron, so you can see. And you push it in all the way and pull it out. Did you hear it pop? That is how you do it. Aaron's turn!"

Aaron and Tommy were very uncertain at this point about what they had gotten themselves into. Aaron was frozen in his place until Kelpie smacked him on the back to take his turn. They all did it. Then Tommy stopped to ask, "So how do you win, Kelpie?" Kelpie sighed, "Ugh, do I have to teach you guys everything? When your thing is not big anymore you lose." There was a crack in the floorboards coming from upstairs. Everyone shuffled to put their clothes back on.

***

Falling asleep typing was not a good habit. Blinking her eyes, Livia woke up from the same nightmare she had been periodically having for almost two years. She was now used to it. She scrunched her face to adjust to the light. Salem had fallen asleep, too.

After putting her laptop away, she turned off the light, put Salem in the bed with her, and they both went back to sleep. Livia enjoyed having Salem in her arms. It made him squirm a bit to have his sleep interrupted, but he put his hand on her cheek, nose, lips – he felt around her face until he found his spot. He always had to hold on to her chin before he could get comfortable.

When morning came, Livia could smell the likes of breakfast being made. It didn't surprise her that Sabrina would hire a chef for the current situation. Sabrina didn't own two restaurants for no reason. Sabrina loved to eat well. Livia did, too. Livia stumbled through the bathroom, not wanting to turn on too many lights. Her eyes still needed adjusting. She splashed some water on her face and freshened her breath.

On her way to the kitchen Livia bumped into Nurse Drake. He was carrying a tray of food for Sabrina. "Oh, excuse me Nurse

Drake. Is the chef still in the kitchen? Did he make enough for everyone?"

"Yes, *he* did. Even for the little one if he eats solids." Nurse Drake laughed and added, "Oh, and no, the *chef* is not in the kitchen anymore. You are looking at him, Honey." He continued walking to Sabrina's room to deliver her food.

Livia didn't really know what to say. A cute nurse that could also cook. She smiled shyly and went to the kitchen to make a plate. She set aside some food for Salem and placed it in the microwave. It was just her in the kitchen, eating alone. The sight of watching Sabrina being spoon fed gave Livia an indescribable feeling.

Livia downed her last few bites then went back to the room to check on Salem. Salem either smelled his mom or the breakfast, because his head popped up when she returned to the spare room. Livia could hear giggling and talking coming from Sabrina's room. Nurse Drake took great care of his patients and him having a sense of humor helped keep Sabrina's mind off of the pending surgery.

Livia picked up Salem from the bed and stole a bunch of morning kisses from him before they both traveled down the hall to investigate the laughter. They poked their heads in Sabrina's room, "Hey, Bri, sounds like you're having too much fun in here."

"Well, somebody's gotta lighten the mood. You certainly dropped the ball on that task!" Bri teased. For a moment they all just stared at each other. Seconds later they all burst out laughing. Nurse Drake sensed a need for privacy.

"Well, Ms. Polk, I'll let you and Olivia have some time. I've got to work on your chart anyway. It has to be ready before your surgery." Nurse Drake smiled, patted Sabrina's shoulder, then escorted himself out of the room.

"What surgery? You're having surgery Bri? You never told me that!"

"Dang. Livia, relax. Yes, surgery. And I did tell you. Did you expect my hands to stay like this?" Bri laughed and waved her lobster-claw-bandaged hands in front of her face. "I was going to ask you to come with me. To drive me. It's minor, but you know how I hate hospitals. Ugh!"

"Yeah, Sabrina, I can do that. You know I would do anything. So...are you... going to... tell me... how this... h a p p e n e d?"

"Olivia. For real? Girl. The way you walked in here yesterday? Looking like you'd seen a dead body? I wasn't sure I should have called you. If you hate seeing me like this, guess who hates it ten times more!"

Olivia just stood there. She wanted to let her tears fly freely, but she knew the last thing Sabrina needed was for someone to cry over her. Sabrina figured if everyone cried, the moment they saw her bandages, it must be worse than it seemed.

After another long stare, Livia went over to the bed and just hugged Sabrina as gently and lovingly as she possibly could. Sabrina couldn't hug back but she pressed her face into the top of Livia's head to return the embrace. Livia could feel the wetness begin to dampen her hair. She didn't know if Sabrina was crying from the pain or the joy of being alive – a survivor. Olivia reached over to the bedside table to grab tissue and dabbed at the tears on Sabrina's face. Sabrina sucked in a huge breath and closed her eyes while starting to trace back what led to her current situation. "It all started at this dinner party Troy was hosting for his friends...."

✳ ✳ ✳

Sabrina was thrilled about the dinner party, but when she got there it did not take long to realize it was a surprise engagement party. Troy had been telling all of his friends about the wedding date and let them know that he and Sabrina had already started trying for a baby. Sabrina could not believe her eyes or ears. Lies, deceit and betrayal filled the space. She was upset by the fact that he would plan such a thing without involving her. She was furious about the claims of a fabricated wedding date and comments about them trying to conceive. But most of all she was hurt that he had not invited any of her close and personal friends and family. She could only take so much of the charade. After mingling and a few hors d'oeuvres, an opportunity provided itself for them to beg off from the party and go to his office in the back of the house.

Troy quickly unzipped his trousers, "Baby, I couldn't wait for you to pull me back here. Yo' ass is feelin' like a ripe tomato in this dress."

Troy assumed she'd lured him into private quarters to show him an act of special appreciation for the amazing party he had pulled together. He took her left shoulder, turning it to the right, his pants at his ankles and bent her over the chair. At this point, Sabrina was not sure if she knew her fiancé at all. She pushed him off and confronted him about the total disregard of her plan to open three new restaurants in Chicago, San Francisco, and Seattle. She wondered how he could be so passé about the most important accomplishment she had made in her life. Having babies at this time in her life was not something she wanted.

"Troy, Troy, Troy. I don't even know where or how to start. First of all, you can zip your pants up, 'cause any part of me that comes near yo' lame dick, is coming to strike, not to please!"

"Sabrina! What the fuck is your problem? You ain't never had no nigga treat you so good? You better check this attitude and get to thankin' a brutha real quick before I change my mind about you."

He began telling her that she should be glad that he was trying to "save her ass" from flopping three new restaurants and putting her existing restaurants in jeopardy. He suggested that she even needed to give up the two restaurants she had, devote her life to his spousal needs, and the labors of motherhood.

"Troy please believe you ain't the first and sho enough won't be the last man, to have a chance with me. You completely blew it with this last act. The lies about a baby and summer wedding I can get over. But if you truly loved me, if you were truly doing this for me, then my close friends would be here. Where are Olivia and Lawrence? Gene? Damien and Aisha? Claudia? Francis? Palmer and Cody?

This is for you, Troy. So, you know what? Go fuck **yo self**! See how you look standing at the altar, by **yo self**. Try having all them babies by **yo self**. Then sit, by **yo self**, and watch me and my restaurants be successful."

"Now girl, you know you don't mean any of that. You better

start taking all that back before I choke the shit out of you. Ain't no threat this time, Sabrina."

Sabrina had no more words for the man. He had become nothing to her in less than fifteen minutes. Tears rolled down her cheeks. Her powder and blush were all smeared across her skin as she tried to flick the tears away. Mascara formed dark, black puddles under her lashes. The idea of spending the rest of her life with a man that couldn't possibly love or care for her as he said he did, boiled the contents in her belly. Sabrina did not even want another second with him.

She rustled through her purse. She loosened her key to his house off of the chain. She loosened her ring, the key to his heart, off of her finger. She gave him one last look, and then was out of the room before the two, now meaningless, pieces of metal hit the floor.

He reached out for her but was too late. He could see some of the guests near the walkway were looking in his direction. Immediately he pulled himself together and let her leave. He rushed back in towards the dining room to address everyone about the delay.

"Carry on everybody! The party is not over. My new fiancé is all excited about this event! She just had too much of the pâté. She'll be back in a few."

Waiting for the valet just increased her frustration. Sabrina slammed the car door so hard, she made herself jump. The smell of burnt rubber and smoke in the air must have given hint to the guests that it wasn't the pâté. She sobbed the entire way home, barely able to see through the watery shield over her eyes. Sabrina wanted to call her best friend. Livia was all that she had, but Sabrina did not want Livia to know she was right about Troy all along. Livia warned Sabrina about Troy's controlling behaviors, but Sabrina just didn't see it that way. If Sabrina couldn't see it before, how Troy acted at the party was more than proof that he wanted to control her life.

Ever since Troy had come around, he kept his distance from Livia. He would make up an excuse to get out of dinner whenever they all had set plans. If Livia was there as a surprise to him, he'd make an excuse to leave. Any time Livia and Sabrina had some girl-time, he would call Sabrina every twenty minutes to interrupt. One afternoon Sabrina was in town and wanted to sneak off to lunch with Olivia. Sabrina agreed to pick her up and then take her to get the girls from school afterwards. They went to their favorite waffle house across town. No sooner than they had ordered had Troy called to find out what Sabrina was doing.

"Yes, Troy, I did tell you I was surprising Livia for lunch…Well, we just ordered our food…Can't it wait? But Palmer's gallery doesn't close until six tonight… Okay…. Fine! I mean, fine, yes, I'm headed there right now," Sabrina slid out of the booth with her purse and phone in hand.

"Uh uh, Bri. You always do this when it comes to him. We can have Palmer open the gallery for us any time! He knows that!" Livia followed Sabrina.

"Yeah, O. I know. He knows, too. But if someone else buys it, he'd be pissed. I really shouldn't make him angry."

Livia rolled her eyes, got in the car with Sabrina, and rode to the gallery. Troy wanted Sabrina to pick out an art piece for the main corridor of his home. But by the time her and Livia arrived, Troy called her back to let her know he went ahead and ordered one he had his eye on a few weeks ago. Livia was not shocked at all. This was typical behavior of Troy. Sabrina gave so many excuses for Troy. She could not see that he would do this sort of thing on purpose. But it was his way of controlling her every move and wedging a gap between any influence Livia could have on her.

Now as much as Sabrina tried to make things work with Troy, her heart was truly set on the one that got away. Angry about how Troy had treated her at their fake engagement party, drove her to think about her charismatic, ex-boyfriend, Kyle.

Kyle had been there for her since eighth grade science class. His mack line was, "You know Sabrina, us being partners in class is just practice for us being partners at baby makin'. You see how well we work together?"

"Kyle Drew, you are disgusting. I will not be makin' any babies any time soon, and definitely not with you, Four Eyes. I did not choose you as my partner. Ms. Mackey did! So, plug your pie hole and give me the beaker."

Kyle laughed out loud and nearly got sent out of class for his outburst. He brought it down to a whisper, "Okay, okay. You are such a Pooh Bear, always bothered. I was just playin' Sabrina. Dang girl." The very next day they announced to their friends that they were a couple. He really knew how to make Sabrina smile. And she did like being his partner, sans the baby making part. They chose the same high school to attend, joined all the same clubs, and senior year they were voted, "Most likely to get married and have babies."

The one thing they could not agree on was the same college. They fought over each other's decision night after night. When they realized there would be no common ground, they settled on a long-distance relationship with the promise of alternate visits each semester and to always come home on school breaks. It really worked out for them in the beginning. However, junior year, Kyle made a commitment to pledge a fraternity and a sorority girl named Taryn had fallen for him during many a Greek event. And Taryn, not knowing Kyle was in a relationship, chose the same weekend as Sabrina to show up to the Frat House, unannounced, in an all-black, crotchless teddy. Sabrina showed up in a messy bun and raggedy sweats.

Taryn had only gotten there minutes before Sabrina, but Kyle had a hard time explaining why Taryn was in his bedroom. His frat brothers had a good laugh about that night. Once Kyle and Sabrina got a chance to sit down and talk about it, he admitted that though he did not have deep feelings for Taryn, he was very much attracted to her sexy side. He told Sabrina, "Pooh Bear, I love everything about you! I been toleratin' all that purity shit you been spittin' in my ear too! But I'm almost twenty-one and you ain't let me get this dick wet once!"

All this time, Sabrina had been letting things go as far as she could without him sticking it in. She heard him out. She really did love him, so she agreed to let the relationship go to the next level. A month after their monumental experience, Kyle confessed to Sabrina that he'd grown fonder of Taryn. He could not resist Taryn's continuous advancements. He imagined it would hurt less to break it off with Sabrina rather than to get caught cheating. Sabrina was devastated but accepted his choice to move on. As angry as she was with him, he always had a place in her heart. She blamed herself for not picking his same school. Shortly after college graduation, he reached out to Sabrina to *rekindle old flames. They hooked up a few times but nothing permanent. They just kept in touch as friends.*

Thinking about Kyle the night she broke up with Troy, seemed to make her situation with Troy worse. Sabrina slammed her car door after pulling into the garage and getting out. Still searching for ways to avow her anger, she marched inside, flipped on the kitchen light, threw her phone on the counter, snatched a bottle of Howell Mountain and continued marching directly to her bedroom. A bottle of wine and loud music were going to have to be her best friends for the rest of the night. Or until she passed out. She bumped her "mad black woman" playlist. The first song to blast through the speakers was <u>Caught Out There</u> by Kelis. Sabrina thrashed around her room similar to Kelis in the video, yanking all the pillows and bedsheets to the floor and throwing things against the wall that Troy had given to her.

Her room that had usually been her sanctuary now looked like the results of a wild, teenage, slumber party. There was a huge king size bed with a canopy and across from the bed, and a 50" flat screen with speakers set inside the entertainment center. Off to the other end of the master suite was the vanity and jet tub with a shower attached. The toilet was in its own room. Only a few songs had played before she was tired and sprawled out in the middle of the floor. Still awake she attempted to take a swig from an empty bottle.

She pranced her way back into the kitchen for a new bottle, still hearing the music from the room. Uncorked bottle in hand and on her way back to the sanctuary, she paused by the phone on the counter. Against her better judgment, she dialed up Kyle's number. The phone rang for a while. She drank a few sips. She just needed a friend. All she wanted was someone to talk to during one of the worst moments in her life. If it was seriously over with Troy, as she believed it was, she couldn't see starting over again for the second time. Sabrina did not want to face being alone. Sabrina waited some years to be exclusive with anyone between dating Kyle and becoming exclusive with Troy.

The phone stopped ringing. She felt the tremble release from her body when she heard Kyle's voice on the other end, but it was just his voice mail. The phone slid back across the counter and she rejoined her date with "mad black woman" playlist and Howell Mountain. <u>Tyrone</u> by Erykah Badu was playing.

Howell and the pâté did not mix well after all. She searched the room for a toilet until she found it, like it was her first visit to the place. She pulled down her panties and sat slowly, anticipating the seat to be cold. After wiping, she reached for the drawer and fished for her box of tampons. Empty! "Great, FUCKING, day I'm having!" Sabrina grabbed a wad of toilet paper prepared to do a waddle through the hallway to the linen closet. She was hoping there was a backup box in there. This was not the greatest time to have to do a late-night run to the drug store.

The lights were mostly off because she was done for the night. She knew her face looked a sloppy mess and did not want to see her reflection in the mirror. Before she could totally rise up from the toilet, she saw a shiny pair of black dress shoes and matching slacks. Without looking all the way up, she griped, "Troy. It's over! Can you please leave? There is absolutely nothing to discuss anymore. Just leave me alone. Put your pee...I mean key! – Put your key on the desk while you're at it."

"Bitch! You think this a fucking game?" Troy roared.

Troy had a lot of issues, but Sabrina had never seen him that angry before. She finally looked all the way up and her nose met, tip to tip, with a very sharp blade. After hanging up with Kyle, Troy snatched up the chopping knife that was on Sabrina's cutting board. She stood up with her panties still around her ankles and tried to push past him, but the bathroom was narrow. She used her forearms to block his attack. He began stabbing in every direction. Sabrina tried her hardest to scream but nothing would come out. She was terrified and attempted to grab the blade from his hand. Troy had a strong grip and sliced through her fingers. Her hands shoved his face and she stumbled back and fell on the toilet when she felt the blade come across her neck and cheek. He walked out thinking it was over.

There was strength in her that she knew could only come from God and she got up from the seat and tried to charge past him. It was an unrewarded effort because he pulled his elbow back and gave her a shock to the face, immediately breaking her nose and spewing blood. She threw her head into her hands, her knees buckled, panties tore near her ankles and she fell to the floor. She was no longer moving, but he stabbed her in the back anyway. He stood over her, blood dripping on her back, a mixture of his and hers. He walked out to the sink and splashed water on his face. Sabrina was still breathing, but she dared not move because she knew he wanted her dead. This was supposed to be the end of her. She heard the bedroom door close and she wanted to get up, but he came back.

She went limp hoping he wouldn't notice her breathing. Troy gave a swift kick to the top of her head and there was no motion. He spat on her, laughed, and exited the room, locking the bedroom door before leaving. Sabrina lay there and bled almost twenty minutes. She wanted to be sure that he was gone. Almost all the feeling was gone from her hands and forearms, but still she found a way to pull herself up from the floor. She pressed her opened face against the screen of the window frame and yelled out to the neighbor for help, but only a raspy whisper came out, "Plea.. hel...cah...9...1..." Sabrina collapsed to the floor again. She passed out from the loss of blood. When she came to, she had no idea how much time had gone by.

✳✳✳

"Okay, Sabrina, how the hell did you survive this!? My God!"

"I'm telling you. Just listen, Olivia."

"I'm trying! It's just...why didn't you call me right away?"

"Just listen!"

✳✳✳

Sabrina had begun to see a bright image and could feel herself fading. It was not as distinct as the shape of a person, but she could see the image reaching out to her and gesturing for her to come along. Right when she started to go towards the image, she got the urge to pray instead, "Lord, Jesus, save me, keep me." She prayed the same words over and over again. After a while she began to sing, "I don't believe He brought me this far to leave me..." It was supernatural; as if the melody picked her up and opened the door for her. She dragged and scooted over to the bedside table and dialed 911, voice still barely audible, "I'm dying...I live at 4...7...2... Clove..." Sabrina closed her eyes. She opened them and saw Kyle standing over her. She closed them again. She opened them and saw a hospital room, flowers, and balloons, all from Kyle. As she lifted a hand to read the card all she could see were bandages.

✳✳✳

"I didn't have my phone or any of my personal stuff. Once Kyle knew I was stabilized, he offered to go to my place and grab everything. He called the insurance company and had the cleaning expedited for me after the police did their investigation. You'd never know this was a crime scene. That's when I got all my messages from my phone and I called you."

"I'm so sorry I was not here for you!"

"How could you have known? You are here now and *that's* what matters."

"So how did Kyle know to come? That's like an hour drive! And how did he get in? Does he still have a key, Bri? I thought he was back with Taryn. I didn't realize y'all still kicked it like that," Livia laughed.

"No, he does not have a key! And don't get me started on Taryn. Anyway!! Let me tell you."

✳✳✳

After Sabrina called Kyle, she left her phone on the counter. Kyle was returning her call when Troy walked in. The phone buzzed on the counter and the screen read, "Ex Hubby." Troy pressed the "send" button and sniffled as if crying.

"What's wrong Pooh Bear? You never call at this hour...Well, not since you became Miss Helen of Troy." He started calling Sabrina *"Miss Helen of Troy"* from the Greek mythology, after he realized how possessive Troy was over Sabrina. Kyle laughed loudly but was met with silence on the other end of the line. *"Okay, I know, not funny, just trying to cheer you up. What'd that young chap do to you now? ...Hello?"* Kyle heard more sniffling on the other end. *"Hey, baby, is it that bad?! I was just leaving a friend's house. You need some Kyle Drew in you?"*

"Mutha Fucka! Ain't this some shit?! Don't you eva call my bitch again!" Troy yelled.

Troy slammed down the phone, grabbed a knife, and went around the house looking for Sabrina. He grew more furious than when he had arrived. Kyle hung up the phone and raced on the freeway doing about 90mph, until he got to Sabrina's house. He wanted to stay with her throughout her recovery. She was grateful that he came. He was always there for her, but she was in no condition to have him back in her life. So, she asked him to return home.

Livia chimed in, "So he just left? Knowing Kyle Drew, I thought for sure he'd go driving around lookin' for Troy's ass. Speaking of...I did not want to ask, but where *is* Troy?"

"Yeah O, you know Kyle Drew too well, but that fool, Troy, had already tried to head for the border. He was dang near Canada by the time State Patrol caught him though. A routine stop turned high speed chase, turned into the arrest of an attempted murderer. I guess they beat him up pretty bad in the struggle to arrest him. I'm just glad they got the muthafucka."

Olivia's fingertips remained pasted to her temples in astonishment. Nurse Drake knocked before reentering the bedroom to help Livia transfer Sabrina out of the bed and into the car.

When they arrived at the hospital check-in desk, an attendant met them with a wheelchair and soon Sabrina was being wheeled away to be prepped for surgery. She asked the attendant if Livia could pray for her before going behind the double doors. She really hated hospitals and hated being operated on even more. While just a simple procedure was being done, it would determine the future use of her hands for eating, bathing, and cooking.

After reciting Psalm 27:1-3, Livia pressed an encouraging kiss on Sabrina's forehead and rolled Salem in his stroller to the waiting area. Not too entirely excited about having her baby sitting in the hospital for several hours, Livia wondered if there was a place near the hospital, she could take him. The receptionist directed her to the Children's Museum a few blocks away. Inside the museum there were endless hours of play available. It was a miniature town filled with everything you could think of – a grocery, a mall, a courthouse, a neighborhood, a farm, a church, a school, a library, a pet store, a gas station, a theatre, and even a hospital.

Livia found a cozy corner on the tiny theatre stage where she could see the whole museum and gave Salem free reign while she continued to write:

Kelpie was nervous about getting caught with his pants down, but no one ever came to the basement door. We had all fallen asleep while pretending nothing was going on down there. Before I could open my mouth in the morning, Cousin Perry was already lecturing me about behaving for the rest of the time we had to stay there. He didn't want to hear too much from me. And by the looks of the boy's faces, I had a feeling I shouldn't tell.

From then on, I just made a vow to wet myself at bedtime to ward off unwanted visitors in the night. Momma greatly disapproved of my behavior, especially since I was at the grade school age level.

She tried everything from cutting off my liquids three hours before bedtime, to punishments for not keeping dry, to making me sit on the toilet before lying down at night to help my problem. But I knew I needed to save the pee. I would let out just a few tinkles to appease her efforts and reserve the rest for the bedclothes.

Unfortunately, it was never enough. It did not take Kelpie long to see through my façade. At night, when he knew I had soiled my clothes, he would still order me to strip naked and place my clothes to the side. He wanted my naked body on top of his duplicate outfit. That was something I could not do. I did not want to get on top of him. Thinking I didn't have the option to completely refuse, I asked to be underneath.

Sometimes I feel like that convicted me, like I was being agreeable to these repulsive acts because I had set up boundaries. I don't know what he was doing up over me. I just balled my fists and arms up to my chest and squeezed my legs so tight. I closed my eyes and made myself to believe I was somewhere else, anywhere else – Sometimes just dead.

At times I imagine it was easier to just stay dry. At least then Momma would bake a strawberry cake for me, to reward a week's worth of dry bedclothes. Then one day I guess maybe his conscious kicked in because he left me alone. One could say I was reaching the age where his tricks and lies could not work anymore. I was getting older and way more articulate in explaining things in a way that could make me more believable. That and we moved to a place where I had my own room. He used to say he didn't want to hurt me; he was just curious about my body. I did not let him use that excuse any longer. I was not afraid of his threats anymore.

I caught him pleasuring himself one day in the bathroom. He was heavy into self-exploration during his middle school years, using his hand or holey objects around the house. And I would not be surprised if he had also found a willing subject in one of his classmates.

Tired of playing with the boys on nights with Cousin Perry, I found a girl down the street to play with. She was a few years older than myself and had all of the fun toys that I could ever want to play with. I wished I could be her. She told me she had no siblings and no cousins and that it had always just been her and her mother. When I and the boys would go to the park, I crossed my fingers that she would be playing there, too. When we were playing out front, I asked Cousin Perry if I could ring her doorbell.

All they ever did was boy stuff at Cousin Perry's. The boys were always teasing me one way or another. One evening, even though the sleeping arrangements were better at Cousin Perry's than before, I just wanted to sleep over at the girl's house down the block. She had asked her mom if she could have company and I was so glad for the invite. Cousin Perry agreed and I felt relief. I was so glad to have a night away from the boys and their stupid games.

Out of all the times her and I played together, I had never been in her house. It seemed a bit dark to be welcoming guests. Her mom was resting on the couch. It was well into the evening. Cousin Perry made sure I ate dinner first, so I did not present myself as a needy guest. I had my pajamas packed and clothes for the next day.

After playing in her room for a while and dancing around in our imaginary music videos, she suggested we take a bath. I felt pretty old to be sharing a bath with a friend, especially her because she was older than me.

She gave me some grown up riddle about saving water and I remembered what Cousin Perry warned me about appearing needy, so I got in. I giggled to myself at the sight of her overly matured bush. I didn't have much myself. It's ironic, for all the early growing up I had to do, I did not really develop until about my junior year in high school.

There we were, in the tub. There were no bubbles and the water was only room temperature, which to me was like ice. Knees and feet fumbling, I began to wash quickly to avoid hypothermia.

"I'm getting out now, it's too cold. Plus, ain't no bubbles or dolls or nothing in here. I wanna just go play." I said.

"Wait, wait, wait Ollie!" She said with urgency. "I can warm you up. Let me just show you how. We don't need toys. How old *are* you anyway? Eleven? And hey, if you get out too soon my mom will think you didn't wash good and maybe just you back in here."

Honestly her mom would have done no such thing. She was passed out on the couch. It was her nightly routine. But I didn't realize it then, so I sat back down in the tub. "I'm nine." As my cheeks hit the bottom of the tub, my heels were overhead.

At first, I thought of how much trouble I'd get into from my hair getting wet and then I felt this wetness between my legs. This was not like the wetness of the bathwater. I was afraid to scream in fear of getting in trouble.

But I knew this was wrong. This was different than anything my brother ever did to me. She gripped my thighs under my knees and tossed and turned her head between my legs. I didn't know what to do so I just sat up.

I hopped out of the tub and ran naked to her room to put on some bed clothes. I got under her covers and tried to go to sleep and forget about it like I had tried to forget about my brother. When she got in bed, she forced me to turn around.

"You didn't think it was over did you, Ollie?"

She was still wet from the tub and had nothing to cover her bare body. She shoved my head down below and smashed my face into her open vagina. I attempted to close my mouth and eyes.

I really wanted to scream, but that would only make it easier for her to achieve arousal. She just kept dragging my head in all directions and pressing so hard that my lips were pulled apart and I could feel slimy, wiry, hair across my teeth. She reeked a putrid smell, having no evidence of the prerinse from the bath we just took. She jerked a few times after she got enough and tossed me to the floor.

I grabbed my things and ran to her mother. All the while I thought she was on the phone, but there was no phone in sight. She had been mumbling to herself. And on the carpet next to the couch were three empty bottles of wine.

I wanted to go back to Cousin Perry's. I really feared the trouble I'd get into for getting my hair wet, letting that monster lick me, and for going outside late at night. Instead, I sat by the front door until morning came and I shot out the front door like lightning.

When Reese opened the door for me, I was shaking and crying. I told Reese the girl was nasty and did some things I did not want her to do to me. And Reese said if things were so awful, I should have come home. That made me feel completely responsible for what had occurred the night before. So, I never mentioned it again.

Beginning to make a comment on the sadness and confusion overcoming my face, Reese grabbed my chin, but then suddenly noticed my shriveled hair, "Ooh, yo momma gone have a fit when she see this hair! Do they have a pool over there?" All I could do is wave my head back and forth and the tears came falling down.

I could hear her trying to calm me down about my hair. But all I could think about was how afraid I was, the night before. I was raped. But my circumstances were like a stripper, in the movies, who accepts a ride home from a boozed customer, gets raped, but lets the guy sleep over out of fear he'd do something worse if she made him leave. Who would believe that stripper? Who would believe me?

I was glad when Momma came to pick us up. I wanted her to comfort me. My one wish was that she would listen to what had happened to me, and what was happening to me regularly. I didn't know how to tell her, or what she could do about it if I did. By the time I had gained the courage to let it all out, it was too late. She had come through the door with fury in her eyes. She smacked me across the face and started to pull me by the ear to the girl's house down the block. All the way there she was demanding I have a good apology.

I didn't know what reason Momma had to be so mad at me. I thought she would be disappointed, but certainly not force me to apologize to my attacker.

When the girl's mom opened the door she said, "There she is! Ran out of here before you thought I would notice huh? Well, no, honey. I count my liquor! My precious lil' girl told me how you polished off my last two bottles and tried to plant them next to me! You are no longer welcome as a guest in my home. And I hope Stevie finds you help for this little problem you have."

After sobbing through the most demeaning apology of my life, I felt so betrayed and hurt and alone. How could Stevie believe this woman? She was obviously twisted.

Mom Overboard

Being back home felt so good for Livia. She really missed the girls and her Guac. Sabrina held an unmovable spot in her heart. It was torture seeing her friend bandaged up and bound for surgery. She hated even more to have to leave only two days after Sabrina's surgery. But Olivia knew Sabrina was in good hands with Nurse Drake.

Once home, it was back to her busy schedule. It was back to cooking three meals a day, preparing countless snacks and lunches, ironing clothes, taking suits to the cleaners, mopping floors, sewing dresses, going to parent meetings, and submitting to Lawrence's needs. That last one she didn't mind so much. Lawrence did know how to handle things in bed. He always had something new to try between the sheets. He reminded her that, "When I am interested in something, I *does* my research. And please believe, I am into my Olivia on a regular, in more ways than one."

One major thing that needed tending to, was Maya's pageant. Yes, Livia is pageant mom and, no, she did not force Maya into it. As a young lady she tried pageants herself and had photos to prove it, but the one thing that kept her from that Miss America crown was lack of experience. Her start and end, in pageantry, was at the shy age of fourteen. Ollie wasn't as prim and proper as the other girls though. There was a smidge of arrogant behavior about her as well. Her infamous pageant speech was riddled with "know it all" notions and quips. Next time she'd know not to use Bradley Stone as help. Ollie's dad had written to her in a letter once, telling her that she was a ham. Having no idea what it meant, but understanding it was a compliment, she worked it into her speech.

Most the judges gave was a few laughs. And with the beatbox-rap as her talent there was no way she could have placed in the running for the coveted crown of Miss Talented Teenager. However, she was able to proudly walk away with scholarship money for maintaining the highest grade-point-average amongst the nineteen other girls. Now if it was called Miss Academic Teenager, that sparkly crown would have been just right for Ollie. Good thing the family took loads of pictures because that was the first and last pageant. It was really discouraging for her to continue. Her disinterest in the ideals of the pageant world, deterred her pageant career as a teenager.

Maya, though, popped out of the womb with the Miss-America-wave down pat. Both of Livia's daughters are the winners of any beauty pageant in her eyes. But Maya was a natural, without affectation. She had the height, the look, the poise and the talent. That little girl could sing. She was like a young Tina Turner.

She had incredible vocal skills and the confidence to match. Livia always made sure everything didn't go to Maya's head or take over her life at such a young age. Claire was passionate too, just in a different way. Claire was a diehard sports girl with her basketball obsession. Her early interest in basketball was the happiest moment for her father. He has been training her ever since she was four. She may not have gotten her daddy's height, but no one would refute her ability to handle a ball.

Lawrence had his passion to share with his baby girl, Claire, and Livia had hers with Maya. There were several pageants that Maya could have entered into. Some of the moms put their girls in two or three pageants at a time to maximize their chances of winning prize money for personal use. But Livia was not trying to pimp out her baby. All of the winnings went into Maya's personal account to be released to her as a college graduation gift.

Quite the future planners they were, and it was Livia's hope that the pageants would continually build Maya's confidence and social skills. Both parents agreed she could only do one pageant per year and, so far, she has been undefeated in her age group. She took home the crown for Little Miss Next at age four and five and if Livia could do anything about it, she would be winning this year for the sixes.

Livia really hoped she hadn't messed up Maya's chances of winning the pageant by being away from home to support Sabrina after the attack. Maya had lots of practicing to do and choreography to learn.

This year she'd be singing *If I Ain't Got You* by Alicia Keys. Maya got the idea that she would sing to her favorite teddy bear, Mr. Wendell. Her Great Grandmother, G.G., had flown all the way up from Texas to hand deliver the bear when Maya was born. Maya and Claire had a very short time with Lawrence's grandmother. G.G. passed away around the time Maya was turning two. Mr. Wendell had been stitched and re-stitched and through the spin cycle more times than anyone could count. He even had a dangling eye, but she loved him with every beat of her heart. No matter how many times Livia washed that thing, Maya always said it smelled like cinnamon. Their eyes welled up every time Lawrence and Olivia heard her say that because that's exactly how G.G. smelled. She was always making sweet potato pie with extra cinnamon.

Lawrence appeared in the doorway to the craft room where Livia had been focusing hard on the pageant details and jotting down random notes to herself to make sure she didn't forget anything. "Hey Liv." She jumped and dropped her notebook and pen to the floor.

"Damn, Baby, ha, ha, were you doing something you weren't supposed to?" Lawrence interrogated.

"No, I'm sorry, I was just making sure I have not been short-changing Maya on my time devoted to this pageant since I've been away checking up on Bri the past week."

"Yeah, I know. Hey, you are a great friend and an even better mother. You hear me? I just don't want you getting too stressed out. Why don't you call up your buddy, Palmer, and have her come help you with some of this stuff? You know this is right up her alley."

"It is, but she is so busy with her gallery and the boutique. I can handle it. But thank you for being helpful. I appreciate you looking out for me."

"Well, Liv, are you able to put the laptop down for one night? We need to be at Xavier's engagement party in three hours. You haven't even started getting ready. Grandma Sugar is on her way to stay with the kids while we're out. And before you turn your face all up, I'm pretty sure there's a hotel. It's going to be a long drive home. I know we're gonna wanna stay late and really have a good time. Plus, you deserve some unwinding time.

This is going to be a romantic evening in more ways than one. Throw some clothes in an overnight bag. And for one night, I'd like you to stop worrying so much."

Livia just sat there and tried to catch her breath for a moment. Lawrence gave her a smile, knowing he'd just left her speechless. Then he walked down the hall to finish getting the kid's things laid out for Grandma Sugar. Livia neatly put everything away so that it would be easy to come back to and pick up where she left off. She walked into her closet and pulled out a blue dress with the tags still attached. It was a gift that Lawrence bought her a year ago as an anniversary present. It was gorgeous and she loved it but didn't know when she'd get a chance to wear it. He just gave her a sweet kiss and said she didn't have to *go* anywhere, he just wanted to see her in it.

The dress was a faint teal. It molded to her frame in all the right places, clinging to her body and stopped just at the knee. She paired it with some killer rhinestone stilettos that had one gentle strap across the toe and one around the ankle, with a rhinestone encrusted heel.

With her outfit and jewelry laid out, she slid in the shower and made sure there was not a trace of hair on her body from the pits on down. She was preparing for two nights, one with close friends and one with her Guac. Her hairdo was simple. She slicked her curls into a bun, shellacked on the scalp, but messy on the bun part. Being the artist that she is, her makeup was done to perfection – modest but noticeable. She sprinkled her body with her signature perfume, moisturized with body butter, slipped into her dress and buckled her shoes just in time to hit the road.

Lawrence walked in the room looking dapper. He was holding her coat and had come to see if she was finished getting dressed. He had recently been growing out his hair so his curls could show. His haircut was tapered and lined just right. He had the barber leave a little of that Hollywood-trend stubble on his chin. Livia liked the way it felt against her skin. Framed by his freshly trimmed mustache were his lips looking smooth and soft.

Lawrence wore a multi-color plaid collar shirt paired with a crisp white tie, fitted grey vest with tailored slacks and a fresh pair of metallic grey oxford Ferragamo's on his feet. If they had stared at each other a moment longer, they would have missed the engagement party altogether. They walked downstairs, then through the family room on the way to the garage and kissed their kids, goodnight. They thanked Grandma Sugar and headed to the car.

An Engaging Opportunity

This was one of those nights when they could leave the family car at home and coast in something completely unkind to children. Lawrence let the Benz out of the garage, and they were on their way to Xavier's engagement party. It was a long drive and Lawrence wanted Livia to be in the mood for the whole evening. He had already downloaded a playlist for the drive. He mixed some of the best "bed you down" music from Teddy Pendergrass, Marvin Gaye, Luther Vandross, and Barry White, all the way to Jodeci, Prince, Case, Maxwell, 112, Usher, and even Trey Songz.

Lawrence was really excited for his friend, but his mind was on Olivia and their private afterparty. He wanted to get her to the hotel suite where there were no kids so he could tell Olivia, "Let's *turn off the lights and light a candle, you sexy little thing, if this world were mine I'd place at your feet all the things that I own*, so *let's get it on*, and I want you to *pump it back*, because I'm about make your *erotic city come alive*, and we'll be playing *sex games till the cops come knocking*, baby *we can do it anywhere, can you handle it - can I go there baby with you*, I want you to be screaming out to The Man Who *invented sex*."

But when he started his playlist, all he said to Olivia was, "Tonight, baby, all I want to do is make love to you. So, don't be surprised if I come up with an excuse to leave the party early."

She looked over at him, grabbed his hand, pulled it up to her lips to kiss it, then she locked her fingers with his and they rode, enjoying the playlist. Lawrence's hotel plans were not as casual as he led Olivia to believe. He had his friend Jordan prepare the room for him. Jordan did the favor for a pair of tickets to see Prince, the "artist formally known as...the artist formally known," at the Dome. And they were good seats, so Jordan hooked their room up. Lawrence knew Jordan would use the tickets to impress the newest lady in his life.

That playlist that Lawrence made included all the songs Livia loved. Livia was having a good time listening to songs she forgot she knew about. She was also thinking about what was on the menu at the party. She hadn't eaten since earlier that morning. As they came up to the neighborhood, Livia touched up her makeup and fussed with her bun a little bit. Lawrence stole a few kisses before she applied her lip-gloss.

He slowly cruised through rows of beautiful homes in the fancy neighborhood, looking for the right house. They finally arrived at the address from the invitation and inched their way up the valet line. At the front of the line, Livia tossed her gloss and powder back in her clutch and grabbed the hand of the valet who had opened her door and helped her out of the car. She took Lawrence's arm and they walked up the steps into Xavier's sister's home. Xavier's sister, Alana, was hosting the party.

Alana spotted guests arriving on the landing, "Hi, you guys! Come on in. So glad you could make it. Lawreeeeeeence! I haven't seen you since our senior year in college." She checked him out from head to toe, cleared her throat, and kept on talking, "Well, don't be shy. Give me a hug, Larry." She hugged him longer than Olivia was comfortable with. "And this must be the illustrious Olivia. I don't think I've ever had the pleasure."

"You *better never* had the pleasure," Livia said underneath her breath.

She stuck out her hand, "My name is Alana; I'm Xavier's big sister. What was that you said?"

Olivia gave a firm handshake. "I'm...ever...so pleasured! I said. To meet you, is also my pleasure. And just, Livia is fine."

"Great then, Livia. You guys, the coat and shoe check are right over there. You can go in socks, bare feet, or have the complimentary booties in the basket. Cute shoes Girl but wait 'til you feel this plush white carpet between your toes. It's amazing! Make yourselves at home!" Alana disappeared into the party and continued hosting. After their shoes were in check, they turned the corner and spotted Xavier and his fiancé at the end of the hall talking to family.

"Babe, remind me of her name again. Quick. Does her whole family speak English?" Livia was nervous about meeting new people. She had the tendency to say the wrong thing **and** say too much of it. Xavier's fiancé was Japanese and there was already an awareness of possible tension. This party was the first time he was meeting a lot of her family and friends. "Here they come. I'll introduce you."

"What's up **Flava Xav**!" Lawrence and Xavier immediately went into their homeboy lingo, giving dap and hugs like they didn't just see each other the weekend before. Lawrence dove right into telling his homeboy how proud he was of him taking such a huge step in his relationship. Livia was steady digging in her clutch for almost two minutes. There wasn't but five things in there, but she couldn't believe Lawrence forgot to introduce her that fast. She just told him she had forgotten the woman's name. Lawrence knew Olivia had a weird quirk about not wanting to ask people's names she had forgotten. It embarrassed her to forget names, but Lawrence lost many debates trying to convince her it would be more embarrassing to pretend like she remembered. This instance potentially was his chance to prove his point.

Olivia spoke to Xavier's fiancé out of nervousness, "It's really good to see you again Girl, tell me you name again." Livia reached out to give her a light hug. Lawrence looked at Livia out of the corner of his eye and smiled proudly at her brave choice. He looked back and Xavier and started asking where Jordan was in hopes that everything went well with hotel set up. Livia was on her own, afraid to put a foot in her mouth, but she kept talking, "Oh, and congratulations, Lady!" Livia spoke loudly then peeked out the corner of her eye and Lawrence did not budge. So, Livia used her sing-song voice to cover up her plunge, "Let's see the stone, Suzy."

Xavier's fiancé laughed, "Livia, stop playing. I know you didn't forget my name. You're so funny!" She raised her left ring finger. She had model worthy hands with perfectly manicured nails. Staring Livia in the face was this uncut, two carat canary diamond ring set solitaire on a yellow gold band sugar coated with baby white diamonds. It was gorgeous. It wasn't modest, but far from flashy. It was perfect and it looked good on her. They both stood there ogling the ring while the guys carried on with their one-week reunion. Then someone called out from the front room, "Mimi! I think your sister is here." Xavier's fiancé, Mimi, excused herself from the viewing of the ring and Livia was relieved. She gave Lawrence a sly look and he shrugged his shoulders and gave a silent chuckle then winked his eye. There was a sneaky suspicion that he purposely let Olivia struggle. Xavier ushered Lawrence and Olivia towards the direction of the dining area. Then he told them to grab a bite to eat, mingle and make themselves at home.

The house's décor could spark many a conversation. It was an attractive layout, although the designer's eye that Livia possessed questioned some of the style choices. There was a huge buffet of food spread out on a u-shaped table configuration. There were lovely Yūzen designed tablecloths and the food was served on golden platters. The tables were adorned with cherry blossom details. It was elegant and classy for what could have come off as cliché.

Lawrence did not eat or drink right away. Livia plopped a few choices of sushi rolls on her plate and snagged a glass of wine from the bar. She found Lawrence out on the beautiful patio sunroom. And that is not even giving it due diligence. Lawrence was already exclaiming about it before Livia could comment. He wanted to add one to their home. Livia stepped outside, onto a heated floor with formal seating in the center of the room. The ceiling and walls were completely glass. The room was the perfect answer to enjoying outdoors in the northwest, where it's not always dry and warm.

It was a romantic area with a clear starry sky. Soft music was being played through the speakers and the flicker of candles reminded Lawrence of his special night he had waiting for Livia back at the hotel. At the same time, he was a bit nervous that Jordan had not shown up to the party yet. Jordan had a history of flaking out and any other night, Lawrence would not have stressed. But this night was different. He wanted everything to be perfect for the woman he loved and adored.

Livia sensed that Lawrence had something on his mind. At first, she thought he was still heated from the flirtation in the car, but she wasn't sure. They were in the sunroom alone and he hadn't tried to make a move, so she decided it was nothing.

They continued through the rest of the house and eventually found their way back to one of the two sitting rooms where the two families were getting acquainted. Lawrence had burned through about two crudités platters and there was still no sign of Jordan and it was impossible for anyone to get reception in Alana's house. Finally, Lawrence decided to grab a glass of wine and get to know some of Mimi's people. Honestly, he really hadn't taken the opportunity to get to know Mimi.

Livia was getting bored out of her mind. All of Xavier's family were having their own mini-reunion and making indiscreet comments about Mimi's people. The children were running around wild and making Livia even gladder she left her kids with Grandma Sugar. People watching couldn't sustain her much longer, plus she was beginning to get sleepy sitting in the living room. Mimi's sister tapped Livia out of her daze and handed her a glass of champagne, "We're doing the toasts now," the sister mouthed.

Trying not to noticeably rub her eyes, Livia sat up straighter in her chair as she listened to the first toast given by Mimi's father. His words were eloquent and meaningful. Coming from a traditional man who had always thought his daughter would marry a Japanese man; he exhibited a lot of respect for Xavier in welcoming him to the family. Most of the room joined Mimi's father in silent tears as everyone toasted and passed the mic. Mimi's sister spoke of her fun times spent double dating with the newly engaged couple and shared some embarrassing stories of Mimi's childhood crushes.

Xavier's parents were still having a hard time accepting the mixed couple so his big sister, Alana, was there to fill many seats. She began her speech with a loving story of growing up with her brother and the many adventures they had trekked. It was a really sweet story of a sister's love for her baby brother. And then it turned hard left into a threat for Mimi to be sure never to hurt him and an insult as to all of the black women he could have chosen to be his wife.

The great thing is that Lawrence was nearby and grabbed the mic simultaneously giving the universal sign for "drunk" behind Alana's back. There was no applause for Alana, but rather a short chuckle at her expense right before Lawrence began his speech. Livia looked to her right and realized Jordan had finally arrived with his new dame.

Livia was shocked and happy at the same time. This girlfriend was four years Livia's junior, while Jordan was pushing forty. Jordan squeezed his way through the crowd to greet Livia. He hugged her and kissed her cheek, "Hey Lil' Mama. Good to see you. I know Xav and L are trippin' that I'm late. Had to make a stop first. You know how that is." Livia hugged back and kept her words short, not wanting to interrupt her man's speech, "If I'm Lil' Mama, your date over there must be Baby Girl, right?"

Jordan rolled his eyes and motioned for his date to join him. Lawrence spoke well for Xavier and gave props to Mimi. He did what anyone who really loved Xavier and respected his decisions would do. Xavier was clearly touched and gestured the mic towards Jordan who refused. His embarrassment of extreme tardiness must have given him stage fright, because Jordan is known as the most outspoken of the three. Glasses clanked and everyone was bottoms up and congregated in the dining area for the main course to be served.

Jordan's date woke Livia up and gave her someone to talk to. The food was delish! And Livia wanted to pile her plate up for round two and three, but definitely wore the wrong dress to have a poked-out belly. She felt that it was really time to get out of there and it was obvious that many of the guests had grabbed a new glass of champagne for each toast in addition to however many glasses of wine or beer they had consumed prior to.

Lawrence made his rounds before he and Livia headed to the car. He was sure to keep her arms warm while the valet brought their car around. He took his time driving to the hotel and once they arrived, he encouraged Livia to have a cup of coffee in front of the fire in the lobby while he pretended to have check-in problems for their room. She was unaware of the elaborate set up. He actually already had the key fob from Jordan and ran up to the suite. It was perfect. A pleasant aroma filled the room. There were fresh flowers everywhere and rose petals on the bed and bathroom floor. There were Belgian chocolates on the nightstand. On the counter there were ripe strawberries with a bowl of whipped cream and champagne – all chilling on ice. The box he entrusted with Jordan was sitting on the bed, wrapped with a huge purple satin bow.

He lit all the candles. The bathroom was beautiful, and the tub filled from the ceiling and along the wall, creating a waterfall effect. He lit the fireplace that split the glass wall between the bathroom and bedroom, and then he put a few drops of lavender and peppermint oils in with the bubble bath. Lawrence loaded his music, but this time it was a mix of his and her favorite jazz collections. No words, just melodic passionate sounds that played lightly through speakers in every room.

He found Livia in the lobby still enjoying the fireplace and coffee, "Hey, Honey, sorry I really thought they'd have lots of availability. I had to take the last room available." Lawrence attempted to deliver believable news.

"Guac, that's fine with me. We haven't had a getaway like this since before Salem. You have the key? Let's go up. It doesn't matter what the room looks like. I am here with you, Baby."

When she got to the room she was blown away. She began kissing Lawrence and softly punching him at the same time for setting her up. Each area of the suite she entered she was lit with fragrant candles.

She came to the bedroom last and opened up her box with the purple ribbon. It was the most beautiful purple, silk, nighty she had ever laid eyes on. Lawrence pulled it from in front of her body and placed it on top of the opened box. He slowly undressed Livia and led her to her spa bath.

"You are too good, Guac. This is almost like a honeymoon, but for one night and without the wedding preceding."

"Yes, I know it's not a special occasion, but I don't want you to think I need a special occasion to pamper my queen."

"Are you getting in too? There's room for one more." Livia suggested.

"I just want you to sit back and relax. Let me serve you." He told her. Lawrence got himself in a ribbed shirt and lounge pants before grabbing the strawberries, whipped cream, and champagne to bring into the bathroom for her. He hand-fed her the strawberries as they kissed and laughed together. They shared a glass of champagne. Then he brought in the chocolates for her to taste and lick off of his fingertips. He washed her hair and massaged her feet as they listened to smooth sounds.

As he rinsed her hair, he was so close to her body that she stole a kiss and wrapped her arms around him soaking his shirt. He whispered in her ear, "You are getting me all wet." Livia quickly replied, "Likewise." Lawrence lifted his arms away from her, stood up, and slightly undressed. He told Livia to take her time and get out when she was ready. Her nighty was lying next to her towel on the bench next to the tub.

When she unfolded her towel, she was a little too excited, "Babe! This towel is large enough to fit Big Poppa! It's like the one's Oprah uses." Lawrence did a small laugh to himself, "I know. I knew you'd like that. Now get dressed and come in here."

She tried to fight back her grin even though Lawrence knew when she was smiling. He didn't have to be looking at her. He was ready to go to a whole new level with Livia that night. Livia walked to the doorway and posed for her man before sauntering over to him and giving a little show.

"Tonight, Liv, I want to give you something I've never given you before." Livia couldn't figure out what he meant. They had shared everything together and had done everything together and their lives were perfect together. Perfect being a relative word.

The couple endured the occasional argument, disagreement, and periods of stubbornness. The bright side was that they always worked through their issues. They often prayed about their differences and always forgave each other to restore grace and understanding. For some reason, though, Lawrence wanted more.

She joined him in bed. They were both turned on before they even started to do anything. He had a firm touch that Livia couldn't resist. Lawrence's palms and fingertips were rubbing her in all the right ways. Their love was pouring out onto the sheets. Lawrence gave her and alluring look and took her up into his arms. Her breasts were against his lips and the heat from their bodies allowed her to slide down with ease.

Everything was right where it belonged. She held on and did not want to ever let go. Livia enjoyed the ride and Lawrence enjoyed giving it to her. The couple reached a high level of satisfaction before falling asleep in each other's arms.

BACK TO LIFE

I n the morning, they had breakfast in bed before they gathered their things to head home. Lawrence reminded Livia that he wanted to give her something. Once they loaded the car, he drove a little further south and cruised down a windy road. She realized they were under the gigantic bridge that connected the two cities. He knew she was curious to see how it would be under that bridge, but he didn't know why she had never gone.

With the car parked as close to the shore as they could get it, they got out and began walking near the rocks. There had been another car parked as well, but by the time Livia and Lawrence reached the dock and looked back, the car was gone. "I hope they don't think we came down here to get it on!" Livia laughed out loud. Then she became a bit more serious, "Did we?" She looked and Lawrence and he grabbed her close from behind and smiled on her cheek, giving her a half kiss. He was quiet, so she was too. They looked out and the ripples in the water and decided it was truly a beautiful scene. He was thinking about their life together, and she was, too.

Lawrence knew Livia wanted so badly to return to Southern California. He looked out and saw the lake, but he looked into her eyes and saw the ocean. He felt like this was the perfect time to let her know what he was thinking, but he wanted to sit down first. He tugged her hand to follow him closer to the lake so they could sit on the big rocks. She was reluctant but when he held her closer, she obliged. He found a rock that was directly under the bridge. Being down there made Livia feel so small and helpless.

She was so scared, but she didn't want to ruin the moment Lawrence was trying to share with her. All she could think about was that the bridge could come crashing down at any moment. The air was brisk, but Livia was beginning to perspire. At that moment she did what only Livia could do...opened her big mouth.

"Baby, don't take this the wrong way, but do you think Xavier and Mimi will ever have what we have? I mean what we have is so beautiful. I wouldn't change a thing about us and look at how long we have lasted and even with three kids. I mean, some people have one kid and can't take it and don't survive as a couple. But we have three and careers, well, I mean you have a career and I have my projects. You know. I just think they are getting married way too soon. I think they should hold off. It's like, I understand they are older, and they feel they know this is the right thing to do, but maybe you should talk to your boy. You know he looks up to you. I don't know. I may be speaking out of turn."

"Yeah, Babe," was all he said and then, "Let's get you back in the car. It's really nippy out here by the water and you know Grandma Sugar is tapping her foot by now and we have a long drive back."

Now Livia felt uneasy. She considered she quite possibly hurt his feelings. His words replayed back in her mind, 'Yeah, Babe.' Now she wondered did he mean, "Yeah, Babe you are totally right!" or "Yeah, Babe I will talk to him!" or "Yeah, Babe you *are* speaking out of turn." Livia did not want to ask. She feared she'd just make it worse. After the night they just shared, she was sure she did not want to have an awkward ride home or get the silent treatment when they got back. So instead of prying, she tried to let it be *water under the bridge*, so to speak.

And Lawrence was absolutely right. Grandma Sugar was ready to go. Not because she wanted to leave the kids, but because there was a huge sale and she liked getting to the store right when the doors opened so she didn't have to get all the stuff that was picked over. The kids always had a blast with their grandmother and knew that when she left, that the spoiled treatment would end.

But they loved Mom and Dad on any given day. They were not the "cool" parents or the "we're lazy so you can do whatever you want" parents. They were exactly what they were supposed to be – parents. The kids had structure and discipline and limits as well as rewards and allowances and all the love and attention they could stand.

It was back to life when they returned home. Grandma Sugar gave a positive report and was on her way to shop her heart out. Salem had just gone down for a nap, so Mom and Dad got to spend some quality time with Claire and Maya.

Mom and Dad weren't gone too long to be terribly missed. The girls filled their parents in on the great time they had with Grandma Sugar and showed off the pillow craft they made with her. The airspace between Lawrence and Livia was on the muggy side after the discussion they'd had by the lake.

Lawrence had to walk by Salem's room to get to his office and noticed his boy was not napping anymore. "Pick-a-up, Daddy," Salem sweetly commanded in his tiny voice when he saw his daddy peering in at him. Lawrence took his baby boy and the basket of toys to his office so that he could prepare himself for meetings he had, concerning The Academy. Salem was an easy baby and sat down while Daddy worked hard at his notes.

Normally Livia would write in the office nook out in the main hallway, but she really wanted privacy while writing. She decided to write in her workroom with the door closed. She cut on some Sade and got comfy in the sofa chair, centered in the corner near the bay windows.

She loved her chair. She did everything in that chair from reading books, to studying her Bible, to sleeping, to nursing Salem. And she had even shared it with Lawrence a time or two. After all, the chair was big enough for two. It had soft, caramel colored lamb skin on the inside with big armrests and a tall back. The chair had sturdy legs and the outer material was chocolate and tan zebra print, trimmed in copper studs.

The chair really inspired Livia a lot whether she was sitting in it or just admiring it from time to time. She got into just the right position with her feet perfectly propped up on her faux mink ottoman. She placed her laptop and its pad on her thighs and hoped she could write with a clear mind after feeling so terrible about insulting Lawrence about his best friend.

Chapter 4
I Like the Boys. I Like the Boys. I Like the Boys.

GROWING UP FOR me was like a full-time job. There was always so much going on in my mind. Being introduced to so much real life, so young, put my brain quite a few steps above the rest. I started my period right before I started the sixth grade. And my mood swings were as crazy as could be. Like I said before, Kelpie backed off from me a couple of years back. For some reason it was like he had some unnatural infatuation with me. It was like, to him, I was not his sister. I was some girl he was on the hunt for.

Time and time again he would make inappropriate remarks or try and persuade me to have sex with him by saying it would help him burn calories. Other times he would try to cop a feel. One day I pulled a knife on his ass. He called Momma so fast. Ha! I had him scared then. He was the one running and crying to Momma for a change. He wasn't sure if I'd actually stab him or not and, hell, neither was I. I told him to keep his filthy hands to himself.

I had my own agenda and my own life to deal with. I was in middle school and even though I was the smallest catch in the lake, didn't mean I wasn't the feistiest. Don't get me wrong. I wasn't one of those girls that just turned into a fast little hoochie momma, opening legs to anyone that passed by.

I believed in God at a very young age. I honestly believe that is why I never took my own life after all I had been through. I valued the life He gave me, and I actually valued the virtue of chastity. Just because I held value in those things didn't mean I mastered healthy boundaries. My attackers did penetrate me. But in my heart and in my spirit, I wanted my virginity back. I believed virginity was a gift. My ability to give that gift freely was taken from me. That loss contributed to my unhealthy relationship choices. I developed a strong sexual desire that was hard to control. I liked the boys.

For some reason the boys did not really like me. It was not about my appearance. They all snuck a look when they had the chance. It was the mature way that I would talk to them, like we were in college and not in middle school. Those mature topics would make them take off screaming. All they wanted to do was to squeeze my booty or even get a peck on the lips. I wanted more. I wanted a relationship. So, I had to skip over all of the sixth-grade boys as well as the seventh-grade boys and head directly to the eighth-grade boys.

I liked those boys and they liked me. They were taller, smarter, and more comfortable talking about relationships. The only thing is that *I* was not as smart as I thought when it came to boys. It took me quite a few runs to realize they liked me, not because of me, but because I was young and naïve and would believe that they really loved me. I got my heart broken many times in middle school.

I would be walking to the eighth-grade hall to bring my "so called" boyfriend a sweet treat. And there he would be, in the eighth-grade lounge, kissing and hugging on his actual girlfriend. This exact scenario happened to me twice! I cried each time. I was surprised each time. I was hurt each time. But I still didn't give up. I knew that there was no way **all** of the eighth- grade boys could be like that. Right?

Well, it didn't matter that I wasn't giving up. They gave up on me. It got around to the whole school that I was a huge cry baby, and no one wanted to deal with that. It didn't matter though. Most of those boys just wanted sex. They settled for heavy kisses behind the portables and I began to explore with my tongue. Whoa. Whoa! Before you go there, *"No. I never. No."* There were no "BJ's" coming from me. Sor-ry. My tongue didn't go below the neck. I was good at ear nibbling and the boys went crazy over it.

Then there came the day I was in seventh heaven. Really, I was just in the seventh grade, but it felt like seventh heaven. The most beautiful specimen of a human being got transferred to my school. This eighth-grade god was the definition of gorgeous! He was tall and slim. He was like all of my middle school crushes put together. He was Tevin Campbell, mixed with Usher, mixed with Ralph Tresvant, with the height and body of Kobe Bryant, and the complexion of a perfect latte. He glowed like an angel. His curly afro tapered to a clean fade that touched his neck so perfectly.

Does it even matter what his name is? He should have been named Heaven. The first student he laid his big brown eyes on, happened to be me. His dimples and straight white teeth captured my attention. Based on his smile, he appeared to like what he saw in me, too. Regardless of the fact that my mouth had to be hanging open and possibly drool slipping off my lip from the fact that he was even talking to me. He was not shy in the least. He needed someone to help him find the classes on his schedule. And I was a more than eager escort.

He assumed I was an eighth grader. I was so familiar with the eighth-grade hall and teachers, but I just wanted to be close to him. My visitor from heaven was 15 and I was 13. So, the downside to all his beauty is that he lacked focus. He didn't have enough credits to graduate from the eighth grade on schedule. He was too embarrassed to go back to the same school to repeat his essential courses to graduate, so his dad encouraged him to find a school where he didn't know anyone and could get his work completed before being transferred to high school. If he weren't so stubborn, he could have been in high school already, but it took him a whole semester to decide he was going to leave his mom in Colorado to move to Washington with his dad. No matter how long the delay, it was definitely to my benefit.

After a day of getting him acquainted with his new school and me, I got it hashed out with the office not to chart my tardies for the day. It turned out fine since the office thought he was coming the following week and hadn't appointed a student-ambassador to him yet. Before school was out, he asked for my number and scheduled a phone date with me, for later that night. Stevie made sure Kelpie and I had our own phone line so we wouldn't interfere with her calls. We didn't just have a special ring and special voice mail; we had a totally different phone number not connected to her line at all.

Stevie got promoted to Night Shift Supervisor at the hospital. Her bigger paycheck moved us into a house. Accepting the promotion meant Stevie had to leave us home alone at night. For me, the promotion meant finally having my own room and my own space. It was still technically a two-bedroom place, but upstairs there was a completely finished attic. That became Kelpie's room and he loved it. At first, I was jealous because he had the same square footage as the entire house, just a shorter vaulted ceiling and no door. All he had was a doorway at the bottom of the stairs where Stevie put up a curtain for privacy. There was no way to knock to alert someone coming up, so the rule was that if the curtain was open, we could freely enter. This was an important rule for me because our phone line was hooked up in his room and Momma refused to spend the money on getting us a cordless phone.

It didn't bother Kelpie too much to share a phone with me because he was gone all the time or in the den playing with his Nintendo. This particular night, I was glad he was at the mall with his friends. His curfew was 10pm which gave me until 9:59pm to be on the phone with my new sweetie and not have him up in my business.

I usually talked on the phone while he was away if it was with a guy because he would be all up in my business saying, "It's my room! I can sit wherever I want to." And where he wanted was right beside me so he could take back what he'd heard, to Stevie.

Momma never got between frivolous feuds with us. We had to work it out ourselves. I guess that was good in some ways. I didn't want Momma saying anything to me about being on the phone all night. Right after I got home, I helped get dinner together, picked out my school clothes for the following day and did my geography lesson. Momma left for work after we ate dinner. Kelpie was still out with his friends. I took a hot shower and made sure I smelled good for my phone date with my beau.

Hearing his voice over the phone was like licking melted chocolate from between my fingers. It felt forbidden. His voice was deeper than most. He knew so much, and I enjoyed listening to him tell me stories about being in Colorado with his cousins and friends.

It seemed like we had exchanged life stories in one day, but of course I left out some of the hard details of my past. Or maybe I just forgot. I think I somehow had to force my brain to block it out so that I could function like a normal person. Anyway, this guy could sense my maturity. I finally told him I was a seventh grader. I didn't want him to start wondering why he would hardly see me in the eighth-grade hall unless it was to visit him.

He said that me being in the seventh grade explained why I was so short. I laughed hysterically at his joke and almost let out a snort. He was so easy to like. I was hooked. When it was time to get off the phone, I made up this rule that in Washington state, if a girl and a guy talk on the phone the first day they meet, they have to give a kiss through the phone to establish the instant connection.

I almost couldn't believe I was saying that to him, but more over I couldn't believe he bought it. But, hey, he is held back currently so some things have simple explanations. He kissed me through the phone, and I felt it. I dreamt about him and that kiss all night.

We were an instant item, holding hands at school all the time. We walked each other to class, and he walked me home after school. Stevie thought he was cool because she didn't know he was fifteen. Kelpie didn't really care. My boyfriend thought that was cold hearted but didn't let it bother him and stayed out of Kelpie's way.

I tried not to show how much I cared because I knew it probably wouldn't last. He was a young man, not a grown man, so he missed his mom. His dad wanted him to at least stay for the summer, but that wasn't going to happen. He told me that he would miss me and that he would write me every week, but I wanted more. I felt like he was really an angel. He was like some perfect human that came down to earth to make me feel worthy. He was a temporary pick-me-up. I promised myself that when it came time for him to move back to Colorado, I wouldn't be mad, but that I would be happy because he touched my life for a short time.

The eight-grade class always had a winter formal dance the week before break. They were allowed to bring underclassmen because sometimes the parents would make their son or daughter bring their little brother or sister so they could get good photos and get both kids out of the house for an evening. The school staff chaperoned the dance each year and it was given at the school. The event started at 6pm and was over at 9pm. They had dinner catered. My school was the only school in the district to have this type of party so many of the students invited friends that were from another school. Needless to say, it was a huge party.

It was the perfect way for me and my guy to celebrate his departure. My only roadblock was that Stevie wouldn't let me go. Actually, I didn't even ask her. If I did, this is how it would go: (–Momma, can I go to the dance with my beautiful angel come down from heaven? –Ollie, I will have to talk to his father.) Boom. And there goes the dynamite.

If Stevie talked to his dad she would find out he was fifteen and that he was really supposed to be a freshman and that I lied about his age and then she'd say that older boys want more than I can give and then she'd say he'd try to take advantage of me since he was leaving. Well, I didn't want to have that fight so I lied some more.

Kelpie was gone. He was out with his friends racing go-karts, as they did most Fridays. Stevie had to work. After my scary experiences with sitters, Stevie realized Kelpie and I were better off home alone, along with the fact that we were getting older. Momma knew Kelpie would be home by 10:00pm. In our new neighborhood, we had become close friends with the people living next door. They had an 18-year-old daughter who was home most of the time with her new baby. She took a liking to me and would check on me anytime I had to be home alone. Sometimes I'd go over and help her with the baby.

I had it all planned out. I told my neighbor what the deal was. She knew all about my "visitor from Heaven" and she was prepared to cover for me if anything went wrong with me sneaking out to this dance. I was cuddled in bed and pretending to watch a movie with my head scarf on when Momma came in to kiss me goodbye. I really felt guilty for lying to her, but it was worth it. This would be my last night to see him before his flight back to Colorado.

Once the coast was clear for a full five minutes, I jumped out of bed, combed out my hair and smoothed out my dress. I was in a pretty pink dress that Bradley Stone, my estranged father, had sent me when he was supposed to be getting married. Stevie refused to let Kelpie and me go, but I kept the dress. And this was the perfect time to wear it.

I acted like it was going to be my wedding, to my beau. School wasn't very far from home and thank God it was not raining because I had nothing to cover me up. I had let him know I would be late because I take so long to straighten my hair. He was waiting out front for me. I felt so bad for missing the dinner part and I could hear the DJ playing, "Tootsie Roll." I wanted to show my moves on the dancefloor, but my boyfriend had another idea.

We snuck past the doors to the cafeteria where the party was being held. The chaperones at the front were on a potty break. Lucky us. He pulled me outside and took me to the stairs of the gymnasium. I had to go up a few steps to reach his lips for our secret kiss. He still was so tall that it was hard to kiss for a long time, so he lifted me onto the railing of the stairs. I didn't even realize what I was doing but I noticed that, all of a sudden, my legs were wrapped around him. I felt like things were moving fast but I was half-way to my fourteenth birthday and the fourteen-year-olds that I knew were doing far more than I had ever tried.

We were kissing and rubbing and hugging and nibbling back and forth. His pelvis was pressed against mine. I knew there was no way that I could be the first girl he ever kissed, and I was wondering would he be the first boy that I gave my gift to. My gift was something I had cherished. I wanted to know the feeling of giving myself to someone willingly. We were in a deep lip-lock.

The time between his pants being buttoned to being dropped around his ankles had passed without my awareness. I felt the softness of his fingertips lifting up my dress. I released from our kiss. A gush of wetness came that almost made me think I was going to pee on myself. But this was not that. I pressed my lips back against his, but we both froze when we heard the cafeteria's side doors slam open.

***

Livia jumped as her door slammed open. She almost dropped the laptop to the floor. Ending the game of hide and seek, the girls came running in and shouting, "She's in here! Daddy Pop we found her! We found her." Livia smiled, laughed, and put down her laptop so the girls could both hop into the chair. Salem inched around the corner too, gripping the wall as he gained confidence in walking. Livia could hear Lawrence's feet, padding in from not far behind. She looked at the girls and said, "What is this all about?" Claire blurted out, "Daddy Pop said you were playing 'hide and seek' and he couldn't find you." Claire took a few breaths, "So, we found you!" Maya chimed in, "He wasn't looking hard enough, huh Mommy?"

Claire did most of the talking, "Daddy said we could go get frozen yogurt if we found you before he did. Let's go, Mommy. Put Salem's shoes on." Livia looked up at Lawrence who was standing in the doorway now and holding Salem. He smiled at her and gave her a wink. That was how he said, "Sorry", "I love you", "I want you", and "Give me a break." Everyone got up and got all of their shoes and jackets on. The kids loved getting frozen yogurt.

When they got in the car Livia played the instrumental to Maya's song. "Practice your song, Baby. I know Grandma Sugar did not have you practice. It's only two weeks until the pageant." As Maya sang, everyone in the car swayed along and gave "oohs" and "ahhs" when Maya sang the tough notes.

Maya didn't sing it better than Alicia, but she did change the arrangement a little bit to make the song her own. The pageant judges championed originality. They always looked for something special to stand out in the talent portion of the competition. They really looked for spark and flare in all the portions of the competition.

Livia felt like it was too close to dinner time to be having a treat, but she knew Lawrence was trying to create peace in the family. They were raised in settings that differed from each other and that was most of the cause for their disagreements. They decided to take the kids to the indoor sand lot where they frequented on rainy days. After having frozen yogurt, they could burn off their treat and work up an appetite for dinner.

While the kids played, Lawrence snagged a couple beach chairs and two sodas so he could talk to Livia about the disconnect that morning. This time it was Lawrence who did most of the talking and explained to her that he did recognize where she was coming from on the marriage of Xavier and Mimi. He explained that at times, she would have to let others make their own decisions, be them right or wrong.

"Sweetie, we are doing good now and no one will say anything bad about our family dynamics, but you were still finishing college when we got pregnant with Claire. We have very little room to judge. You know Xavier is like my brother and I will always support him, whether I agree or not."

Livia clenched her teeth and listened to the lengthy lecture. All along she knew he was right. She felt horrible for speaking out of turn about Xavier's relationship. She agreed with Lawrence, apologized, and found a way to segue the topic to the pageant for Maya and a birthday party for Claire. They got some solid ideas noted down and once the kids had been playing for close to an hour, they were all ready to go back home.

Livia immediately started dinner while Lawrence had the girls get cleaned up and into their pajamas. Livia still did not like the idea of siblings taking baths together after the age of two. Although Maya and Claire were both girls, Livia insisted on them bathing separately.

Claire, wanting to be more like a big girl, would take a

shower. The girls had their own bathroom. It was decorated in deep shades of mango orange and watermelon green. The accessories were stars and rainbows, which the girls loved. The water was running in Lawrence and Livia's tub so that Maya could take her bath in their room while Lawrence got all the kids' bedclothes together with Salem in tow. Picking out a pair of footie pajamas for Salem was easy. He got washed up and before long, Salem was smelling fresh and clean with loads of baby lotion and powder. The girls dressed themselves and Maya shuffled behind Claire to follow the smell of Livia's famous smoked salmon and mushroom fettuccini.

The girls sat quietly, and Salem was clinging to his daddy. "Should we have done dinner first?" asked Livia. "You all look like you are about to pass out." All she got was a couple nods and grunts. They did eat and very shortly after the kids had all gone to bed.

"Honey, that pasta was hittin'! You hooked that up. As always. Do you get your recipes from Sabrina or does she get them from you?" he giggled. "Anyway, I refilled the bath and it is all ready for you." He got close to her face, "There are the bubbles and oils you like in there. It's kinda like the hotel. You deserve it. Don't worry about the kitchen. I'll clear the table and clean up. Go ahead and relax."

And she took advantage of that offer while he hand-washed some dishes and loaded the dishwasher with the others. Once the kitchen was sparkly clean, he stepped in the shower in the guest bathroom near the entryway and wrapped a towel around his waist when he was done. He poured two glasses of wine and treaded lightly past Salem's room. Passing Livia's workroom, he peeped lighting coming from the laptop. He noticed that it had started a scan and was prompting a reboot so the updates could take place. Patiently, he hit the button, took a seat, and waited for it to cut back on so that he could log her off and shut it down properly. The time must have zoomed by because he was still sitting there thirty minutes later, reading her story. Livia grew tired of waiting and came hunting her prey, wondering what could be spicier than their warm bed.

Her eyes blinked and she began to feel a wave of heat come across her forehead as she watched him reading her naked work. "Lawrence! Are you reading my stuff?!"

"Baby! At first...I was just doing the scan. I mean scanning for viruses."

"That scan doesn't take that long. Then what?"

"I didn't read it."

"What do you mean? Lawrence. You are sitting here, reading my private stuff."

"Okay. I am sorry I read it, but if you wanted to keep it private, why didn't you close it and password protect it?"

"So now it's my fault? Should I keep a lock on my journal too just in case I leave it on your side of the bed one day and you just happen to read ten pages while you carry it back to my nightstand?!"

"Look. Look. I am sorry. I messed up. I should have asked. Yes, I did read it. I just thought you were turning this into another one of your silly hobbies. I didn't know you would be writing a whole book."

"Excuse the fuck out of me! Are you serious right now?! I cannot believe this! Me keeping your house and your kids together a silly hobby too? Me decorating and creating gowns? Is that silly? Oh, me cooking gourmet meals for my family. That must be silly too. This was my homework from counseling and it's really helping. Did you forget Dr. Luke was *your* idea?!"

"You know that is not what I am saying Olivia! I just thought you needed to write to get some things out of your system. I did not think you were serious about making it a book. That's all! I was wrong!"

"Well, you can seriously stop talking to me right now! You are dead ass wrong!"

Livia stormed out of her workroom. Lawrence felt awful. Despite the argument about her ability to stick to one thing, Lawrence was proud and impressed by her dedicated writing. Livia was fuming, but deep inside she was glad to have an opinion posed about her writing. She was unsure whether she should research getting an agent or if she was in fact just writing to get some things out of her system.

After a few days had passed, and she refocused her attention on Maya's pageant. She had forgiven Lawrence and he agreed to ask before doing anything like that again.

✳ ✳ ✳

They finally found parking at the Tacoma Arena. Salem was with Grandma Sugar and Claire came along for support. Maya had suitcases and hanging bags full of her gowns and costumes as well as props and accessories. She had a lemon-yellow gown for her opening wave. With that dress she wore the straight wig with a side part. The curly wig was for the talent portion so that she could bounce with personality while singing her song and dancing in circles with her bear. There was a purple gown and a pink gown in case they spotted someone with a duplicate. All the girls had to bring their issued uniform for the group routine and Maya wore the pigtails wig for that.

Mirrors, outlets, and tables were set up for the girls to share. Livia kept a close eye on Maya's things. Moms and other participants had been known to sabotage and steal. Maya had jewelry and eyelashes and makeup. She had shoes and her music and spray tan. She didn't need the color, but she wanted to glow. Her mom bought the spray tan with body shimmer.

Each girl was given a couple minutes on stage to go over blocking. Maya became nervous when she saw that most of the girls had coaches.

"Mommy why didn't you hire me a coach?"

"Haha. Aw, honey, I'm your coach."

She had never asked for a coach before and had never needed one, but she was older this year and nerves were getting the best of her. Lawrence stepped in and gave her that last minute pep talk before show time.

Lawrence and Claire stayed backstage while she got prepped for her first appearance and then they took their seats. Livia stayed behind to do all of the costume changes and prepare Maya for each section. She also packed extra snacks for Maya.

"Mommy, I really wish Grandma Sugar could be here!"

"Me too, Baby, but you know these events are too much for Salem and Grandma Sugar still does not agree with these pageants, so they have to keep each other company."

"Well, maybe I should pick something that Grandma Sugar likes so that she can be proud of me."

"Maya Jane! We are all proud of you! Especially Grandma Sugar. She would want you to do whatever made you happy."

"Okay, Mommy, I'm ready to win this thang!"

They slapped hands and gave a tight hug. Right after she got Maya set in her first outfit, she ran out to seating to get an audience view. The stage managers were familiar with the girls and their routines and directed them on to the stage at the right times. Livia always got a special workout this time of year from all the running back and forth from backstage to audience and back again between each set, but she didn't mind it.

Maya nailed her routine and hit all the right notes. Her dresses had great glitz and her wigs were styled to perfection. This year the prize for 1st place was $500 cash, a laptop, and a Toy Store shopping spree. All the girls in Maya's category were lined up and Maya was dressed in her purple dress with white Mary Jane shoes and white socks with ruffle. Livia put the big curly wig on Maya's head to make sure her crown would fit just right, and she was now waiting in her seat with the rest of the family to congratulate Maya. Lawrence was recording because Maya liked to look back and watch her winning reaction.

Maya would practice her surprised face in the mirror at home. Since she always won the pageants, she wanted to make sure she always looked genuinely grateful and amazed at her winnings. Not that she was trying to come off as being a faker, but she didn't want the other girls to think that they didn't stand a chance against her. Judge Anderson announced the third-place prize to Allie Holmes. Allie took home a 3rd place sash and trophy, as well as a $100 cash prize and a complete Pocket Dolly play set.

Next for 2nd place was Jade Jones. She took home a sash, trophy, $250 Amazon gift card, and a shiny new bike with the works – helmet, pads, streamers and horn. Maya watched these two girls as they jumped around and screamed with delight for their winnings. Maya decided she was going to display a quieter reaction to her winnings. First, she was going to lift her eyes up to make sure she heard her name. Then she was going to cup her hands over mouth and nose. And lastly, she would drop her hands to her side, shake them out, gain her composure, and then slowly walk up to receive her crown with her award-winning smile.

Maya's family was ready too. Lawrence had the camera zoomed in on Maya's face. Claire and Livia held hands. They had her bouquet ready. Judge Anderson also had a bouquet ready. On top of the cash, laptop, and the shopping spree, they gave the ultimate winner a bouquet of two dozen pink roses.

The lights in the Arena dimmed and there was a spotlight on Judge Anderson. And when he called out Maya's name, she just knew that a spotlight would shine on her as well. Judge Anderson spoke in a slow calm voice, "And our 1st place crown goes to...winning the ultimate prize...and newly added this year, the Toy Store shopping spree, thanks to our new sponsors who have also provided $50 gift cards to ALL of our participants...so girls, remember you all did amazing, everyone is a winner...our

1st place goes to...let me get this tricky envelope open...it's really sealed...Ha ha ha...Little Miss Brittney Ford! Brittney Ford everybody!"

When the light brightly shined on Brittney, she curtseyed and waited for the crowning. Maya was crushed! After all, Brittney simply recited a poem for her talent portion and wore her *own* hair throughout the entire pageant.

Maya really wanted a recount. Lawrence shut off the camera and immediately ran to Maya to pick her up and comfort her. Livia sunk low in her seat, thinking about how Maya worked incredibly hard on the routine.

Livia allowed Maya ample father daughter time while she gained composure. She then walked over to embrace Maya and gather her belongings from backstage.

Once everything got loaded in the car, Lawrence got behind the wheel. They took off for a long silent ride home. On the way home, one of the other mothers, familiar with them from other pageants, texted Livia. And it read:

[Sorry Girl. I really think your baby should have won. My daughter is good, but we all know she can't hold a note the way Maya can, so we don't mind 3rd place. Anyway, my cousin knows one of the judges through a friend of hers and that judge, I can't say their name, but that judge said that this Brittney girl has been winning a lot of pageants! She is way from Eastern Washington. She has been going all over state and word has been getting out about her. The judges like her because she is new and different. They have seen dancing and singing, and all the instruments played. This whole poem thing is really winning it for this girl. They are categorizing her as "The Actor." Well, anyway, I thought you'd want to know that. See you at the next one, Girl!]

Lawrence pulled through the drive-through closest to their house, hoping Maya would have an appetite by now. Happy Meals always cheered her up. Not today. Livia wasn't really in the mood to eat much either. Livia just ordered a coffee knowing she would have to be up late with Salem. Grandma Sugar usually allowed Salem to nap all day. She had a special song she would sing and no matter what time of day, it could make him doze off. Claire wanted to band together with her sister. She felt really bad for her, except her stomach was growling. She and her dad had only shared a Cola and large popcorn at the Arena. Claire ordered the nuggets. Lawrence ordered nuggets too.

Maya stared out the window. When they got home, she let her mom take her makeup off. Normally all of the makeup and clothing and wigs got put away at the end of the pageant, but Maya wanted to leave that place immediately.

Once her face was clean and her wig and gown were taken off, she pulled on a night gown and got into bed. After Claire finished eating, she got cleaned up and dressed in bed clothes, too. She climbed next to Maya in bed and cuddled with her sister that night.

Lawrence followed Claire's routine before going to find Livia. She was playing around with Salem in the middle of the living room floor, letting him tumble and roll all over her.

"Honey, let me take Salem and put him in the playpen with some toys. I'd like to speak with you in our room for a moment."

"Okay...that's fine I guess," answered Livia.

When Lawrence walked back to their room where Livia was waiting, he pulled the door shut behind him. He began speaking very passionately, but at a low enough level not to alarm the kids.

"So now do you see why my mom doesn't like this stuff?! I hate to see our daughter feeling this way. You push her to do what you couldn't do and now she is hurt. She sings a song for every pageant. You know I've begged you to let her do some poetry or a monologue. Yes, yes, I got that same text you did! That lady practically texted every parent today! This is it, Liv! You goin' on trips to see your friends, you're spending time designing homes for other people, making gowns for these high school girls, and on top of all of that you're now writing every minute of the day. I was surprised to see you even playing with your son, to tell you the truth. Be a mom and not a roommate!" Lawrence paused for reaction.

"Who the hell do you think you are, Lawrence?! You are in support of the pageant until our daughter loses?! You could have put in extra time practicing with her as well. You're always doing stuff with The Academy. Isn't that why you hire people to run the school for you? So, you don't have to be there so much? You are not those boys' father! Show up to their games and support them. Fine. But you don't have to still coach! And, you know what, thanks for all your support in me writing my book. You know you can try spending some time being my partner in all of this instead of being Judge Livingston. They got enough middle aged black male judges on television. We don't need another." Olivia scoffed.

Livia got up from the bed and pushed Lawrence out of her way, oblivious until down the hall that her little tiny shove, knocked Lawrence back into the dresser. He was a big guy, but her push was so surprising to him that he lost his footing. At first Livia felt bad for pushing him and she almost turned back to apologize but her pride was too strong. It won over.

She stopped by the kitchen and grabbed the fresh tub of her famous celebratory guacamole, the whole bag of chips, and stormed down to the den. She turned to the made-for-TV, movie channel and stuffed the entire tub of guacamole and chips down her belly as she watched.

Lawrence had been left upstairs in a fuzz. He was not really sure how to handle what just happened. After a reflective moment, he thought about how long Salem was left playing alone, and then rushed to give him attention. He found Salem cozied up with his big bear, feet propped up against the mesh walls of the playpen, snoring away. It looked as though Grandma Sugar did not let him sleep all day after all. He got Salem out of the playpen and secured him in his comfy crib and kissed him goodnight. He started cleaning up the floor in Salem's room and in the midst of toys was Salem's First Baby Bible. There was a scripture about God's grace and mercy on the cover, and Lawrence felt led to pray.

Lawrence had been praying for a while and felt like asking not only God's forgiveness for the way he came at Livia, but for hers also. In the girls' room Claire was half in bed and half on the floor when Lawrence came to check on them. He lifted her into her own bed and kissed each of the girls on their foreheads before going downstairs to check on Livia.

He walked downstairs into the den and didn't know if he should laugh or be upset with what he set his eyes on. Olivia had fallen asleep on the sofa, dreaming about the last passage she wrote:

✳✳✳

"Olivia Stone!!! Get your fast ass down here right now!" I knew it couldn't be good to hear the cafeteria doors slam open while I was making out with a boy, but the last person I expected it to be was Stevie. Stevie walked up to me and slapped my eyes crooked.

She almost slapped my angel, which now I was starting to think of as my naughty devil.

But instead of slapping him she said, "I have already called your father, little boy, and he's about two minutes behind me."

Still I cannot decipher whether Momma walked me out around the perimeter of the school to save me the embarrassment or to save her own. Without Momma noticing, I looked back to check on my angel.

I didn't know what else was going to happen to me yet, but from the looks of it I could tell my angel should have pulled his pants all the way up before his father got there.

His dad was whooping his bare butt. I quickly snapped my head back front and continued walking with Momma. Momma's punishment was too harsh to ever be spoken of again. Let's just say the next time I attempted to open my legs to a boy, I made certain Stevie was far, far away.

WEDDING BLISS or WEDDING PRISS

He tried to quietly walk downstairs to the family room and let Livia know he was coming in peace. But the way she was snoring would have taken more than some heavy footing to wake her. He couldn't help but to burst out laughing. She still didn't budge; garnished with guacamole hanging off her lip as she snored.

There were chip crumbs scattered about as if the chips were live prey. Livia's left hand was tucked neatly in her waistband. The TV flickered with scenes of *after dark* movies. She and Lawrence lacked opportunities to connect as often as they'd desired to with all of the latest situations getting in the way.

Lawrence removed the bowl of empty guacamole from her lap and balled up the bag of air that used to contain chips. She licked the food from her lip and smiled and turned over. "This girl is still sleep!" Lawrence breathed out. He sat down next to her and just watched for a moment. He could never understand how she could sleep so hard. But he admired this woman who still took his breath away after so many years. In his eyes, all he could see was beauty every time he looked at her. It didn't matter if she was asleep, drooling, farting, or snoring. It didn't matter if she was 40lbs heavier while pregnant with each child. He thought it was kind of cute to see her with some meat on her bones. With her being so short, she looked extra thick and he rather liked that. But after each child she snapped her body back into shape within months. Skinny or chubby, he loved him some Livia.

"Baby! Wake up. Can we talk?" Lawrence pleaded. Livia grumbled some unrecognizable jargon and rolled over. This roll almost had her face plant on the rug. Lawrence gently grabbed her arm. She let out a huge gasp as she opened her eyes and saw carpet. "I'm right here; I got you. I always got you." Lawrence comforted her. She looked up at him and started crying.

"Lawrence, you don't have to say a thing. I agree with what you said. You are right and I was wrong. Grandma Sugar was right about the pageants, too. Once or twice was enough. If she didn't think it was so important to us, Maya might have stopped a while ago."

Lawrence carried Livia back up to their bedroom. She basically weighed as much as the girls put together and he carried the both of them often. But this was a romantic carry. He gently settled her on their bed and wiped the rest of the food off her face. When he stepped in the closet to change his clothes, she grabbed a swig of water from the nightstand and tried to straighten her hair a little. He came out the closet in some briefs. Livia pulled back the sheets for him to join her in bed and they both enjoyed making up until sunrise.

Several weeks had passed where things were actually normal at the Livingston house. It had been peaceful. There were no homes to be decorated. No dresses to be made. Livia hadn't even been to visit Sabrina. Sabrina was doing well. She would frequently video chat with Livia and the kids from New York and Paris as she was getting her restaurants established. Livia had even slowed down writing. She set up writing appointments with herself to give Lawrence and the kids more of her time. Coach Livingston had a break from coaching and had more time with the family as well. And with The Academy being on break, he only needed to spend a few hours in occasional meetings.

But the wedding of Xavier and Mimi was near. Lawrence was pumped for his friend. Livia just loved seeing her man in a tux. When they arrived at the venue that weekend, reality set in. Xavier was finally getting married. Rehearsal day was overcast, nothing new for the Great Northwest. Livia was quizzical of the fact that anyone would have an outdoor wedding in Washington state, because of all the rain.

To her amazement, the wedding day was perfect. It was 78 degrees with wispy, thin, white clouds feathering the sky. There was a gentle breeze causing fluttering leaves. Wooden bento boxes filled with fruit jellies held the programs down in each seat. Getting married in a botanical garden saved lots of money on décor. The landscape was a visual gift. A grand tent was set up with lights and seating for the reception and a gazebo was equipped with a D.J., for dancing.

Livia was questioning her shoe choice, although she looked hot in her Alexander McQueen's. There were enough paved pathways not to sink into the grass. The issue was she'd already been in the shoes for three hours. She and Lawrence had already been at The Westin for the traditional Shinto ceremony Mimi's parents insisted on, so her feet were beginning to throb. Livia wanted to fast forward to cocktail hour. Weddings were not on her top ten list of favorite things to do. Her philosophy was – call the pastor, get a Bible, grab a few witnesses, and party big in the Bahamas. She knew Xavier and Mimi felt the need to include everyone they have ever met in their entire lives as if they'd lose 300 family members and friends by eloping. Maybe that had some truth to it, but Livia was happy enough to just be included in the line for the Sake bar later.

For the less traditional ceremony, Mimi wore a white gown made entirely of lace. She was wearing only a spaghetti thin t-strap panty underneath and flower petal stickers to cover her nipples, no garter. Her wedding gown, though enticingly transparent, went halfway up her neck with a scalloped edge. The sleeves bellowed past her wrists. At the hem, Tiffany blue, peep toed wedges peeked out from beneath the lace. And the lace train trailed a few feet behind her. Her train was lined with satin, permitting it to glide effortlessly. Beading cascaded down the back of the dress and her hair did not have one loose strand.

Her father wistfully escorted her across the short bridge, and they floated down the stony steps. Xavier knew a few people in high places, which allowed Mimi's procession to be accompanied by Miri Ben-Ari. Once Livia was off her feet and enjoying her fruit jellies from the dwarfed bento box, she finally understood the reason for all the fuss. She shoved the last of her jellies in her mouth so she could give full attention to the bride.

"Where do I put the box? This was dumb. What do we do with these awkward little things? Whose idea was this? I don't want to litter..." Livia ranted to herself in a not so whispery whisper.

"Lift! Fold! Stick it in your purse," instructed her neighbor in a more whispery whisper and slight hint of irritation in his tone.

"Oh...that's kind a cool," Livia remarked.

Everyone's neck stretched towards the bride. Xavier's pastor was short and pudgy and stood with him at the end of the isle. Xavier had to use his handkerchief multiple times while watching his bride get nearer. He was definitely the emotional one of the two. Mimi's makeup was airbrushed on flawlessly. Instead of holding a bouquet, Mimi and her bridesmaids held fans. When Mimi felt a wave of emotion during the vows, she would turn toward her sister to be fanned. It was quite sweet. The pronounced couple kissed to solidify the agreement.

Cocktail hour arrived. It had only taken twenty minutes before everyone was cleared out of the ceremony area and Livia was already smacking the Sake off of her lips and returning for more. She grabbed a few miso-tofu bites with black sesame seeds from the server as he passed by with his tray. She wondered when the tray of hot wings was coming back around.

"Babe, we have photos! Come on," Lawrence beckoned.

"I'm not family. I'm not in the wedding party..." she turned back towards the Sake bar.

"Olivia...even Jordan's girl is over there in the photos...c'mon now. How's that look? Me posing without you?" Lawrence was practically begging. He knew how stubborn Livia could be. He tried his best not to seem domineering or passive all at the same time. He was shooting for reasonable. The Sake was taking effect and she was becoming more pliable. Livia caved into reason and scurried off to the gazebo with a miso bite in each cheek and

125

Sake cradled in her grip. She slowed her feet as she noticed the hot wing tray coming into view. She thought to stop but Lawrence had looked back to make sure she was still trailing closely behind.

The pictures didn't take long and since Lawrence was the best man, Livia was amongst the first served for dinner. It was a surf and turf spread with some American and some Japanese favorites. Livia was relieved she went with the more conservative, yet still sexy, wedding attire. The way her dress flowed allowed room for food baby.

Afterwards there were more toasts similar to the ones everyone heard at the rehearsal dinner. Mimi and Xavier gave a wonderful "Thank You" speech and then the cake was devoured. That left the dance floor and there was not a quiet foot in the house. The D.J. had a Karaoke stand set up per Xavier's request, which gave room for a few drunken ballads to be inserted between the dance grooves.

Feeling the perfect opportunity to steal Livia away, Lawrence led her to a private waterfall several yards beyond the bridge Mimi came across during the ceremony. He found a large rock to sit on and guided her to sit on his lap.

"What's all this about, Lawrence? Are you glad this is finally over and you can chill after all this wedding bliss?" She said with a trail of sarcasm.

"Olivia, believe me or not, I like all of this...wedding bliss. It reminds me of the time I first fell in love with you and I knew you'd be my wife one day."

"Lawrence..."

"Look, Baby. I just want to ask you a question and I want you to be honest with me."

"When have I not been honest?"

"You know what I mean."

"If this is your romantic way of trying to get us to have another baby..."

"Naw...Shoot, with the way you been eatin' tonight, minus the Sake, I was wondering if we were having another baby. But that is not why..."

"Okay, well what? Are you trying to get all sexy under this waterfall?"

Livia tensed at the clip clap of wandering footsteps closing in. It was Jordan.

"Aye yo, L! You back here bruh? I been looking all over for you. You can hook up with this hot honey later. You know Xav got all of us rooms at The Westin for tonight...Hey, our song is up! You gotta bless dis mic! Karaoke bruh! Come on."

Livia got up, off of his lap, "Honey, go with Jordan. You know he lives for this sort of thing. He's right. We *do* have The Westin."

Reluctantly, Lawrence got up and gave her a deep kiss. He held her hands and guided her over some of the rocks as they followed Jordan back to the gazebo. Everyone's stomachs were splitting in two when the guys got up and did their song. They performed a tribute to Xavier of *End of the Road* by Boyz 2 Men. Mimi and her family were having a good time watching these grown men display their affection for Xavier. Xavier had to pull out his handkerchief again. He was honored that his boys had so much love for him that they'd embarrass themselves in front of hundreds of people.

For the bride and groom's dramatic exit, they had changed clothes in the dressing tent. They spent an extended amount of time in that tent. It was a task getting Mimi out of her dress. They booked a red-eye flight to Turks and Caicos Islands for their two-week honeymoon. All of the guests were waiting on the big bridge over the pond with sparklers for the newlyweds to run under on their path to the limo. It was a great send off and the beginning of a beautiful marriage. They packed into the limo with luggage and boarding passes headed to the airport.

At The Westin, Lawrence and Olivia were awed to find their room had been set up like a honeymoon suite. Actually, Lawrence was aware. Xavier got the room as a package deal for the all the rooms they had reserved for their guests. He knew they were leaving right away for the honeymoon, so he gifted the room to his best man. There was champagne and chocolate covered strawberries in the sitting area. The bathroom had a step-down Jacuzzi tub.

They moved the champagne and strawberries to the tub and peeled down out of their wedding rags and enjoyed warm bubbles and cool bubbly. Livia was so relaxed.

"Oh, Guac, when we're 90 years old doing this, we won't have to worry about the water wrinkling us."

Lawrence paused for a moment and then they both burst into laughter.

"So hey, what did you want to ask me at the waterfall?" Livia asked.

"Huh? Oh...nothing Baby...you kinda already answered my question."

Livia gave a seductive look and leaned in towards Lawrence with a strawberry in her fingers. She slid the strawberry into his mouth, and he caught a taste of her thumb.

He pulled her in close against his body and their lips touched. She licked the dripping strawberry juice from his lip and a trace of chocolate. She rubbed her face against his stubbly chin. She loved that he never got a close shave. His hair sent her to the moon.

Lawrence took his last sip of champagne and then took Livia's glass. She looked in his eyes and it felt like bliss. A bit of champagne spilled on her shoulder. Lawrence couldn't resist kissing every drop of champagne that landed on her velvety skin.

One thing led to another, the jets of the tub had timed out, and the sounds of the room were like that of the ocean under a midnight sky. Water was crashing back and forth and spilling over the walls of the tub. The heat in the room was intoxicating. They were lost in the moment.

Lawrence wanted the night to last forever. Lawrence got out of the tub and helped Livia to get out so they could move to the bed. Their feet were dried by the bathmats and towels that had fallen onto the floor.

Livia woke up in bed, not remembering how she got there. Lawrence hugged her tightly against his chest and guided her back to sleep, "Checkout is not for another six hours, Baby."

"Good," she said, leaning in closer to get snuggly and warm.

By the time Livia was fully awake, Lawrence had showered, dressed, packed, and ordered a breakfast for them to eat before leaving the hotel.

BACK ON THE SCENE

Xavier's wedding and Lawrence's birthday were days apart. Xavier, Jordan and Lawrence were close friends. They made it a point not to miss each other's events. Since Xavier and Mimi would be gone for a couple of weeks, Livia had planned a grown and sexy event for when the newly married couple touched back down in the States. For Lawrence's actual birthday, Olivia had a simple dinner at home with him and the kids. She prepared smoked salmon and mushroom fettuccini alfredo with steamed asparagus. Livia made a decadent chocolate cake, and everyone had an adventure following in Salem's footsteps by eating the cake with their hands. Livia was snapping photo after photo and Lawrence loved being with his family.

In the morning, after Livia had finished making the final reservations for Lawrence's birthday party, she helped Lawrence and the kids out to the car. He was taking the girls to their swim lesson and Salem was tagging along for the ride. Claire and Maya were cool with swim lessons. But the best part about Daddy taking them to swim lessons is that he would treat them to tacos afterward and sometimes they even stopped by the park.

The rest of the family had gone, so Livia pulled out her laptop to take advantage of some quiet. She hadn't written in a while and she decided to read back and see what was going on in her own story. Some parts made her laugh, and some made her shed a tear. Livia knew what had to come next. More laughter, some danger, and some things she dreaded having to revisit. She hesitated as she wondered what her therapist, Dr. Luke, would think of her process. After all, writing out her past was the homework he assigned to her. The assignment was meant to be her path to mental healing. She was committed to seeing it through, and decided to label the next section of her memoirs, *Skate Date*:

Chapter 5
Skate Date

AFTER I GOT caught kissing outside the eighth-grade winter formal dance, with my angel turned little devil, I wasn't allowed to do much. He was now thousands of miles away, in Colorado, at home with his mother. My life turned pretty boring as I entered into eighth grade myself. I didn't participate in many school activities. My eighth-grade year was supposed to be exciting and adventurous but with Stevie keeping such a close eye on me, I could barely turn around without her being in my face.

At dinner one night, Kelpie announced his camping trip with his classmates and that he'd be gone over the weekend. This was the perfect set up for me. I had been hanging out with this girl I met during the Homework Rescue after-school program.

Homework Rescue, after-school program, was available to all students. For some students, it was an alternative to stay out of trouble long enough for their parents to get home from work. Other students received necessary assistance with time management for getting assignments done and turned in on time. And a select few solely there for the socialization and snacks. I didn't ever figure out why she was there and never discussed why I was there.

She had been invited to a skate party by a ninth grader from high school. She expressed wanting to go to the party but not by herself. When she asked me to go with her, I just knew Stevie would not approve. My time was not wasted on asking a question I already knew the answer to.

Stevie did not let me do parties. Stevie did not know this girl. Stevie did not know this girl's parents and it was not going to happen on her watch. Except now that Kelpie would be gone on a camping trip, I would not have to worry about him telling on me for sneaking out. With him on that trip I could ask to stay at the neighbor's house. I could go on about how I would rather not stay home alone and be bored while Momma worked late hours.

It was set. As soon as Kelpie finished unloading all of his details about the camping trip checklist, we were done eating dinner. He immediately headed off to his room to see what he already owned in order to determine what extra items Momma would need to buy that were on the list. I lagged behind and helped with kitchen clean-up.

This was not beyond usual. I was silent, not knowing how to finesse this operation. Stevie was clever and on edge for anything suspicious. My pondering disposition led her to believe I was jealous of the trip, "I know you wish you could go Ollie, but some things are just for your brother. When you get to high school, which is only a few months away, you'll have plenty of outings, events, and activities to participate in, too. And maybe by that time I can trust you to do the right thing."

I started to talk but decided to stay in listening mode. I was curious to see where exactly Stevie was going with this speech. There was no way to be sure if this was going my way or hers. She kept on, "But...you can stay at the neighbor's house. I don't want you here alone getting into trouble."

This was great! She just gave me the green light. All I needed was to figure out how to get a hold of some extra money so that I could really have a great time at the skating party. I still hadn't said anything in reply to the scenario Stevie was laying out. I continued to wash the dishes and focus so that I would not grow a devious grin on my face.

Stevie came behind me and grabbed my shoulders, then kissed me in the hair, "Good night, Honey. I'm headed to work. I'm doing my best to get a day shift again." She left the kitchen. I could hear her grabbing her keys and purse and putting on her raincoat. Then she called into the kitchen, "Oh yeah...come Friday, don't forget to grab some money from my jar for pizza and a movie rental or something." The door closed and she locked it from the outside.

I waited a beat or two and then used the support of the sink to jump up and click my heels. I was grinning from ear to ear. This was such a perfect plan. There was no way Stevie could think I was up to anything since she engineered it all.

I couldn't wait for school the next day to tell my friend in Homework Rescue that I was down for the party. It would be so easy to sneak out of the neighbor's house. All I had to do was eat whatever dinner had been cooked and play with the baby until she fell asleep. Everyone in that house slept like rocks and I'd have the pizza and movie money to pay my way through the night.

My friend was so glad to hear that I was coming. She even suggested we wear matching outfits from her closet. My week at school went by so fast because all I could think of was this high school skate party with so many cute boys.

✳✳✳

Finally, Friday came and all that was on my mind was the party. On Fridays, Stevie pulled a double shift. She worked it out that way so that she could have Sunday with us as a family. Each Friday we had just enough time to get home from school to see her and she'd be gone until Saturday afternoon.

Saturdays were her days to rest. Stevie would come home every Saturday from work and make sure our chores were done, that we had dinner plans, and that any homework was done before we got on the phone or watched television. After that she would sleep the whole day and be rested for Sunday.

Being that my friend lived on the west side of town and the party was two cities away, we had to be creative in our travels. My friend had way more freedom than I ever had. To this day I don't know where her parents were or what they did for a living, but she always told interesting stories of sneaking out. Now it was my time to have a bit of fun. She waited at a park near the school where a lot of the other kids would go to smoke and drink and play dice. Honestly, I was a little scared to walk over there in the dark, so late at night, all by myself. Determination to have a story to tell, overrode my fear.

Things didn't go exactly as planned at the neighbor's house. This is the one day that no one seemed to be tired. The baby was not feeling well so there was battle as to who could care for her the best. Running out of time, I came up with a new plan. I made up an excuse that I was extremely tired and that I was not feeling so well either. I convinced them that I'd be much more comfortable at home, in my own room in my own bed. I assured them that I was safe in the house alone and that I'd be going directly to bed.

I walked back to my house and called the neighbor. I put on a groggy voice and thanked them for keeping me company. I stayed by the phone for a grueling five minutes just in case they tried to call me back. When it looked as though they had carried on with their evening, I left out the side door.

My friend was still waiting. I was so glad she did not leave me. Since it had taken so long to get free, we ran out of time to go all the way to her house to change. Instead, we walked four blocks to her cousin's house. Her cousin let us borrow a couple of miniskirts. This was not the original plan, but we definitely looked like high schoolers. Her cousin gave us dark lipstick and mascara and we left. I was still wearing my sneakers since my feet were too tiny to fit any of her cousin's girly shoes. I made my friend keep her sneakers on too, so that it would look like we did it on purpose.

Outside of her cousin's house, a cab waited. I knew I did not grab enough money from Stevie to cover our cab fee. I just assumed that my friend was going to cover it. Once we were about three blocks away from the skating rink, my friend told the cab driver to pull off into a residential area. She told him she was lost and had forgotten the way. She asked him to slow down so that she could look at the house numbers. She squeezed my hand really tight but would not look in my direction. All the while she kept squinting through the window. So abruptly she shouted, "Stop! I think this is it, but I can't see the house number from here. I have to get out and look closer."

As soon as the driver stopped, my friend flung the door open, yanked me out of the car and whispered for us to run. I was so appreciative of my sneakers! The driver got out of the car and starting yelling after us. I could have sworn he was chasing us, but I never looked back to find out. We just ran. Part of me wanted to be mad at her for not giving me fair warning. It was at that moment I realized I didn't know how to get home without her, so I sucked it up and tried to air out my pits. We were just across the street from the skating rink and I had to refocus my mind on the birthday boy.

Our skates were on and the party was packed. The first thing on my agenda was nachos, licorice, popcorn and a huge soda. Those were all of my skating rink must haves. I slowly glided my way to the concessions. I looked back to see if my friend was done lacing up. She was busy making her laces all pretty. With the outfits we were wearing, no one would give a care about our laces, but she insisted. I turned back around and landed smack dab in the middle of the birthday boy's chest. A long time passed since I had been so close to a boy. His cologne was pleasant, and he was very tall. Most of the middle school boys were still my height, waiting for a growth spurt. Not the birthday boy. He was at full sprout. Lost in my thoughts I tried to move my feet, but they had gone numb. Before I could retain my balance, I stepped on his skates. We both fell down and I landed on his chest. My legs straddled his sides. At first, he grabbed my butt and put my skirt back in its proper place. And with his muscular arms, he lifted me off of him.

He said, "Your skates weigh more than you!" I laughed and used whatever body weight I had to help him to his feet. He thanked me and asked, "Where's your friend with the big booty? Didn't you walk in together? You must be one she was telling me about."

Right at that second, I felt her skate up and put her arm around me, "Girl, you tryin' to steal my man!?" I hesitated a little and then realized she was teasing. She pointed to a boy at the water fountain and suggested, "I think that's the guy you want." I looked at them both and the birthday boy smiled, nodded, and then gently pushed me in that direction.

Ok, so I was a little disappointed, but I knew Birthday Boy was not for me, although he did feel good for a few minutes. Water Fountain Guy was loud and clumsy and not quite as tall or as cute or as cut as Birthday Boy. I just went with it. Water Fountain Guy ended up being super funny. I pretty much stuck with him during the entire party. The rink was about to close, and my friend was still somewhere gone with Birthday Boy. Someone said they had turned their skates in and went outside to talk. I knew they weren't talking. I was not invited to many parties like this one, but I did know that no one left the party to go and "talk."

Water Fountain Guy and I waited for almost an hour. The parking lot was practically empty, my soda was empty, and I got irritated. I began to fuss and cuss, and Water Fountain

Guy tried to cheer me up, "Hey, hey, hey, you know my boy is just tonguin' your girl down and grabbin' on that fat ass booty she got. We could be doing the same thing and we wouldn't even notice they were gone..."

"First of all, I don't even know you like that to be lettin' you all up in my mouth. You make me laugh and all, but I am not like that. We just met three hours ago," I reminded him.

He got a strange look on his face and snickered, "I was just fuckin' wit chu, a'ight? Here, drink somma dis. I see your soda been gone."

He handed me his soda, so I wiped off the straw and started guzzling. Immediately I started choking and coughing. I pushed his arm hard and asked what he was drinking. He explained to me that he had poured some vodka in it to make it taste better. I admitted that I sort of liked it and so I slowly took a few more sips.

Before long I had finished the entire cup. I quickly started loosening up. Water Fountain Guy noticed I was beginning to be affected by the night air. I left my jacket behind in order to show off my cute outfit. His coat stood open like a matador's cape and motioned for me to snuggle in. Hesitation was winning at first then my concern with warming up aggressively took the lead.

Within a few minutes my head lay on his chest and suddenly his body seemed taller than before. It was quiet and everyone had left the rink. It was just the two of us waiting. I looked up at him and under all of that silliness was quite a handsome young man. Something made me lean up towards his face. I wanted to kiss him. His lips looked inviting. He already had a touch of fuzz framing them. Warm hands worked down my back and ruffled my skirt a little. He pressed my body into his. This was a feeling that I had felt once before. I was expectantly curious to know what should happen next.

"Ooooh. Y'all nasty!" My friend blurted out as her and Birthday Boy came walking back. The kissy face couple had remembered to come back for us. Just on time to ruin the moment. I asked my friend if she had called a cab to pick us up. She explained to me that cabs did not come this late and that she planned for us to catch the bus home. I looked at the guys, "Don't y'all drive?" They both looked back at me and waited for me to answer my own question. So off we walked to the bus stop. It wasn't that far away but the bus was not scheduled to come for another twenty minutes or so.

We all walked across the street to the Burger Joint where it was warm. After sitting and chatting for about five or ten minutes, the owner came over and asked us to buy something or leave. We smacked our lips at him, but we did not want to wait in the cold. I was the last to order. Everyone waited for me to get ketchup and barbeque sauce for my fries. As we pushed our way out the restaurant, we saw the bus closing its doors and pulling off.

We were only a parking lot away. We ran, yelling and screaming, towards the bus. I dropped my fries and everything, trying to make the bus. The driver did not even look our way. He drove off. That was the last bus for the night. It was almost 1:30am and the next bus line was three miles away. There was no other option than to walk. At least the road was at a decline. The bottom of the hill was a busier highway with buses that ran more frequently. On the walk down the hill, it was spooky and dark. The temperature was dropping as well. My new guy friend had taken off his coat for me to wear and that helped a lot, but I just looked naked with an oversized bomber jacket and sneakers. None of us wanted to admit how scared we were. A group of young teenagers on a dark road with a cemetery on one side and unlit homes on the other. We didn't speak for a couple of blocks.

We all were visibly nervous. Bushes were rustling and only one car drove by about every five minutes. Birthday Boy tried to talk about his party to take our minds off of the creepy road, but that didn't last long. Water Fountain Guy decided to inform us of a story he'd watched on the news about a serial killer in the area. Initially we weren't fazed, but with each cold and dark step, we began to believe the possibility of being stalked.

I made the wise storyteller hold me as we walked. I wasn't really afraid, but just in case, I held tightly until we got closer to the streetlights. Everyone seemed to be a bit more at ease when we reached the streetlights. There were more cars and fewer potential creeps. The bus schedule noted that the bus would arrive in the next thirty minutes. We waited for forty-five. No buses came.

Well it's after three a.m. at this point and Water Fountain Guy made his way back inside his jacket with me. He couldn't hide being cold, and the extra body heat didn't hurt either. With none of us really wanting to call our parents, Birthday Boy came up with a plan. He went down the street to the phone booth and called his mentor to pick us up.

His mentor was not happy to get up in the middle of the night, but he did rescue us. We all slept on his floor until the morning bus came. By the time I got home I was exhausted! I had truly experienced an adventure and I was on cloud nine. With it being broad daylight, I had to make sure the neighbors didn't see my sneaky arrival. I wouldn't have to worry about Stevie for a couple more hours, but a sighting from next door would blow my cover for certain. After hitting the shower and before going to bed for real, I checked the machine to see if the neighbor's called to check on me. There was a message. It was Stevie...

✱✱✱

"Give a kiss to the birthday boy, Baby." Lawrence said playfully to his lady. He was pumped for his birthday celebration at the billiard lounge. He and Livia walked into the venue looking like a celebrity couple. They went straight for the bar and grabbed a drink, then headed to the back where Livia had rented out a private dance floor and pool table for the evening. Everyone was already feeling the groove and it heightened the excitement when Lawrence stepped in.

Xavier arranged for bottle service and soon their table was lit with sparkling bottles. Jordan started up a round of pool and the party was jumping. Livia and the ladies were getting it going on the dance floor. The party continued to grow as a few of Lawrence and Livia's other friends happened to be there. They were all invited to join in on the celebration. With everyone having fun, the time arrived that it was time to head to the entertainment portion of the night. The guys did another round of shots. The ladies topped off their drinks, and they all headed to their reserved booth for the comedy show in an attached venue towards the back of the lounge.

During the comedy show, Funny Mike had everyone in stitches. He even snapped on Lawrence for a few jokes off the top. After the comedy show, Lawrence was hugging, kissing, and thanking everyone who showed up. Laughs were still lingering as people were repeating jokes from the show. Jordan walked up to Lawrence and told him, "This ain't the end of the night, Bruh!" He fanned out some passes in his hand. They were for backstage access.

After the backstage introductions and pictures, the crew was invited to hang out at Funny Mike's penthouse. They hung until about five in the morning, when Funny Mike had retired to his bedroom with a couple of groupies from the show. That was everyone's signal to leave. There was a breakfast spot within walking distance from the hotel. Lawrence, Livia, Xavier, Mimi, Jordan and his new girl all had breakfast together. Strolling to the parking lot after they left the restaurant, Lawrence dared his buddies to top his birthday celebration. Everyone had a good laugh as they began to recount their evening.

They were giving hugs and saying goodbyes before everyone got into each other's respective vehicles. Not even to the car yet, and Livia started in with what the routine would be when they got home and a list of things for Lawrence to do.

Lawrence gripped Olivia's arm tightly. She was expecting him to squeeze her in for an embrace of gratitude but instead, Lawrence clinched his chest and took a knee to the concrete. Jordan turned back when he heard Livia yell out, "Xav! Call 911!" Xavier was closing his wife, Mimi, in the car when the screech of Jordan's cry pierced his ear. Olivia felt this was the most serious moment of her life, while waiting for the ambulance Livia was reminded of her own life events she was writing for the sake of therapy, and how it all came to this point. She was about to lose Lawrence.

✳ ✳ ✳

Chapter 6
A Strong Measure of Pleasure

STEVIE NEVER DID let on that she knew I was at that skate party, but I think she had an idea. With the neighbor's baby being sick, I wasn't planning on them calling Momma to fill her in. Stevie lived on the philosophy that parents should pick their battles. She was happy that I was home safely, and she partially blamed herself for not being home during the time that Kelpie and I needed her most.

During the summer, she lifted the reigns a tad and came to the realization that I was going into high school. Her fear was that if she was too heavy on the rules and regulations, the more I'd want to oppose them. That was one intelligent woman. I honestly wasn't too mischievous a teen, but I often tended to get entangled in sticky situations.

At our community center, which was a safe summer hang out, I met Bronson Palmblen. The community center offered free lunch and classes as long as you were registered. They offered knitting, sewing, basketball, dance, tennis, and other classes I couldn't care less about. I think Bronson Palmblen was in a music class they ran. He'd always be singing wherever he walked. It was sweet to hear. His voice sounded really professional. There's a possibility I just had a small crush on him, so it didn't matter if he was beat boxing or whistling or twiddling his thumbs, I'd think any of it was cool. Bronson Palmblen never hinted that he was aware of my presence. The whole summer had almost flown by before we had an exchange. The music teacher had to end classes early for the summer program and the center didn't have a last-minute replacement. Instead of joining a new class like the others did, Bronson Palmblen just sat at the piano for that hour practicing an original song someone had written for him.

I pretended to have to use the bathroom while he was at the piano. Then I pretended that bathroom was out of order so that I could have an excuse to walk past the piano again. Then I faked like I was looking for something. All of that commotion and the boy just kept on singing and playing. I eventually just sat on the couch next to the piano and yelled over his volume, "I like the way you sound!"

He smiled at me and kept singing. My ears listened for a while longer and he stopped looking at me, so I went back to sewing class. I waited around until after the last class of the day to see which way he was walking home so that I could incorporate it into my own route. Unfortunately, he got into a car and drove off. I never saw him drive before that day. A boy came behind me, fake pushed me, and just stood there.

"Stooop," I nagged. I was not interested in his constant bugging. "I see you been stalkin' my boy Bronson Palmblen! Dang girl. Let the guy come after you," he said. I rolled my eyes, but he was so right. It was just that I had waited the whole summer, almost, and nothing.

"You know I got his number. Plus, I could hook you up," he kept on. He was tall and musty and, in my opinion, a bit husky for a ball player. His hair was never cut, and his shoes were always dirty. I hated that he had something I wanted so I thanked him and held my hand out to write down Bronson Palmblen's number. "Aw, naw naw naw. You got ta earn this, Shorty Doowop."

I was entirely disgusted. He was puckering his lips. He had sloppily wet them with his tongue, but they were still crusty. I wanted the number though so I puckered for a quick peck, but he clinched on and forced his tongue in my mouth and there was no way I could free from his lip-lock. I stomped his feet and he only kissed me harder. I tried to knee his balls, but he blocked me, knocking me to the ground. He tore up the number and threw it at me. Right at that instance Bronson Palmblen's car cruised back into the parking lot. He parked crookedly in front of the steps and came flying out of his car, to fight the guy.

"No! NO!" I yelled, coming to my feet swiftly, in attempt to hold Bronson Palmblen off. I thanked him as "Mr. Hot Lips" laughed and walked off with his basketball under his arm. I looked at my hero with inquisitive eyes. I couldn't believe he came back for me. He gently put his arms at rest on my shoulders. My eyes searched his mouth as he began to speak. He simply moved me aside and said, "Sorry, Girl. I just came back for my notebook."

My jaw dropped low, as I watched him turn his back and walk off. I lowered my head to begin walking home while feeling utterly crushed. Just then he turned back around and held me against his jacket right as the tears went pouring out my eyes and said, "Don't cry! I was just playin'! I was trying to be funny… For real though, I am mad at chu."

"Mad at me?!?!?!? You don't even know my name! You don't even look at me! I get pushed to the ground and you mad at *me*?"

"Ollie," he said with confidence. My skin began to glow. He went on, "I know you and everything you like. I even saw you watching me drive away. I was looking in my rearview mirror. As I turned the corner, I also saw that chump walking up behind you. I was gonna go home and act like I didn't care but I ended up turning back. I couldn't let him win."

I was so confused. Bronson Palmblen went on to explain that he was shy and that he was trying to find a way to approach me all summer. When he had mentioned it to his friend, his friend joked about liking me too and commented that he had the balls to do something about it.

When the guy saw how much Bronson Palmblen was really digging on me, he offered to get my number for him. Bronson Palmblen agreed to the help but in the back of his head he thought it might not go over so well. That's when he turned his car around. He could have turned sooner.

Now that our feelings were out in the open, he started driving me home at the end of the day and asked me to be his girl. I made him let me out on the corner by the blue house, so Momma wouldn't see I was getting out of a guy's car.

Bronson Palmblen and I would kiss every day after that. It wasn't hard to tell that he was ready to move beyond it. It's what boyfriend and girlfriend do. The close encounters of exploring sex before him, had me losing my mind with curiosity. To *willingly* give myself to be pleased was becoming a strong desire of mine.

So, like any curious teenager would do, I went after my desires. Bronson Palmblen told me he loved me. I felt like I loved him too. Two weeks after officially becoming a couple, he suggested I come to his house so that he could teach me something.

At first, I thought it was going to be about music. I don't know why I thought that. The weird thing is that he did not want to pick me up from our usual spot. He told me how to get to his house, but I took a longer detour to make it seem like I was actually walking to the center.

His directions upon my arrival were to let myself in and quietly find his room. He said the front door would be unlocked and that his room was the first on the left. The door would be closed but unlocked.

The room at the end of the hall was his mom's and she worked nights like my mom, so she would be asleep, he said. I walked in his room and gently closed his door behind me. Bronson Palmblen was sprawled out on his queen-sized bed with only basketball shorts on. He had the lamp on next to his bed and his stereo was playing soft music.

"I thought! —

"Shhhhh!" he hurriedly came to me by the door and pressed his fingers against my lips.

"My mom is awake." He said in a soft tone.

"Well why? —

"Don't talk. I have to teach you something," he shushed me again and this time his body was right up against mine, pulling me away from the door.

He touched my face. His half-naked body was warm. He took off my sweater and kissed my shoulder. I was so nervous his mom would barge in the room, so I kept looking back. He pulled my chin towards his face and looked into my eyes. I knew this would be the time I was waiting for. My shirt was off, but not my training bra. The skirt and knee-socks I was wearing remained on too. Bronson Palmblen was on his knees and licking my tummy as I stood in the middle of the floor.

I felt it natural to rub his hair and his muscular shoulders. He grabbed my butt with one hand and pulled my panties to the side with the other and his mouth kissed me so passionately. I was glad I wore my grown-up panties that were low cut and solid colored. Not like the high waisted floral ones with the thick white waist band on them.

We moved to the bed but before I could get on top of him, he jumped back up. We could hear his mom's door open. He darted to his door and was out of it, closing it behind him. Muffled talking was going on and I contemplated getting dressed, or hiding in the closet, or escaping through the window. I was nervous. I got under the covers – just wanted him to return.

As the doorknob turned, I tightened up. Something about the danger drove me wild. What would I do if it was his mom? Thankfully it was just Bronson Palmblen entering the doorway. This time locking the door behind himself. He told me he asked his mom to go to the store and get him some medicine for an upset stomach. He acted like he was going into the bathroom until she left out the front door. He locked it behind her, came back in the bedroom, and joined me under the blankets.

He tossed me on top of his body with my thighs clenching his ribs. His shorts still on, head back, his eyes closed, and his palms on my hips as I moved to the music. I liked it and I was content in his hands. Of course, he wanted to go all the way. Bronson Palmblen was going into the eleventh grade and I was not going to be his first pony ride. He was accustomed to the usual progression of teasing to pleasing. He called me a tease, but he was not angry with me.

I was afraid to round home plate, so I stopped him from taking his shorts off. I asked him if I could leave and he simply put his hands behind his head and nodded towards the door. He smiled and I got dressed to leave, praying not to run into his mom on the way out. I felt so in charge. I felt in control and I loved it. I opened his front door with a huge smile on my face and there she was on the doorstep. I was face to face!

MILE HIGH RECOVERY

F acing mortality while waiting for the paramedics was not how they expected Lawrence's birthday party to end. Xavier's wife, Mimi, was searching her purse for an aspirin. She thought for sure that Lawrence was having a heart attack. Livia was at his side and the paramedics arrived in a flash. They checked him out and said that he was not having a heart attack but that he should go directly to urgent care for further evaluation.

Lawrence was a healthy guy for the most part. He had a few drinks with guys from time to time, but he worked out regularly and Livia cooked healthy food. What Lawrence had experienced was a panic attack, also known as an anxiety attack, which can range from light to very intense heart palpitations. Dr. Garret advised Lawrence to take it easy for a while and engage in relaxation activities.

He talked with the doctor about things he could do to relax. Relieved that the diagnosis wasn't life threatening, Olivia left the exam room to find the restrooms. That allowed Lawrence the privacy to express his stressful issues with Livia in more detail.

Lawrence admitted Livia's writing assignment her therapist assigned was indeed helping Livia to address unresolved issues of her past, but the lengthy healing process was affecting her relationship with the kids and him. Lawrence also mentioned to Dr. Garret that there was something he'd been wanting to ask Livia and he was afraid of her answer. Dr. Garret revealed some alarming facts to him about how untreated stress can wear down the body. Dr. Garret warned him that if he held off talking with Livia any longer, the palpitations could intensify.

Livia worked her hardest to make things comfortable back at home for him. It was overwhelming experiencing one scare with Sabrina, and shortly after, encountering another scare with the love of her life. Lawrence meant the world to Livia and she had not entertained the idea of ever being without him.

It was refreshing to know that Lawrence's condition was manageable. With a large cup of tea in her palms, Livia snuggled into the oversized sofa chair in the living room. She wanted to do some reflecting. The kids were out of the house and Livia was spiritually worn out. Looking out the grand picture window over the bag of pistachios Grandma Sugar brought over for Lawrence, her eyes lightly closed with her face soaking in the glow. Lawrence was getting much needed rest back in their bedroom.

Livia began asking the Lord to speak to her. She wanted to truly know His purpose and His will for her life. To know His plan for her life would tremendously boost her being. Sometimes Livia prayed and *"searched God's kingdom and His righteousness,"* while at other times she recited fatal thoughts of, *"To be or not to be."*

It was becoming clear to Livia that she wanted to stop running from the Lord. She knew it was time to join a church family to increase her spiritual health, and not just occasionally attend. She really felt led to set a stronger foundation for her children.

Lawrence was already a member of the church. Claire had gotten baptized there a year ago and joined with her dad. Maya wanting to be like her mom, was waiting for Livia to make the move.

Just as Livia was finishing thanking God, in advance, for His revelations, she noticed her phone was going off. Rushing up to the counter to answer it without disturbing her Guac, she was able to see "SISTER" flashing on the home screen.

It was Sabrina. She hadn't had contact with Sabrina in a several weeks and was glad she got the message to call.

So much had happened since this pair last connected. Livia had the pageant for Maya and the wedding for Xavier. Livia was also occupied planning Lawrence's birthday which Sabrina was usually a part of, but Sabrina had been staying away from people since her scars were extremely noticeable from the attack.

But Sabrina had used her attack to propel forward in a major way, she'd redirected her time to dominating the restaurant world rather than sulking.

Sabrina had not let being a victim of attempted murder slow her down in the least. She had been going high speed at opening her restaurants and keeping focused on her successes. Using them as a huge healing factor in her life. They both talked about how much they missed each other.

Livia updated her on Lawrence's health, and all of the new things the kids were doing and saying each day. Salem started walking and adding more words to his vocabulary. Claire was becoming more independent and finding new interests. Maya was satisfied with not doing pageants anymore and glad to have more playtime.

"Yeah, but Lawrence gave us a pretty bad scare, Bri. Almost losing you, then Guac?!?! I just could not maintain. But glad you both are okay."

Sabrina was worried about Lawrence. She and he were like brother and sister and Lawrence called Sabrina on an occasion or two to get advice on how to handle certain situations with Livia. Livia knew that Lawrence and Sabrina talked occasionally, but she was not threatened.

Sabrina felt badly for Lawrence but tried to be supportive of Livia, too. Sabrina would advise her friend to hear Lawrence out and give his ideas a chance. Livia would listen, but still would keep her ways – mostly.

Sabrina liked catching up with her favorite family after not talking with Livia for so many weeks but called because she had huge news to share as well. She wasn't sure what Livia's reaction was going to be, but she wouldn't be able to hide things for much longer.

"Well, I called today to catch up and it was so good to hear how my favorite family is doing. I do actually have new revelations to share with you as well. No matter how it may sound coming out, this really is positive news."

"Bri! What is it girl?! You pregnant? Have you been messing with Kyle again? Isn't he still married to Taryn? Tell me. Is it Kyle?"

"Damn, O! I cut him off. I really am through with him. I know that wasn't healthy. And just because you brought that up, I should tell you there are times that people do shit. Not to hurt anyone, not for anyone, but people do shit. Okay?"

"I'm sorry. I am sorry. I don't mean to be judgmental. What do you want to tell me?"

"Well...the thing is...what I wanted to tell you is...I'm getting married."

"What, Sabrina?! To who? When?"

"I'm marrying Nurse Drake. Well, Drake Brandon Louvier."

"Oh! Wow. Okay. Sabrina, Sabrina, Sabrina. Congrats, Boo! But..."

"Listen, I know you thought he was gay, but he isn't."

"I never thought that! Okay...well just for like a split second. Anyway, I am so happy for you! Just surprised. I wish you nothing but the best. I am truly happy you found love."

"Thank you. It feels good to have your support, Liv. Drake and I really connected through my recovery and we have been inseparable ever since we met. I love him Liv! Plus, his family is from France and he made opening my Paris location go seamlessly."

"What? Paris? I didn't realize that location was open already."

"I know. I know. I wanted to tell you sooner, but everything happened so fast. Look, I know this is short notice, but we want to send for you all to come to Toulouse, in the south of France, for the wedding. It's in two weeks. You can stay in Drake's parent's home. They have several extra rooms. Drake and I will be temporarily staying there as well. The wedding will be on the roof top of the building my new restaurant is in, just a short flight from Toulouse. It's stunning girl. I can't wait 'til you guys get here! I'm gonna book your flights and send your itinerary."

Livia didn't get a chance to say "yes" or "no", but she knew she had to be there for this momentous occasion. Especially since Sabrina was already purchasing the flights. Lawrence, Livia, and the kids would probably be the only family and friends Sabrina had in attendance for her big day. With Lawrence still managing his stress, Livia was nervous the trip to Paris would add to it. She still couldn't understand what was stressing him so intensely. They led a successful life. But whatever he might be dealing with, she didn't want to make it worse.

The ladies exchanged endearments and hung up the phones. Livia jumped when she watched Lawrence come from around the corner. She was already looking in his direction, but she didn't plan on having him appear.

"Guac! Did I wake you?"

"Oh, I have been up a little bit," Lawrence said. "What's this I hear about Paris?"

Livia was in a tight situation, facing off, and not sure what to say. Just like where she'd left off writing in her book, about that day at Bronson Palmblen's house:

$$* * *$$

I couldn't believe we were face to face! After being Scott free. After not even really doing anything bad and deciding to leave, here we are facing off. How did she even know I was here? Or was this a coincidence? No. Trying to figure out the words to say, I just wanted to run. I didn't run though. That would be silly. She was looking just as nervous as me. What was I supposed to say?

Would Bronson Palmblen be coming out to check? Most assuredly he was watching out the window to see me walk away. Would his mom be back soon? There was no way I could let this standoff continue. Somehow my neighbor had found me. She must have followed me from home.

"Are you following me?! What are you doing here!?" I yelled in a whisper.

"Look little girl. I don't know what has changed you, but I can't cover for you anymore. You come with me down these steps and explain to me why you are over here instead of at the Center?" she scolded.

"I said – *How did you find me?!* Are you a spy?" we began our march down the steps.

At this point I was triggered about Ms. Palmblen's eventual return. I pulled her arm as we started walking away from Bronson Palmblen's apartment. Figured once we crossed the street we'd be in the clear of his mom.

"Look girl, your mom saw me leaving the house to go on a walk with my baby and asked if I could run your backpack to you. You forgot your bag! I was right behind you calling your name on the way. You didn't even flinch. When you passed up the Center I just decided to try and catch up. I was hoping maybe you were meeting a friend to walk with, but when you didn't come out for almost 30 minutes! I came hunting. Do you want to be like me with a brand-new baby?" she interrogated me like a criminal.

"I can't trust you anyway." I concluded. "That's why I stopped coming next door to help with the baby. Anything I want to do; you will tell Stevie!"

"Hey girl. I don't need to go telling on you. I am trying to save you. You don't want this. Don't you know? That boy has a girlfriend already!"

My eyes squinted. My arms folded. Now she is just being mean. Why would she say something like that about Bronson Palmblen? How would she know? "I am his girlfriend and he just told me he loves me. I know he is going to be a junior, but I am only a few weeks away from high school myself. We are only two years apart, but I know Stevie won't understand. That's why I hide it."

"Okay. Ollie. I didn't come to make you upset. Here is your bag. I gotta go."

She walked away and I didn't want to return to the Center. Not after what just happened. I had to though. If I didn't show, without an excused absence, they would call home. I stopped by the Center and told them I puked on the way there and that I am probably contagious and should go home. They picked up the phone and dialed my mom. I said, "No! I mean. No." I warned them she had a long shift and would not want to be bothered. I lied that I had bothered her enough by first puking at home and begging to come to the Center since it was the last week.

After an awkward moment of convincing, they let me walk out and I prayed they didn't call Momma. Instead of going home, I took the long route to the park where Bronson Palmblen and I would go for lunch sometimes. At the park, I sat under our tree near the water and wished I was in Bronson Palmblen's arms. His scent was fresh on my nose, still. I could feel his soft touch. I could even hear him telling me to open my eyes over and over and over again. Just letting the warm sun beat on my face was enjoyable. My dream was disrupted by my neighbor's words, *"Don't you know? That boy has a girlfriend already."* Was I not his only girl?

"Olivi-AH. Open your eyes," not loud but just direct.

I opened my eyes to see Bronson Palmblen, kneeling in front of me. I must have fallen asleep holding my knees. There was an immediate urge to ask about his having another love. The opportunity passed though. He kissed my cheeks and then we laid down in the grass together.

No words were exchanged. We looked up at the clouds that now tucked in the sun. Staying a bit longer was my only option. In my mind I toyed with why we hadn't just done this to begin with instead of meeting at his apartment. Either way, I knew things had to be real with him. He came after me. I don't think he would have done that if he'd had another girlfriend. He told me it didn't matter if I didn't want to go *all the way*. He just wanted to be close to me.

Shortly after our summer program ended was the commencement of the new school year. Finally, I was a freshman. Being in high school changed my life. Having control of my body and the things I did and the places I visited were my choice. Stevie nearly backed off completely. Kelpie decided to take a different route than high school graduation. Cousin Perry owned a car repair shop and gave

Kelpie a job. The money was consistent, and Kelpie had been into cars as far back as my oldest memory of him.

Momma didn't fight Kelpie moving out at a young age. One day Kelpie was living there with us and the next day he was gone. I remember telling Momma about Kelpie taking advantage of me but don't recall ever there being a punishment. Maybe this was his punishment. Maybe Kelpie was being banished from the family.

My new life had no room for Kelpie, but he would call and talk to Momma almost every week. My routine had weekly occurrences too. I altogether stopped talking to the neighbor.

Sitting on the couch with Momma one night I dropped in on a phone call that the neighbor might be moving in with her boyfriend in order for him to help with the baby and allowing her to get a job.

Funny how swiftly life can take a turn. I turned into a woman. No more raisins filling my training bra; there were full breasts. They were A cups; but they were full A's. Everyone in school knew Bronson Palmblen and I were the cutest couple. His close friends were jealous of our relationship. They accused me of wanting him for his money. It was news to me that he had any.

Towards the end of the school year it had become plain to me that his friends wanted his future riches and didn't want to share any spillage with me. Bronson Palmblen's music career was rapidly taking off.

He had always won the local vocal contests and talent shows. He also picked up a guitar to add to his list of musical instrument conquests. Once he tried teaching me piano. I concluded my fingers were just too short.

Waiting up one evening for our daily phone conversation, my attitude kicked into high gear. It was like I felt something in my gut that was not going to end well. Although Bronson Palmblen and I had hot and heavy make out sessions, we had never completely rounded home base, so I knew pregnancy was not the feeling.

While my mind was drifting, waiting for my call, I wanted to know how long third base would satisfy him. My phone rang and I dropped the receiver. It accidently hung up. I had to call back. Usually, I liked him to be the one to call so my heart was sure he wanted me, and that I wasn't chasing him.

This particular call was like the most exciting phone call of my life so far. My boyfriend had landed a record deal! He was going to be famous and I was going to be a famous guy's girlfriend. Giving the life changing news was shortly followed by disappointing news. Our time would be cut short. All of the late night and weekend rehearsals were going to increase. He was leaving our school. It was almost summer again anyway, but his plan was not to come back senior year.

Studio time was being booked, interviews were taking place and the album was soon to drop. The limited time we had to see each other between classes and during lunch were no longer available. Too much time had passed since we last kissed and caressed each other. My phone calls were coming less and less. I wondered what he was doing, who he was meeting, and what the celebrity experience was like for him. On a late night he called to remind me I have his heart and to think about him while I lay in bed at night. Doing that was a given. There was no way to go without thinking of him and his body and his lips and his voice. One night he sang me a sample of a song he was working on. Someone else had been hired to write the song, but he said it reminded him of me. The song is called, "Under a Tree."

His voice was so effortlessly beautiful as he sang to me, *"I wrapped my arms around you, laid you on your back. (Under a tree.) I kissed your cheek and neck and then you kissed back. (Under a tree.) I don't care if they watch and even if they did, all that matters is - it's you that I'm with. (Under a tree.)"*

His singing made me feel the same way I do when we're together. I wanted to be happy for him. But I missed him so much, I began to cry. He told me not to worry and it started an argument. His point argued that if the current arrangement was too much for me to handle then I would be worse off when he had to travel for concerts and tours.

"Aren't you getting ahead of yourself Bronson? Tours? We don't even know if your album will sell," I blurted candidly.

It was a heated situation. The following week we both apologized but I could sense there was something different in the way he addressed me. I got over it because few weeks after our blow up, he was being interviewed on the music channel to talk about his new album and to promote his new brand. His new album was titled, "Just B."

Every time I called him Bronson, he corrected with an, *"It's just B."* The first couple of times I laughed, but then it got weird. I called him Bronson because that was short for Bronson Palmblen which was how I had referred to him for most of our relationship. Everyone in school called him Bronson Palmblen including the teachers. One time he snapped and griped, *"Aimee can do it! So can you."* I was like,

"Who the heck is Aimee?" Apparently, Aimee was one of the assistants that got their lunches and all of that stuff. Aimee, to me, was just a name.

Not being able to talk to Bronson daily was the worst part of my life. Since school was now out for summer break, the days seemed longer without him. Stevie knew I didn't want to return to the Center for their summer program, so it was up to me to find a replacement. Turns out the neighbor's boyfriend kicked her out for his boyfriend to move in and she was back to the drawing board. At least she had a job this time to make a living of her own. So, while she worked, the baby hung with me. There was a small stipend for the job, but anything paid more than the Center, so I didn't complain.

The minute the neighbor stepped on her porch; I was handing her baby off. It was THE night. It was Bronson's, *"Just B's"*, interview and missing it was not an option. Cozy on the couch I shared a bag of popcorn with Stevie. Originally, she didn't approve of our relationship. But eventually she gave in and supported my "puppy love" for the boy. She had just enough time to catch the interview before jetting off to work.

Wow. My eyes practically jumped out of my head. Bronson Palmblen looked like a different person. He had bulked up and was wearing a white, ribbed, a-lined tank, baggy jeans and Timberland boots. A genuine leather bomber jacket topped off the look. There was more hair than I remembered on his head and face. Was that a goatee?! A few months had changed him drastically. Even his voice had dropped an octave. I noticed on the phone, too.

Proud of my *"Just B"* and grinning from ear to ear had Stevie smiling too. She was accepting her daughter being happy. Her joy probably coincided with the fact that he was so far away and therefore unable to be under my sheets at night. But she jerked me out of euphoria in time for me to hear him give a shout out to his girlfriend. Momma even became noticeably giddy.

For the first time ever, we held hands. She gripped me with anticipation of hearing my name on TV. The prospect of your daughter being courted by a millionaire might make a person dream many dreams.

I turned the volume up and prayed my friends and classmates were watching. I was getting my "15" minutes of fame. Nerves came from not really knowing what picture they would show on the jumbo screen.

The yearbook photo wasn't bad, but I had changed so much since then. Having the nation think he was dating a little girl mortified me.

Bronson's mom often took pictures of us on her camera. Any of those photos had me looking mature and not as stiff as a yearbook snapshot.

A camera on Bronson zoomed in close to his face for him to speak right into my television set. I got close too.

I may have even said, *"Yes, B?"*

"I owe so much to my girlfriend. We have been together since I can remember and I know she is genuine, she real, she my everything. She used to sit by the piano and listen to me play. I love you Boo Boo."

I interrupted and with appreciation to his giving me a new pet name, "I love you too, Bronson Palmblen." Momma chuckled at me talking to a TV screen.

He continued, "You stay by my side and I bring you everywhere with me. You so ride or die, you here right now. Come out Aimee!"

Crackling could be heard from the tiny broken pieces of my face and body crumbling to the floor.

"Aimee?? BITCH!"

Stevie smacked me in the arm before pulling me in for a hug. No tears poured. No sadness, only fury. It was me! I had been there. I was ride or die. I WAS his everything. It was rare for Stevie and me to connect which is why I let her keep hugging me. My heart told me it was done months ago. Clapping in the distant background of my angry thoughts meant that Aimee had joined him on set. I opened my eyes.

As Aimee spoke, there was mention of her having a duet with him on the album called, "From A to B." Before the segment was over, she also brought up her work as a writer on the album for the track, "Under a Tree." I was hurt.

Shut the television off – done by me. Shut the front door – done by Stevie. For a mom, I wanted her to have more to say before leaving for work. My neighbor and I weren't close anymore either; I was simply the sitter. Journaling was my only outlet and those lined pages held my life.

Anytime Bronson's video would come on or he would have an interview, he would steal an eye to the camera and lick his lips.

This was always our unspoken sign for each other that meant he wanted me. I ignored it. After the interview came loads of phone calls that were left to ring. Finally, a letter came. Bronson explained the whole thing with Aimee was just for publicity, and that everything he said about her, he truly meant for me.

I didn't believe him. I moved on without him. That summer was a lonely season. So, in fall of my Sophomore year, I joined every club possible to keep my mind off of Bronson. One of those clubs was Black Student Union. Our BSU President, Tre, kept us late one evening while planning a Spoken Word event. Panic flooded my face as I walked out the library doors and it was dark outside. I was supposed to have been in the house before she left for work on a school night.

I wanted to ask someone for a ride, but I wasn't really friends with any of the members of BSU. Showing up to the meetings was my outlet. I started the 20-minute walk home in the dark. Then before I reached the main road, Tre pulled up with his window down and told me to hop in his car.

"Come on Olivia. It's just four or five blocks, right? It's hella dark out here. It's late and it's my fault. I owe you," he insisted while driving two miles per hour beside me, "You gonna walk then?"

I wasn't responding to anything he was saying. In my mind I was like, "Tre is talking to *me*! Tre is *talking* to me. *Tre* is offering me a ride in his car. OH MY Gosh."

"Olivia?" he said, still waiting for an answer.

"Uh, yeah, Tre. Okay... I guess you can just drop me down the street. I am not supposed to be in anyone's car my mom doesn't know."

Tre looked at me and grinned sideways to himself. The ride was nice. His car was an all-black '86 Mustang, with new black leather seats, a custom spoiler on the rear, and a loud sound system. It wasn't playing for my ride home, but I noticed when he came and left school it was bumpin'.

The stop lights were long, and the trip was quiet. At the corner of my block, my hand motioned to pull off at the blue house. Dark interior in a strange vehicle and I couldn't find the latch to exit.

Tre reached over with no regard to my sitting there. Our bodies brushed causing physical static and his jacket button got caught in my hair.

"Oh shit, sorry Olivia. I am not doing this on purpose. I'm for real. Your hair. My button. It's stuck."

My burst of laughter was reaction to a comically awkward moment mixed with a smidge of flirtation. Every girl in school wanted Tre.

His girlfriend, Sarah, that went to the *all-girls* private school most definitely wanted him, but he was on *me*. Hair loosened; I still was lost for the door handle. When I located it, the darned thing wouldn't open up.

"It's broken. Only opens from the outside," he confessed.

"Well then why were you reaching over like you were going to open it for me?!" I demanded.

"Dang girl, I didn't want it to look like I knew my door was broke and didn't fix it. So now you know."

I blushed, "Tre I don't care your door is broken. That just means you have to be a gentleman and let me out."

"Oh, yeah. Haha. Hey, why you don't got no boyfriend?"

167

Let's see, I'm locked in a car and this fine boy is talking to me, and he has a girlfriend. How do I answer this, "Because you're taken?"

"You mean, Sarah? She broke up with me like a week ago because I won't apply to Morehouse. She's into Spellman and wants me near her. I'm sure she'll get in but I ain't leaving this state. And if I were, it'd be Howard. Howard's tight! My homey go there. His dorm be havin' hella...Anyway, my parents are giving me the furniture shop to run after graduation so they can retire. Hey, I'm just not a college guy."

"Oh yeah, the furniture shop. Your mom donated that wooden bench we have in the courtyard at school, huh?"

"Yup. Like I said, they want me to run the shop and I like that idea. I can work on my art and continue my family business."

"Tre, you're not what I thought."

"Oh really? Come here and see if this is what you thought?" With his eyes closed and lips floating my way all I could think of was Bronson. I pictured Bronson's face and Bronson's lips. My and Bronson's special time shared under the tree was popping up in my head. His faint voice haunted my memory.

From far off I could hear, "Ollie!" then closer, "Ollie!?"

Opening his eyes before our lips met, "Hey! Is that Just B?!"

My skin turned grey. Just B walked up to Tre's car, accompanied by my mom. Bronson must have told her about the blue house. A local radio station was doing an interview

THE MONSTER IN MY ROOM

with him that week. I heard. All of us had heard. Given the history of our breakup I can't imagine what brought him to my neighborhood. Leave it to me to be busted in yet another compromising predicament.

Stevie's screaming accusations penetrated the passenger side window, "Is this how all your BSU meetings go?! Is that man your classmate?! Have you just been sitting here all night?! Get out this car!"

This is obviously not how I wanted my door opened.

BOOKER

TOULOUSE OR NOT TO LOSE

The cabin doors to the airplane opened for boarding. The idea of going to France was cool with Lawrence. He just thought his first trip to France would have been a romantic vacation with just Olivia and not to marry off her best friend. Olivia felt similar to Lawrence but knew they were the only family Sabrina had.

Missing the wedding was not an option. The bonus was that Sabrina's future in-laws covered the air fare for Olivia and her family to fly out which made it rude to refuse Sabrina's invitation. On the flight to France, Olivia had a lot of time to think about the passages she had just written about Tre and Bronson. Especially since she left her laptop at home so that she could focus on Sabrina getting married.

Toulouse or not to lose a friend that was drifting away? *Toulouse* or not to lose an opportunity to travel the world? *Toulouse* or not to lose an argument with the man you want to spend the rest of your life with?

Livia had become drenched with emotion concerning the abrupt wedding overseas. Not always understanding her friend's adventurous lifestyle, Livia would always come through for Sabrina, no matter what. Olivia let go of her anxieties as the plane descended. Though she had never been a Bridesmaid or

Maid of Honor this would be the easiest job of the sorts – all she had to do was show up. Planning was done. Venue acquired and lodging arranged for all attendees. Nurse Drake's family possessed myriad cars, bedrooms, and love to share with Sabrina's special guests.

Among the list of those that did not enjoy the flight to Toulouse were all five members of Olivia's family. They all hoped the drive to Louvier Manor, would be smoother than the flight. Livia was surprised to see that the French drove on the right. Lawrence chimed in with a fun fact, "Honey, this is not Australia. In fact, France and America were the leaders of right-side driving in the 1700's. They controlled the horses with their whips in right hand, while keeping eye on wagons passing on the left."

"Oh no, kids," Livia joked, "We brought the 'college professor' along with us again! Let's ditch him."

Livia pretended to open the car door. The kids roared with laughter and Lawrence joined them. The driver dropped them off at Louvier Manor. It was clothed in ivy preceded by an iron gate and an enormous fountain. The kids took to the fountain with a blast of energy.

In groups of two and three, the people flowed out of the front doors and pooled together as a welcoming committee. Livia and Sabrina jumped into each other's arms and rocked back and forth. Lawrence and the kids were in need of an introduction. Next there were bursts of Bonjours from papas, mamans, soeurs, and a drone of other family members and friends with pleasant greetings.

The Louviers stood out as an attractive pair. They loved their son, Drake, and openly doted on their soon to be daughter in-law, Sabrina. Claire, Maya, and Salem quickly adopted Grand-mere Louvier. A prepared woman, Mrs. Louvier, had purchased toys for all the children, eight in total. Mrs. Louvier was very loving towards the children.

The week leading up to the wedding was magical. On the evening of their arrival to Toulouse a huge feast was prepared, and everyone got better acquainted. The entire guest list was staying at The Louvier Manor, totaling thirty-two in all. Mrs. Louvier was similar to Sabrina in that her family was not represented well in the course of celebration. Besides Mrs. Louvier's sister, nephew, and Drake's siblings, everyone else were relatives and friends of Mr. Louvier and Drake. The attendants included Mr. Louvier's parents as well.

The chemistry filling the room was momentous. Sabrina was elated and could imagine no other time like this in her life. After the feast, they all danced on the patio under the soft outdoor lights. They sipped wine, cocktails, and beer, long after the children had worn themselves out and nodded off to sleep. Pair by pair, everyone retreated to their room assignments. Each person slept well past 10:30am the next day.

Euphoric was the best way to cap the previous night's events. Half the guests woke up around 1:00pm to get the rest they needed. Almost every night going forward, they stayed up past 2:00am. Day Two in Toulouse was more relaxed. The women and men split up. The garden presented a wonderful tea party for the women while the men headed off to play pool and grab a drink at the pub Drake's cousin managed.

Livia was soaking in the moment. The sites were phenomenal. They visited vineyards and museums. Sabrina was able to show sister-friend the part of France she had grown to love and possibly call home. Livia had brought her dress but joined in with all the women for their final fittings of the dresses they ordered. Sabrina looked breathtaking during her fitting. The final alterations had been completed so she could take her dress home.

The gown was satin, embellished with tiny pearls. It was fitted, mermaid style, no train. The front of the dress presented a classic sweetheart neckline with sheer off-the-shoulder sleeves. On her chest rested the same diamond pendant her mother wore on her own wedding day. In her hair she displayed a tiny owl pin once belonging to her father.

Mrs. Louvier pinned Sabrina's hair in an updo for the fitting. A veil which was hand made by Mrs. Louvier's sister was brought to the fitting as well. It accented the dress marvelously.

Livia allowed a skinny stream of tears to flow down her face. Here was her best friend, finally getting the wedding and husband she truly deserved. It was less than a year ago that her friend's heart could have stopped forever. Now it beat with passion and desire like living out a fairy tale.

Before flying out to Paris where the actual ceremony was to take place, the entire wedding party came together one last time to shower the couple with gifts and toasts of affection.

It was out of tradition to hold the reception before the wedding but that is exactly what they did. The couple would leave from Paris and then travel on to Italy for their honeymoon. The guests would leave from Paris and return back to their respective homelands. The day before the wedding, Livia flew up to Paris with Sabrina. Livia loved the restaurant and the studio apartment above it. On top of the restaurant and apartment was rooftop seating that was transformed to accommodate the wedding ceremony.

After the grand tour, the two of them had an old-fashioned sleep over. Hanging out in their pajamas with a few bottles of champagne, they reminisced and looked back at old photos from their college days. Livia spotted a series of photos with her old roommate and Sabrina's old friend, Gene.

"Oh my gosh, Bri! Look at the three of us. You couldn't tell us nothin'!!!" The two of them slapped high-fives. Livia continued, "Gene would have loved Paris, but I totally get her not wanting to fly out here with a newborn baby."

Sabrina replied, "When our schedules line up, we should fly down to Cali and go see her and the baby. Wait, I guess if want to pick up and go somewhere, now I'll have to first ask my husbaaaand!" Sabrina reminded herself. They both cracked up, toasted their champagne glasses, and kept looking at photos.

The next day was the morning of the wedding and they headed to the spa for a full makeover. They started with massages, followed by mani-pedis. After makeup and hair, they returned to the studio apartment to get dressed.

They felt like it was the last time the two of them would see one another for a long time. In effort to keep tears from ruining their makeup, they did not make eye contact for most of the day. Livia joined up with Lawrence and the kids on the roof after getting dressed. Lawrence looked especially handsome in his grey tux which complemented Livia in her pale-yellow gown. Salem slept through it while Claire, Maya, and one other girl sat cross legged around Sabrina's dress in the grass while tossing rose petals throughout the ceremony. Those photographs promised to be timeless. Directly after the ceremony, there were formal pictures and a farewell to the newly married couple as they rode off to the airport in a rented, classic, blue 1941 BMW 327. Of course, Papa and Maman Louvier followed behind to make sure the car was properly returned.

For many reasons, the flight home felt especially long. Initially Lawrence was complaining to Livia for the cause of them missing their annual Hawaii trip due to the time off from flying to France, but Hawaii was far off in the back of his mind. Drake and his family were easy for Lawrence to fit in with. Being able to witness Olivia's face during the past week gave him more satisfaction than Hawaii ever could.

Right as the captain announced the landing of the plane, Livia woke up in a cold sweat. She locked eyes with Lawrence. "The nightmare?" he asked. "On the plane?"

Livia nodded and closed her eyes, but not to sleep. The plane safely landed, and she kept her eyes closed. They patiently waited for everyone else to disembark the plane before even trying to move a muscle. It was useless to try and maneuver with three children and several bags amidst the narrow aisle way and crowded ceilings. Once the aisle was clear, they gathered themselves with the help of two flight attendants, were off the plane, and on their way home.

It took Lawrence three trips back and forth to the car to get all their bags inside the house. Salem helped, or rather watched, as his Mommy unpacked the bags and while Lawrence unpacked the drive-through food on the kitchen table for everyone to eat.

After the late dinner, Lawrence gathered the kids downstairs in the family room to watch a movie. Livia popped some popcorn and brought the large popcorn bucket down to the family room to join them. Lawrence let her get settled while he went back upstairs for drinks, napkins, and a DVD he had found at the store.

"What movie is it Daddy Pop?" Maya wanted to know. "I bet it's Toy Story! Or Maleficent! Is it Maleficent, Daddy?"

Claire jumped in, "Alice in Wonderland is scary Mommy! Do we have to watch?!"

"Claire, I'm sure Daddy wouldn't pick something scary." Livia looked over at Lawrence with a scrunched forehead and he furrowed his in return. She laughed.

"Scayy-wee?" asked Salem. "No Buddy Boy, it's not scary." Livia hoped she was telling the truth and now met Lawrence with wide eyes, "Is it Guac?" She demanded, as more of a threat than a question.

"Nooooo! You guys need to relax more. Maya, it's a movie Mommy loved when she was a girl. I hope you guys will love it, too. I really got it for Mommy, but we can all watch with her."

At a whisper, "Crooklyn? Guac, are you sure they are old enough for this movie?"

Lawrence wrapped his arm around his lady as the kids munched away at their popcorn, eyes glued to the screen. Soon after bellies were full and everyone had cuddled together on the oversized couch, they fell asleep. All of them were snoozing long before the movie concluded. Somehow, the credits rolling had magically caused Livia and Lawrence to open their eyes at the same time. Livia started to clean up, but Lawrence handed Salem to her and told her to head upstairs. He cleaned up and carried the girls to bed before joining Livia.

With Salem tucked away in his crib and the girls knocked out, Lawrence found himself feeling around under the sheets for Livia's smooth body. His fingertips traced her hips down to her thighs. His body rolled over so that he could begin using both hands. Livia moaned in agreement to his soft caress. Her body arched and slow danced beneath the sheets. Both hands slid underneath Livia's shirt to gently massage her back. Keeping one hand on her back, he moved the other hand down her spine and continued to glide past the waistband of her leggings.

Olivia shifted onto her back and grabbed at Lawrence's hair. They enjoyed a connection that they hadn't been able to visit the way they wanted to while abroad. Olivia tugged at Lawrence's arms to remove his shirt and clawed into his biceps. He enveloped her bare body into his.

Olivia's hands and fingers pressed every inch of his back as they both arrived at a place of familiarity. Lawrence kissed at her neck and shoulders before rolling on his back and tossing her on top of his chest. They laid nose to nose and he asked, "How much do you love me, Liv?"

"Guac. To the moon and back." She wanted to say. But the traveling and staying up late had taken a toll on her. When she opened her mouth, all that came out was a terrible cough, "Ackakakcughg Ahgggg uck uck hgggnah."

"Baby! You're sick! Aw, Babe. Why didn't you say something?" Olivia smiled at Lawrence and wanted to reply but she knew that would make her cough again. They looked into each other's eyes and Lawrence knew exactly what she wanted to say. He gently laid her on her side and grabbed a warm towel from the bathroom for her as well as a fresh pair of pajamas.

He disappeared into the kitchen for five minutes and came back with a warm heat pack for her neck and her favorite mug filled with hot tea.

By morning, after she rested, he had her propped up with comfy pillows. He also placed a pair of warm fuzzy socks on her feet. Her personal, in-house, doctor kissed her on the forehead and left the room.

Lawrence set the pot on the stove to heat her up some soup and poured a glass of orange juice to serve to his patient.

The kids were dressed and ready for church the best way Lawrence knew how. He promised to take them out to eat afterwards to be sure that Livia could get optimal rest in a quiet house.

Before heading to church, Lawrence ran Livia a steamy bath with bath salt plus a few fresh squeezed lemons to help rid her body of toxins, just like she'd do for him when he was sick.

Livia also added some eucalyptus and lavender oil to her bath. She was able to relax for half an hour before the bath started to lose heat.

Livia got out, moisturized her skin with lotion, and sank into a long, cozy, robe. She heated another can of soup in the kitchen. Feeling like she had a little more energy than the early morning and attempting to take advantage of a quiet house, Olivia grabbed her laptop and settled into penning a few more lines about her post-meeting hang-out with the high school BSU president.

✳✳✳

Stevie pulled me out of Tre's car. I was beyond embarrassed by having my mom and ex-boyfriend rescue me out of the malfunctioning vehicle of my new love interest and walk me inside the house. At the same time, I was feeling flush. This flush feeling, I hadn't felt since the last time Bronson Palmblen and I were together.

That wasn't surprising given the fact I was just about to hit up a major make out session with Tre. But I couldn't shake the image of B in my mind. I was definitely confused now. Not only because B came to my house looking for me, but also because I couldn't tell if I were flush over B or over Tre.

I mean, I was definitely attracted to Tre. Who wasn't? He was very muscular. I'm judging his physique is from countless hours spent in his parent's shop building stuff. Or maybe he dedicated himself to a gym routine. I really didn't know, but God had indeed shined upon him. The hair on his face was thick and full for an 18-year-old boy, but it was incredibly sexy.

He was cocoa brown. His hair was dark and curly like mine, but a lot thicker. The sides and back of his hair were tapered and faded down low until reaching his bearded face.

To most, he'd be classified as short, but to me he seemed just right. Just right like I was Goldie Locks, but the black version. I could imagine myself fitting perfectly in his strong arms. With the casual way he dressed and the apparent dirt beneath his nails I could tell he was rugged.

Although B and I had come very close to intercourse, we were only having what I had come to call "fake" sex. I had no idea what "real" sex was, and I wouldn't know until Tre taught me. Now that I think of it, I was most definitely flushed over Tre.   Possibly Tre was unaware of his drop-dead gorgeousness.

I was all *too aware* of it, which made it really hard for me to concentrate on what B was saying to me. But not too hard for me to say to B what I needed to say to him.

My mom, Stevie, was furious from walking around with Bronson looking for me, when I didn't come home on time. Above all else, she was glad I was safely home. Since she was late for work; waiting around for me. So, she did not devote a great deal of time scolding and lecturing and punishing my reckless behavior. Furthermore, she actually left me in the house alone with Bronson.

"Ollie, I don't know what else to do with you. I may need to call your father on this one. Look, I have to go to work. You STAY in this house the rest of the evening. I cannot believe I am saying this, but I'd rather leave you with Bronson than that overgrown boy in that car. Olivia... Just look, you know you are not supposed to get in anyone's car I haven't met! And I might as well say it. If you are going to have sex..."

"Mommy..." I never call her Mommy.

We aren't that affectionate. I didn't even know what I was going to say to follow that, but I had never had the "sex" talk with her and I surely didn't want to be having it in front of B.

"Ollie. Listen, I was your age once and I know what teenagers do. Like I said, I'd rather you do it here with someone I know. I can't be with you every minute, but I hope that I raised you well enough to trust you to abstain from sex. I am leaving now. But Bronson waited two hours for you to get home. I might not have found you if he didn't tell me about the blue house you used to have him drop you off to instead of in front of ours. So, he can stay for a little bit. But I will call you when I get to work, and he had better be gone."

"Yes, Momma."

The doorway she had been standing in was now closed and locked. Bronson took me by hand and walked me to my room. I wanted to do all the bad things Stevie told me not to do just to spite her, but I hadn't heard a word of what B was saying because I was thinking about Tre.

I was wondering if Stevie had the chance to get to know Tre the way she had known B, then maybe she would let Tre stay over the way she was letting B stay at this moment.

If only Tre were sitting on my bed, picking up where we had left off in his car, I could enjoy this bit of freedom Stevie granted. B was standing in the middle of my room, declaring his love to me.

Here and there I could pick up a few topics he was touching on, like him talking to Stevie about letting me come travel with him on long weekends and school breaks.

I thought there was no way Stevie would agree to anything he was saying unless she was getting tired of me. Unless she didn't know what else to do bring us closer together. Maybe, instead of losing me to an argument, she would let me free like a bird in hopes I would return happily and not drift further away.

I wanted this freedom, but it was clear to me now that I wanted this freedom with Tre. Even if I didn't know the truth about Sarah, I still wanted *him*. And now that I knew there was a possibility of Tre also wanting me, I had to let go of B. My mom was wrong about Tre. I was gonna prove it to her.

Tre and I could grow old together owning *our* carpentry shop. I was so far into my fantasy that I was allowing B to have a one-sided make out session. His hands were under my shirt and his tongue flopping around in my mouth and, me, I was flush all over again, but once more it was for Tre. I was daydreaming that my mouth was on Tre. When I opened my eyes, I knew it was completely over between B and me. I just didn't know how he would take it.

"Wait," smooch, "I can't," smooch, "do," smooch, "this." I pushed Bronson back from me and pulled my shirt back down.

"But you heard Stevie," he reminded me. "She practically said, 'happy fucking!' and left for work. Ollie don't do this now. You don't have anything to worry about, your own *mom* said it was ok."

"That's not what she was saying Bronson."

"Yeah, but we can take that and run with it. I want you and if you don't want me gettin' wit' other girls on the road, you're gonna have to give me more. More than...*this*. Look, I don't care about that guy Tre. Our love is stronger than that. He's cool, I know him. And I know his girlfriend, so I believe you that he was just giving you a ride home. Anyway, with me gone, I know you have needs. I have needs, too, but now we don't have to get it from other people. Your mom just gave us the GREEN LIGHT. Now *come on*. Open up for me."

"I just can't Bronson. Okay, I did miss you at first."

"At first!?"

"Yeah, at first. And it's just the distance and well, maybe a little about the fact that you may be already seeking *needs* elsewhere. You dumped me. For music! I just don't love you anymore."

"So, who you love? You love Tre?! I just told you – he got a bitch. He gon' play you just like he played her. Girl, you got one more chance. I will forgive you because I have been gone a long time and I know you don't like being away from me. Winter break is coming up and I already bought you the ticket. Come to New York for a week with me. I have a video shoot, photo shoot, and a few interviews. You can see the life I can give you. Tre can't give you none of that!"

"Bronson, you are trippin' talking to me like that. You need to leave."

"You'll change your mind, Ollie. You just mad, Baby. I'm here through the weekend." He threw a set of keys at me that I caught against my chest.

He explained, "I brought you a gift too. You don't need no dude givin' you no rides. You don't need no bus. You can drive your mom to work. You need me, Baby. You need B."

In disgust, I let the keys drop to the floor.

"Just leave, *please*."

Bronson grabbed his jean coat with this new arrogance about himself and walked up to me and reached for my chin. I flinched a little because this was a Bronson that I didn't know, a Bronson that my Stevie left me alone in the house with.

I can't imagine what he had told her to get her to agree to New York. He forced his lips against mine and gave me a toothy kiss and walked out the front door.

That was possessive, I thought. That Bronson would just throw money, plane tickets, and literally car keys at me and then take a kiss? He violated me and believed he could buy me with his new money.

I stood there, frozen, and in need of a hug. I needed a *mommy*; the name I had accidentally called Stevie and now maybe I wanted it to be true.

The phone rang and I jumped in place. I was thinking Bronson was coming back to take me because he thought that he owned me, that he had paid for me and I was his merchandise.

Fame had definitely changed B. And although I was glad that this was probably the last time, I'd ever see him, I did wish him the best. I was in love with him once, but I could never win against fame and fortune.

The phone! The phone was ringing but I was still frozen. It wasn't Bronson coming back to take me. It was just the phone.

I figured it was Stevie. She'd be calling to tell me she had made it to work and that Bronson had better not still be at the house.

"Hi, Stevie. He's gone. He just left." I chanted in a monotone voice. "And – I'm not going to New York, so I hope you're happy."

"Who is Stevie? Is Stevie your other man? I thought you didn't have no boyfriend when in fact, you got a few," Tre laughed on his end of the line.

"Hello?! Who is this?!" I asked. I ran to the kitchen to check the caller I.D. It wasn't Stevie. It wasn't the hospital. The caller I.D. said *Tracey Collins.*

Chapter 7
Calling Collins

I WONDERED AT first how Tracey Collins had gotten my number. Then it dawned on me. I had written it on the sign-in sheet at the very first BSU meeting. Immediately after that thought, it occurred to me that I had had his number all this time, too. I know I would have been nervous after he picked up the line on the other end. It's just the realization; knowing I had a way to connect with him all this time.

Anyway, he did have the guts to call me! Suddenly I began to wonder why now and how did he know to call? He must have known I was in trouble for the way Stevie had snatched me out of his car. From the way Bronson hugged me when I got out of the car, Tre must have concluded that I did, in fact, still have a boyfriend. So, like anyone else would have done, why didn't Tre just go on about his night and forget I even existed?

"Tre? Is that you? Is Tracey your mom's name? Are you named after her?" I just couldn't find any other words to come out of my mouth at the time. I mean, I know how I felt. Being that I just kicked a millionaire out of my house for this guy, he had to hold some weight.

This is the guy I was sweating over and I didn't know what to say to him besides, *"Are you named after your mom?"*

"No. My mom is Sonia. I'm Tracey or Tre; for short."

"Oh, cute." Why did I say cute?! "Stevie is my mom's name. It's short for Stevonia. How did you? Why did you? I mean, not that you can't call, but...you saw me walk off with my mom and Bronson... Wait. Where are you calling me from?"

He laughed a cool laugh. It was low and scruffy.

"Slow down Baby Girl. Look, you know we like each other. Let's just say that. What happened was, my car ran out of gas around the corner from your house. I saw your mom walking to the bus stop. Then I saw your boyfriend drive down the street like twenty minutes later. Look, I'm just sayin' if *I* had you to myself..."

"He's not my boyfriend. Hold up, so are you stranded? You have a cellular phone? How you gonna get home?"

"Baby Girl. I'm a man. I got this. But it's cute how you care so much about me getting home. I called my dad too. This is a company cell phone. All the shop employees have one. Employee perk, I guess. Anyway, my dad is on his way with a gas can, but he was at the shop which is like 45min away. So, when I assumed you were home alone, I called to make sure *you* were ok."

I turned to mush right there on the kitchen floor. The phone was lying on top of a pile of mush because that is all I was at the moment. My mush lips mumbled, "How did you know my dad wouldn't pick up the phone??"

"If you had a daddy, *he* would have been dragging *me* out of my car instead of your *mom* dragging *you* out."

"Okay, you gotta point there. So, are you cold out there waiting?"

"I don't have to be. You can come and wait with me."

"That would take me walking outside in the dark, this late, by myself to find your car. Uh uh. Isn't that why you offered me a ride in the first place? So, I wouldn't be walking in the dark alone?"

"You're right, I did. That's why I am actually at your front door right now. So... I was wondering. Could I wait inside...with you?"

"Creep! How long have you been at my door?"

He laughed an adorably cute laugh, this time with a slightly higher pitch than before. I could tell he liked me.

"Baby Girl, I am not at your door for real. I'm just playin'. You didn't let me drive you to your door remember? But if you tell me, can I come be with you, where it's warm?"

"You're funny. Well, I guess you can come inside. It's the house with the rose garden and the long porch, three doors down from the blue house. But come through the back, I have nosey neighbors."

It took three minutes before Tre was inside my house. How did it come to this? Oh yeah – I remember. It was dark out. My bus had stopped running. I was new to his car. I was locked in his car.

I was going to kiss him, or he was going to kiss me. My mom and ex-boyfriend barged in on us and in a flash, he was history. Or so I thought.

He wasn't history. This was the beginning. In the three minutes it took him to come to my door I had gone to the bathroom and brushed my teeth. I didn't want the remnants of Bronson on my breath. I glossed up with my tube of Lip Smacker's lip gloss and sprayed some of Stevie's perfume, then straightened the comforter on my bed.

And he was in my house now. No one else was there but the two of us. We skipped pass the living room and went directly to my bedroom. I know what he wanted, and he knew what I wanted. And he was more than willing to give it to me.

He wrapped his arms around me, low on my back and I held him the same, putting my arms underneath his. He looked into my eyes and I felt like I was exploding with curiosity of going all the way with him.

We kissed and kissed and kissed and kissed and he laid me down onto the bed. He was so strong the way he picked me up without me even knowing it. We were in my bed when he asked me.

"Do you have...," he began an awkward question.

"What, a condom? Aren't the guys supposed to have those?"

He started his question again, "Do you have love for him still?"

I was irritated he picked this very moment to ask about B.

I sighed with irritation, "Do I have love for who? Bronson Palmblen? No! Why is he coming up right now? Is he your friend? He did say he knew you. If he is your friend, then me and you being together this is weird, I get it."

"No. He's not my friend. But...that brand new car parked behind your house...is that his? Did he buy that for you? Because if it was your mom's, she would not be bussin' it to work right?"

"Uh...long story. The car is getting returned tomorrow. It was a misunderstanding. Just like you, having a girlfriend. I misunderstood that, right? You don't have a girlfriend, do you?"

"It's a long story too, but no, I don't. I want you. I want you to be my girl."

It kept playing in my head over and over. I wanted to be his girl, too, but I didn't respond. I just stared into his eyes for a while and he stared back. I put my head down and nuzzled into his neck and he kissed my forehead.

I must have fallen asleep. I turned over to adjust my body in my bed. It was uncomfortable laying there in full clothes. When I reached out for him, he was gone.

I reached for my clock and strained my eyes to read 1:23AM. That was funny I thought. It was like the time I woke up and the time was 12:34AM. That happened after the first night I met Bronson Palmblen. But this was without the four.

Was this a sign telling me to 4-get Bronson?

Being with Tre was easy as 1-2-3. He knew to leave before my mom got off her shift and she had no idea he was ever there. I wrote Stevie a letter. She was asleep when I left for school later that morning.

~~Stevie~~ Momma,

Sorry about last night. I lost track of time. It won't happen again. I didn't have sex with B. Please send his car back. I'm not going to New York. We broke up.

Ollie

I walked to the bus stop for school and waited. But before the bus came, I saw Tracey pulling up from a distance. He stopped at the curb and got out to let me in on the passenger side. We exchanged no words. It was happening how it was supposed to be. We naturally went together. I was his girl. He was my man. When he got in on his side, I kissed him, and we drove on to school.

As we pulled up to school, the other students watched. They looked at the new couple. I was the girl that had gotten dumped on national television, and now I was with the school's benchmark for "Cool Guy 101." Tre didn't care that I had gotten dumped. He didn't look down on me for blowing it with a superstar. He was glad that he had the chance to show me what real love was like and I believed he would never treat me like Bronson did.

However, I failed to realize, and Tracey neglected to warn me that while Sarah had been attending the *all-girls* school, her best friend since the first grade went to our school. And her best friend was worse than the FBI and CIA put together. I couldn't know she had watched us pull up to the campus together. I couldn't know that she watched us walk through the double doors together. I couldn't know that she was trailing us down the hallways and that she noticed how he walked me from classroom to classroom the whole school day risking being late to all of his own classes.

I couldn't know that Sarah's best friend turned secret agent had watched Tracey as he handed me his car keys first thing every morning so that I would know he wasn't going anywhere without me. I also couldn't know that after a week or so of watching us, this secret agent had been calling Sarah each night and telling her what was going on. She was building a case. She couldn't merely go off of one day of scandalous behavior, she needed a history of misconduct.

Tracey didn't lie to me about Sarah. They had broken up indeed. But that long story, that long story that he hadn't gotten around to telling me was about to be revealed. It was going to be revealed in front of everyone at the school and even some of the staff and security. It was going to be revealed during an assembly.

The Black Student Union had been working on a project to get a panel of police officers to talk to students about racial profiling and the affects it was having on the community. My worst nightmare actually happened as the assembly was letting out. Tracey and I were shaking the officer's hands and thanking them for truthfully answering the hard questions. It was loud in the main foyer, which was to be expected with any school assembly, as all the students walked back to their classrooms. The odd thing, though, was that no one was actually heading back to class. The foyer kept getting stuffed beyond capacity.

Tracey and I had finished up with the panel and were on our way through the crowd when some girls shouted, "There they go now!"

BOOKER

AN ENGAGING DISCUSSION

Months had gone by with no weddings, pageants, or formal dances to occupy Livia's time. She prided herself in staying fit by working out and eating right. Jogging was a daily routine for her and coming up with newer healthier recipes to feed her family was a welcomed challenge. She regularly prepared meals ahead of time for the family and kept the kids busy with after-school activities.

Claire and Maya liked taking tap dance class together and all three kids were signed up for swimming lessons. While the girls and Lawrence were in school, Salem stayed home with his mommy. There was a huge, wooden, play structure in the back yard. But on days when it was pouring rain, they would drive to the Indoor Sandbox to keep busy.

As Salem got older, the more mobile and inquisitive he became, and Livia had to find more stimulating activities for him to do. She often wished Salem had cousins his age or that she could find him some friends. She did come across moms with other one-year-olds at the Indoor Sandbox, but she would rather be spending time with Sabrina and Palmer than those ladies. However, Sabrina and Palmer were career women and weren't available for regular play dates.

They had something that Livia wished she had. They had the

drive, power, and ability to start and run successful businesses. Sabrina had the restaurants and Palmer had the art gallery and clothing boutique. Even her roommate from college, Gene, had success as Senior Director of Engineering for a software startup company.

Lawrence's friend, Jordan, had two children in middle school. Xavier had just begun his marriage as had Sabrina. Palmer and her husband Cody were completely content raising and breeding pit bulls, or four legged babies as they liked to call them.

This train of thought led Livia to the hole in her heart for her nephews, Kelan and Kelvan. She often thought about them. She imagined they were into cars like Kelpie. She wanted to know how tall they'd gotten and how they were doing in school. Livia's visits with them were far and few between. Livia feared the notion the twins would ever find out what their father had done to her.

Livia preferred to be evasive when it came to Kelpie, rather than reveal how the abuse she endured affected her relationships as an adult. How she preferred having sex with her eyes open to avoid flashbacks of abuse. How she struggled to love Salem, for fear he'd grow up to abuse women. How she was extremely protective over Claire and Maya, never letting them get close to friends. Livia often believed it to be her fault that she allowed herself to be abused for so long. As a child, no one took action against the repeated abuse she endured. That made her feel like no one would help her through it as an adult.

Livia lived with guilt for not fighting harder to be heard as a child, and shame of the notion that anyone would see her as less than the innocence that was stolen from her. Often, she was conflicted by the sisterly love she had for her brother. In her younger years, she read in the news and watched on TV about how child rapists and child molesters went to prison for a lifetime. She couldn't bring herself to charge her own flesh and blood with a life sentence, behind bars. And because of that, she, herself, was serving an internal life sentence of shame and humiliation.

Livia prided herself in the love she was blessed to experience with Lawrence, a man who was able to make her feel like no other human being could. She delighted in the children she bore that loved her unconditionally. However, she had to bury herself in a pile of hobbies and activities to keep her mind off of the unmentionable. Livia was a seamstress, interior designer, mother, lover, cook, chauffeur, jogger, yoga enthusiast and she did not hesitate to add to the list. She began writing and it was at this point in her life that she truly found her outlet and began feeling free.

It was a constant struggle for Olivia to rid her mind of the horrid scenes that would play continuously in her mind throughout the day and wake her up from sweaty nightmares at night. With her eyes closed or opened she could not detach from the sexually abusive events of her childhood. She wondered what would become of a tainted girl. Self-destruction seemed like the answer to her feelings. Each day was a new day to encourage herself to live and not perish by her own hand. Even with a family that loved her and was always by her side, Olivia imagined it would be easier to cease existing rather than to continue living her life with this debilitating dark past.

Olivia knew of women who sold their bodies because they did not believe they were worth more than twenty dollars or had anything more to offer after suffering abuse as a child. She knew of women that had taken to drugs and alcohol, heavy partying, and reckless behaviors to drown themselves in anything that would make them forget about their abuse. There were times that Olivia contemplated finding refuge in those lifestyles for herself.

Protecting her daughters from harm and fearing her son would harm another continued to keep her soul at a tug of war from feeling complete in life. Olivia's mind was trapped by these haunting thoughts that leaked like a broken faucet. To Olivia, it seemed there was only one way to shut the faucet off.

She and Salem were still in the back yard when Lawrence arrived home with the girls from tap class. He glanced out the window and noticed Salem napping on the slide and Olivia was hunched over her knees in the lawn chair. It was odd to him they were separate since they always napped together.

As the girls changed into lounge clothes, Lawrence rushed out back to check on his other two precious loves. Salem was safe and sound asleep on the slide.

Lawrence moved him out of the direct sunlight and laid him on the padded bench in the shaded area. Next he rushed to Livia's side and cradled her in his arms.

"Did something happen? Baby? Baby, why you cryin'?" Lawrence could see the girls peeking out the window and he gave them the "OK" hand gesture and waved them off. Olivia spoke through the gap between her knees and didn't lift her head.

"I don't want to be here anymore."

"Well, you can go inside. C'mon. I'll help you to bed and come back for Salem."

"No, Lawrence. On earth! I don't want to be *here* anymore."

A well of tears flooded Lawrence's eyes and immediately poured out.

"Olivia, don't talk like that. You're scarring me, Liv. I am here with you. Just tell me what to do. What can I do to fix it, Baby? I wanna help. We just can't...this would be nothing without you here with me...and the kids.... We want you here. God wants you here."

"God doesn't want me, Lawrence. God doesn't care about me. Why do you think I don't go to church that much? If God cares about me, then why did God let these things happen to me?! Why did God leave me by myself?!"

Lawrence cried with her for a few minutes and then he told her all the reasons why God did love her and all the reasons why he and the kids loved her and wanted her to be around for generations to come. He told her she was wonderfully made, and that God had not forsaken her or forgotten her. He reminded her there was no greater love than the love Jesus showed by His shed blood when He died on the cross. He also reminded her of God's servant Job that had everything stripped from him including his family, possessions and health, but was restored. He reminded her of the woman with the issue of blood for twelve years that was healed just by touching the hem of Jesus' clothing. He reminded her of all the promises of God. He could not tell her why those things happened to her. But he did tell her how he was inspired by how God had brought her through. And that, if not for God, he didn't think she would have made it this far.

Lawrence then confessed that he read her story when she began writing almost a year ago and how he had been sneaking to read whenever he had the opportunity. He urged her to go on with life because not only did he and the kids need her, but because God needed to use her to reach others. God needed her to help reach the women that did sell their bodies and the women that did take to drugs and alcohol; to help the women that continued to seek abusive relationships that had not found their worth; to help the woman that was holding up on the outside but crumbling on the inside. And ultimately, to help save the woman that was ready to step off the ledge of life because she didn't know her own value.

"Look at me Olivia." He held her face in his hands and asked her if she believed that God had brought her through.

"Yes, Lawrence," she responded like she was afraid to admit it, "I do but, it's just so hard to deal with all of this."

"Only the Lord knows the plan He has for you. But His Word says He plans to prosper you and not leave you but to give you hope and a future. Romans 10:9 says that, 'if you confess with your mouth and believe in your heart that Jesus Christ is Lord then you shall not perish, you shall not perish, you shall not perish but have everlasting life.' I want you to believe *for* yourself. And I want you to believe *in* yourself and know that we can conquer this together with God's help. Do you believe that?" Lawrence knew this was the moment he'd been waiting for.

"Yeah...," Olivia answered.

"*Do you?*" Lawrence repeated with a crack in his voice.

"I do," Olivia confirmed with more confidence.

"Then please marry me, Olivia. I know that you've always had God in your heart. I've just never heard you say it. I will always be here to support you through this. Whatever it takes. But I no longer wanna be in this relationship as your '*baby's daddy.*' I wanna be with you as your *husband.*"

"Oh, Lawrence. You keep asking me to marry you, knowing my fears about marriage…. You know I love you. And I know how badly you want us to be married, but I also know how hard it is for you to deal with my depression and anxiety. I want you to be able to freely walk away from me when you've had all you can handle."

"You are more than that to me! I love YOU and that means loving ALL of you. But my prayer will always be that you will honor this relationship by becoming my wife. I want to publicly unite with you in front of friends and family. I know that this is hard for you, but we are in this together. I want to make this commitment to show you that I never plan on walking out on you, no matter what hardships we might face. So that I know that you believe in our future too and that you plan on spending the rest of your life with me by your side. So that I know we will be holding hands as our children get married and start their own families one day. I want to know we will be sitting on our porch someday, watching our great grandchildren play in our yard. Will you be there with me? Will you marry me, Olivia Shania Stone?"

Olivia's perception of marriage shifted drastically with Lawrence's heartfelt proposal. She began to let down her guard and be open to vulnerability.

"Yes, Lawrence, I will."

The two of them sat holding each other tightly, both bawling in happiness at what was to come. A nudge came from under their elbows. It was Salem awake from his nap.

"Don't cwy Mama. Don't cwy Dada. I wite here. I no lost."

"Hey Buddy!" Lawrence exclaimed. He'd almost forgotten that Salem was napping on the bench. "We know you're not lost. We are just crying happy tears. Wait here with Mommy. Give her lots of hugs. I'll be right back."

Lawrence went into the house and found the girls who had been watching cartoons. He told them to turn off the TV and come outside with him because he had something for Mommy.

They waited in the hallway while he went in his room. In Lawrence's nightstand, he kept a tiny box wrapped up in a bag. It was tucked in the bottom drawer all the way in the back inside of a black sock. Urgently he pulled it out of the sock and unwrapped the tiny box from the bag. Quickly Lawrence opened the box to examine its contents and a gorgeous, gold, antique, diamond ring was nestled there, in a velvet grip, waiting to be placed onto Olivia's dainty hand. The ring was specially made to be a replica of the ring Olivia's great grandmother had worn.

Livia had one picture of her great grandmother. Her GG Pearline was in a beautifully simple dress with her hair perfectly in place looking pleasant with a Mona Lisa smile, legs crossed and one hand atop the other. Each time they looked at the photo, Olivia went on about how perfectly stunning the ring was and how she wished she could have tried it on just once so that she could feel closer to her great grandmother. Stevie always spoke highly of GG Pearline, too, which contributed to Olivia's memory of her. With a lot of help from Sabrina with logistics, Lawrence was able to copy the ring almost exactly.

"Daddy Pop. We're waiting..."

Suddenly Lawrence re-appeared in the hallway, helped Maya onto his back and rushed with her and Claire downstairs and outside. They caught the tail end of Patty Cake between Olivia and Salem. Livia had just "put it in the pan" and Salem was cracking up, laughing and wriggling around in her lap. They both ended up laughing really hard when Salem tried to tickle his mommy. Then she looked up at Lawrence and the girls with her face still a bit worn from crying.

"Hey guys! Should we have dinner outside today?" she said with delight.

Lawrence held out his hands for Salem to come. No sooner than he was with his daddy did he reach for Claire to hold him. His arms were wrapped tightly around his big sister's neck and Lawrence's arms were free to reach for Livia and pull her to a standing position. Right when Livia came to her feet, Lawrence went down on one knee. Immediately tears began to roll down her cheeks once more. All three children were silent and had their eyes glued to their daddy. Lawrence's hands were shaking as he held the tips of Livia's fingers.

"For this day I have waited over ten years. I asked you to marry me the moment I fell in love with you, but you wanted to finish school. I asked you to marry me when we found out we were pregnant with Claire, but you thought it wasn't the right time. And when we moved into this house and had Maya and Salem, I asked then, too. I wanted to ask you again, that day under the bridge, but I could tell you were still afraid. I even tried to propose to you at Xavier's wedding near the waterfall, but the timing wasn't right. So, right here and right now at our home and in front of our children, I want to ask you properly." He took the ring out of his pocket and placed it on her finger. All of them were dripping with tears. "Olivia Shania Stone..."

"Yes, Guac?"

"Will you please do me the honor of becoming my wife?"

"Yes, Baby, I will!" Livia declared.

Lawrence stood up and Livia jumped into his arms with her legs wrapped around his waist. He swung her around and around. She whispered in his ear, "This is exactly like GG's ring! I love you so much." He gently let her down and the kids ran up to hug their parents.

"Hey! We can still have dinner outside, but not here. This is cause for a celebration. Girls, go and put on a fancy dress. We're going out to eat!" Lawrence decided.

Everyone went inside and Lawrence called the restaurant to make a dinner reservation. In the room, Livia already laid out her dress and was halfway done putting Salem in a little shirt with clip-on tie. Lawrence walked up behind her and held her by the arms.

"I am excited to plan this wedding with you but promise me one thing."

She put Salem down on the floor and turned around to respond, "What?"

"First, you will finish your book."

"Deal," she said, sealing her promise with a kiss.

Olivia wanted to share the news with Sabrina first, and called her on the way to the restaurant. The two sister-friends were already discussing dates and venues. Next, she called Stevie. Then she called her friends, Palmer and Gene.

The hardest call she had to make was to Bradley Stone. She hadn't spoken with him in over a year. A scary thought about weddings for Olivia was her parents' involvement. She often wondered what it would be like to have her father walk her down the aisle.

As she dialed the number, Lawrence pulled up to valet and was getting the kids out of the car. The attendant let her out and she put her hand over the receiver and told them to go ahead of her. She stood outside the restaurant and promised to only be a few minutes.

A voice answered on the other end of the line.

"Hello?"

"Brad...Daddy. It's me, Liv," she said, not knowing if he'd saved her number.

"Oh, hey Ollie! I knew it was you, Princess. I'm on the other line though. Hold on while I finish this call and I'll click right back over to you, Ollie," he assured her.

Hearing her childhood name was a trigger for Olivia. While waiting on hold, she began thinking about the last guy she told Bradley she was in love with. In her book, *"Ollie"* was getting busted by that guy's girlfriend, Sarah, in the school foyer.

✳ ✳ ✳

I couldn't believe I was surrounded by almost the entire school. Sarah approached us and was looking me square in the eye, though all of her comments were directed to Tracey.

"So, this the bitch you fuckin' wit now?! Her little burnt toast ass lookin' self. Her ol' African reject lookin' self. Do you feed her? She look anorexic. I can't believe this is what you want over me!"

Sarah was a beautiful exotic looking girl. I later found out that her mom was Filipina, and her dad was mixed with black and white. Her long, light brown curls cascaded down her shoulders and back. Her physique was tall and curvaceous. And her lean finger was waving in my face. I must have been in a daze because next she said, "Girl, do you hear me?" I heard everything but she technically wasn't talking to me, so I didn't respond. Instead, Tracey stood up for me.

"Sarah. I'm done with you. Olivia is my girl now and you better fuckin' respect that. I don't love you anymore. I only love this girl right here. Only thing between us is that baby inside of you, and that's *if* you keep it!"

I couldn't believe what I was hearing. I had no idea how to process it. Did this change the dynamic of my relationship with Tracey? I thought I loved him. I thought I had finally found my true love. How on earth could he not tell me he had a baby on the way? Was it because he was ashamed, or afraid I would judge him? Was it because she really might *not* keep it? I cringe at the thought of that. I wondered then at the possibility that she could be lying about the baby just to make him love her. She certainly didn't look pregnant. They had been going back and forth and I could see the security guards pushing their way through the crowd behind us, so I bolted. I forced my way through the other side of the crowd and found the private bathroom in the nurse's office. I cried my eyes into a blur and tried to get over it so I could finish the rest of the school day.

Tracey was supposed to take me home. Three minutes before the last bell rang, I needed to make a choice. I heard Sarah had been escorted off of school property. I assumed Tracey was given a detention slip but wasn't sure. Either way, I needed time to gather my thoughts before going home. The bell rang and he wasn't at the classroom door waiting for me. I looked in the office for him. Didn't find him there which meant he was either in detention or waiting for me by his car. Stevie expected me home right after school. But I needed more time to investigate, so I asked the secretary to use the office phone.

I called Stevie and made up an excuse that I'd be trying out for Dance Troup from 3:00pm to 5:00pm. She gave me the "okay" but demanded I bring home a note to prove I was really at tryouts. I'd have to figure that one out later.

I figured I could at least sit at the park and go over the emotions I encountered. I walked out the side entrance of the school which was the opposite of where the student parking lot was located. I got about halfway to the end of the block and touched Tracey's keys that were hanging around my neck. "Shoot!" I thought. I ran around to the other side of the school since the side doors don't open from the outside and noticed Tracey's car but no Tracey. Going through the front entrance I had to explain to the security guards why I needed reentry, "Uh, I have to pee!"

They let me in, and I went around the corner the long way to the cafeteria, which was past the bathrooms. I looked through the window in the cafeteria door and could see Tracey sitting at one of the tables with his head in his hands. The other kids were doing homework. Detention was another fifteen minutes so I hid out in the girl's bathroom so I wouldn't get caught roaming halls after hours.

The moment I heard voices in the hall I came out of the bathroom to see if Tracey was there. And he was. He was just leaning against the wall outside the cafeteria. The teacher that ran detention must have left right away thinking the students couldn't wait to get as far away from school as possible. His head was still down and his face in his hands. I wanted to yell at him. I needed to cuss him out. The act of throwing his keys in his face also seemed like a great idea. But at that moment all I could express was love for him.

I walked up and grabbed his face and kissed his lips. I was so drawn to him even more than before. Something about seeing him in a vulnerable state made me want to be intimate. I wrapped my arms around his neck and began passionately kissing him. He held my little body against his and I didn't want him to stop for anything.

"Hey! YOU!"

The security guards were coming. Tracey grabbed my hand and we ran like hell out the back door and all the way around to the student parking lot. I tossed him the keys and he ran a little ahead of me, since he was faster, opened my door and then jumped in his side to start the engine. No sooner than I had closed my door, he had peeled out of the parking lot. I snapped my seat belt on as fast as I could. We were both reeling. It was the funniest thing ever! There was so much adrenaline and endorphins running wild. I didn't even say any words. I just rode.

I was leaning down to gather my backpack since it was about the time we should've been pulling up to my house, and I was contemplating inviting him in since Stevie had probably left for work already. But when my head popped back up, we were getting on the on-ramp to the freeway.

"Tre! Where are you going?! You passed my house."

"Baby Girl, do you trust me?"

I didn't know if I trusted him. I just sat there wanting to ask him if the things Sarah claimed were true. I wondered if she was really pregnant. I didn't really notice a baby bump, but she was wearing a big sweater that made it hard for me to see details. Maybe she had lied to him. I wished she were lying. I believed she was lying. I was convinced.

She was too tall for him anyway, and too light. I complemented him in a way that she could not. And either way, I was head over heels for this guy, so I tried not to let Sarah bother me. I didn't answer him though. I didn't know the truth. I had a hard time trusting anyone. So, I sat quietly. He looked at me, but I kept looking forward. He turned on his music and put his hand on my thigh.

Timbaland and Magoo's *Clock Strikes* was playing. I loved that song. I put my hand on top of his and five exits later we were getting off the freeway.

After exiting the freeway, I asked, "Why y'all live all the way over here?"

He smiled and drove two more blocks and pointed out the furniture shop his family owned. It was nice from the street view and I wanted to go in, but I wasn't ready to meet his family, yet.

Both his parents' cars were parked outside the shop. We drove five more minutes and pulled up to his place. He drove his car around to the back where there was another house, like a mini house. He stopped the car there.

"Come on." He said when he opened my car door.

He walked me inside and it was just one big open space with a huge bed in the middle of the room. Off to the side there was a mini kitchen and then a door which I was pretty sure was the bathroom. He took my coat and backpack and set them in the chair. We both gazed into each other's eyes and were standing super close. He put his hands in my hair and said, "She doesn't mean anything to me. We were broken up before she told me about the baby. I don't even have proof it is mine. She probably messin' with other dudes behind my back. You see how pretty she is."

I rolled my eyes and pulled back, but he held me closer and kissed me, "But you! You are more than just pretty. I can talk to you. You are smart and there is something about you that I can't stop thinking about you when we're not together. And I know you are not like her. Sarah?... I know for a fact other dudes that got that ass before me. But you are pure and untouched. She doesn't mean anything to me like you do. I got bored with her. All we did was fuck."

"Okay. That's my cue to leave. Please take me home now, Tracey."

"No. I mean, please stay. Damn, that came out wrong. Look, it's like – I like you! You make me not want to just fuck. For real. It's like, like – I love you, Girl. And I ain't never said that shit to nobody. Like – if *you* was having my baby, I would tell the whole world!"

"Oh, wow. Well, I am too young to be having babies and so are you. But I really like you too. I guess I love you too. I just want to know that I can trust you."

"You can!"

He kissed me and sat me down on his bed and held me. After a moment we laid back just holding each other. Then he told me to get undressed and get under the covers.

"What?! Tracey!"

"Baby Girl, not like that. I just want to make you feel good. I want to give you a massage. Have you ever had a massage before?"

"No. And why do my clothes have to be off for a massage?"

"Because it will feel better that way. Leave your panties on if that makes you feel better. It's gonna help you relax, that's all."

I did want to feel relaxed and I was beginning to trust him. I told him to go in the bathroom while I got undressed so he couldn't see me. I did keep my panties on and glad I had decided to wear cute ones that day. I laid my head in the crook of my elbow and yelled that I was ready. I heard him come out of the bathroom. My eyes were closed but I could tell he turned off the light. Music came on but was soft enough for me to hear the sound of the curtains being closed. K-C and Jo Jo's *All My Life* was playing, and on the bed, I felt that Tracey had joined me.

He pulled back his comforter leaving just his sheet to cover my back. The touch of the softest hands in the world began to rub my body. I know that he just wanted me to feel good. It was definitely working. I was totally relaxed and almost asleep when he asked me if I was too warm. I was very warm. I responded, "Mmm hmmm."

He gently started pulling the sheet down to my waist and stopped there. Then the smell of baby oil reached my nose and before I could react to it his oiled hands were on my back. This made my body quiver. I turned over so that I was facing him. As I opened my eyes, I saw his bare-naked body on the bed with me. He glided his hands over his chest and mine to get the rest of the oil off of his hands. Then he climbed on top of me.

He began kissing me while the music continued in the background. He asked, "Do you trust me?" I nodded yes. Next he asked, "Do you want to be with me?" I nodded yes. Finally, he asked, "Is this okay with you? I won't do it if you don't want me to." I nodded yes and then closed my eyes tightly as he gently pulled my panties to the side and guided his hips forward. We resounded audibly in unison. He asked me to open my eyes. So, I looked at him. He buried his face into my neck and continued, going slowly. But after a few minutes I asked him to stop. He rolled over to lie next to me and held my hand. We didn't speak for almost ten minutes. I wanted to confirm, "Did we just do it?"

He clarified, "Have sex you mean?"

"Yeah." I braced myself for his response.

"Yeah, we did," he carefully replied.

"How far did it go in?" I was curious.

"Like half-way," he said with encouragement.

"Really?" I was impressed, "Because it felt like all the way."

"Nope. Trust me, Ollie, you'll know when it goes all the way. I'll play a different song for you when that time comes," he chuckled. "When it *'seems like you're ready'*," he sang.

"I don't know if I want to do that again, Tracey."

"You don't have to. I will still love you, Baby Girl."

"You should probably take me home and write a note for me!"

"A note?! Saying what? For who?"

"For my mom. I told her I had dance tryouts, so you need to make it look like Ms. Harmon signed the note. Everybody knows her hands shake. Anybody can forge her signature but just not me, Stevie will know if it was me."

As Tracey began to answer, someone tapped on the window. I almost peed my pants. Well my panties since my pants were on the floor.

"Tracey...! That little girl's mom know she over here?!"

"MOM! Yeah. Privacy!"

His mom didn't respond, so I jumped out of his bed and threw my clothes on.

"Tracey! Your mom is here?!?" I was interrogating in a whisper, "I thought she was at the shop! What is she gonna' think of me? Oh my god. Let's go."

Tracey mumbled, "Fuck. She is always in my business. I'm thinkin' bout gettin' my own place. The shop pays me enough. I'm too old for this shit."

We walked out the door, and Tracey's mom was standing right there with the cordless phone in one hand. Her other hand pressed against the receiver so that whoever was on the line could not hear what she said next.

"Little girl, I know your mom from way back. Your mom used to shop at our store all the time. She's even been to my house a few times. Tracey here has had a crush on you since then, but I keep telling him you're too young for him. I don't need no grand babies! Ya hear? Now I don't want to see you back here again. Next time I'll call up to the hospital and speak with yo momma."

Chapter 8
Calling Off Collins

BREAKING IT OFF just wouldn't do! For weeks now, I had been hiding my relationship from Stevie *and* Mrs. Collins, because I absolutely adored Tracey. I was madly in love with him; or maybe it was just infatuation. Maybe I was in a state of euphoria because I had experienced things with him that I never had before with anyone, willingly. Even Bronson and I hadn't gone as far as Tracey and I did. The hard part was not sneaking around with Tracey, it was getting rid of Sarah. She just would not give up.

I had a huge project coming up in Mrs. Holmes' geography class and it was just as I'd imagined that all the good research books were either checked out or not in our school library catalogue. The public library, a few blocks away, was gigantic and there were tons of resources. I used to visit the public library a lot to get away from Kelpie. It was a place I knew Stevie would approve of me being and I always came back with proof that I had actually gone there.

Mrs. Holmes always chose an interactive approach to learning for her students. Most of our projects entailed classroom demonstrations or presenting speeches about the topic we were studying. This current project I was working on involved us having to draw a country out of her hat. I picked Brazil. Well, actually I didn't pick Brazil, I was the last student to grab a country because Mrs. Holmes thought it was a great idea, fair if you will, to let us pick in alphabetical order of our last names. I was last. After we picked a country the project guidelines were to:

- Embrace your country as though you were a native
- Research your country's history
- Find one highlight about your country to diagram
- Prepare a written essay
- Give a 3-minute speech from the content of your essay

So, I decided to focus on the rainforests. I realized I had checked out entirely too many books when I left the library.

Before I could unhook my bike from the rack, the strap on my bookbag snapped. One of the big books fell on the foot of the girl standing next to me.

"I am so sorry. My bad. Good thing you have on sneakers and not flip flops, right?" I tried to laugh it off. After I gathered my last book and tied the straps together to make the bag still work, I noticed this girl was still standing over me. I had already apologized and it's not like she was severely hurt, but she was still hanging around. There was nothing more I could do for her. I threw my leg over my bike and situated my bags in order to take off.

"Hey Darkie! Your memory as bad as your judgment? I know you know who I am so don't play dumb!"

I was looking at her. My eyebrows went up and my lips twisted to one side. My head was about to tilt so I could tell this girl that I did not know her and that she better watch it so I could get this heavy bag back to the house. Right as my long blink was turning into an eye roll, my cornea focused on her attributes. Quickly my brain catalogued key details – fair skin, curly hair, tall legs, amazing lips, and an OVERSIZED SWEATSHIRT, "Sarah?!?"

"Bitch, don't play me Boo Boo. You stop fucking with Tre or Imma fuck you up."

A few things raced in my mind at this point. Number one, I didn't know how to fight and if I did it would have been difficult to do so while on my bike with a ton of library books. B) I didn't feel like fighting over a boy. And lastly, I was beginning to think that the Tracey Collins era was coming to an end after all. I didn't know what made her want him so badly. My mind was taking forever to formulate the words that were eventually going to come out of my mouth. The pits of my shirt started to tingle so I could tell I must have been sweating. "Who Tre?!" I said, being snarky.

"Yeah Tre! D-Did I stutter?!"

She kind of did stutter a second and I don't think it was fully intentional. In any event, I finally did answer, "I been dropped Tre. He didn't tell you?" As I was finishing my last sentence, my wheel had already been turned and my foot already kicked me off to a peddling start. No way was I looking back until I got all the way to the corner. Two reasons: A) If she was chasing me with those tall legs, I needed to keep momentum. And secondly, with my bag all Geri rigged, I couldn't risk toppling over. At the corner, the light was red, so I stole a glance. I saw reverse lights of what must have been her white Jetta pulling out of a parking spot.

In the house, an aroma of fresh casserole filled the hallway. Momma had left for work. The baked casserole was left on top of the stove, still a tad bit warm. It only took a total of five minutes to scarf down a plate of the easy but thoughtful dinner she prepared for me. Next it was to the books. A good twenty minutes of my study hour had been stolen away by time spent trying to process what had just happened at the library. I took a deep breath, said a little prayer, and blasted my music. The only way I was able to focus on my work is if I had my music loud.

To no surprise, the moment I learned the colors of the country's flag and found out Brazil is the biggest country in South America, my front door was being pounded on. I gathered that it was urgent because the first or second time probably wasn't heard over my blaring music. Placing my pointer finger and thumb in the shades allowing a peek to the front porch, I was able to see Tracey. He stood hunched over, sopping wet from the rain showers that started up the second I walked in my house.

"Baby Girl, come on, open up!"

He wasn't totally yelling; I had just shut my stereo off before I walked to the front to answer the door. Tracey walked in then kicked his wet boots off to the side of the door mat. Our eyes stayed locked as I pushed the door closed behind him.

I could feel his breath on my face. My hands crept inside his jacket to slide it off and I let it drop just to the left of his boots. He gripped me by the arms and then gave me a full-on hug. I hugged him for what had to be almost two minutes standing in front of the door. No words had been exchanged but he knew that I knew that he knew what had happened between Sarah and me that day.

He interrupted my study time, but it never had the proper beginning anyway. Every Brazilian woman in the book reminded me of Sarah's pretty face. She was prettier than me, taller than me, and probably more sexually experienced, based off of what Tre said.

But when he looked at me, he had a way of making me feel like I was the only girl in the whole world. It was easy to be with him. He stood up for me and complimented me. We always did everything I liked to do, and he always made sure I was having a good time. We were a great team. So much so that Stevie started to notice it and even lightened up about our age difference.

I had so much to say to Tracey, but the words would not come out. Tracey fell asleep in my bed with me cradled in his arms as I looked up at my glow-in-the-dark stars on the ceiling. I didn't want him to let go of me but a little voice inside kept urging me to call it off. Did I listen? No!

Once I realized I had fallen asleep too, I sprung up to a sitting position in my bed. Stevie might have been okay with knowing Tracey and I held hands at school and went to the movies together. Maybe she was even cool with us kissing. However, Stevie didn't know that Tracey would have spent the night with me most nights out of the week. I was forever thinking we would get caught. Even though he would set his watch to go off at 2:00am, he was always gone well before then.

That next day at school was the same as any other day. Tracey picked me up, walked me to my class and gave me a kiss as he handed over the car keys for safe keeping. During lunch period, we usually took his car to the park to talk and eat lunch but this time he had forgotten to wait for me outside of math class. I walked to his car and waited several minutes and every guy that walked through the corridor continued not to be him. We technically only had 50 minutes if you counted the tardy bells, and with all this waiting, there wouldn't be enough time to get to the park and back to school on time for me to avoid getting a tardy slip.

Instead of being angry I walked to the school library. I considered he might have a few huge projects on his plate, too, being a senior and all. He wasn't in there. I checked the cafeteria. There was one time that he waited for me there because he knew I really liked when they would make corn dogs. All the way to the cafeteria I figured I would have remembered if it were corn dog day. At a glance, the menu calendar showed that corn dogs were not for another week and a half. Then, feeling silly for worrying that he might be up to no good, I returned to the car in hopes he was just running late from changing out of his gym class clothes. I did pass the gym, though, on the way to the cafeteria and it looked totally empty.

He was not at the car and I missed my lunch and went to 5th period super hungry. Mrs. Green sent me to the office for trying to sneak and eat a bag of chips from under my desk. My stomach was growling, my boyfriend was missing, and I got pulled out of class before I could turn in my homework. This was one of those days Monica used to sing about. No one wanted a grade deduction for turning in late work and Mrs. Green didn't play around. If your work wasn't in the basket before the bell rang, she took off half a grade. Since the stipulation for being sent to the office was having to remain for one full class period, it was a done deal.

Sixth period was a blur. The bell rang. Still no Tracey. I dashed to the car, pushing people in the hall and maybe even knocking one girl's book out of her hand. All of that rushing through the parking lot to again find the car sitting there alone. My head whipped around about to storm into the school yelling, "Tracey Collins! Get out here right now!"

My nose was the first to notice the stinging sensation after I had collided with the man missing in action. "Hey Baby Girl!? You almost gave me a black eye with that big head of yours. Where were you going? I was at your class. You wasn't there."

"Don't say Baby Girl to me! Where have you been all day?!"

"What? Damn! Don't even ask me if I am ok. Just start accusing me of being somewhere that I wasn't."

"No! I asked *where* have you been?"

"*Where* have I been? What do you mean *where* have I been? You **know** where I been!" We started walking towards the car.

"I don't Tracey. Stop playing me. I looked everywhere for you and you didn't show up to lunch; you weren't there when I got out of class."

"I was here! At school! Where do you think I could go when you have my keys?"

"Well, you have legs! I couldn't find you. I looked in the gym, the cafeteria, the library... If you were here, why didn't I see you?"

"Man girl, you trippin'! Did you look in the nurse's office too?"

"No! Why would I look there?"

"So, then I was in there...Because that is where I was...being sick."

"Tracey! I know you. You drive home when you are sick."

"Yeah, but you had my keys and I was so sick to where I couldn't make it up the stairs to where your class is. Didn't Joey give you a letter from me?"

"No! Well, I did see him in the hallway trying to wave me down, but he does that every day and I, today, I didn't have time for that."

"Well you should've made time. I know you see him every day in that hall, so I told him to give you a letter for me."

"Well I didn't get the letter. And I had to sit in the office because of you! I got caught eating in Mrs. Green's class."

"Oh, yep, because he came to tell me you didn't stop for him, so I told him to go to your class to tell you I was sorry, but you wasn't there."

"Well I am still mad at you. He could have still given me the letter. I just walked right by him to come out here."

"Well, how fast was you going because he probably figured he should throw the letter away since school is out."

I rolled my eyes at him as he opened my door. Something about his story was off but I chalked it up to me just being paranoid at the time. He crossed over into the right lane to get on the freeway. That meant he wanted me to come over to his house instead of going straight home. Stevie was still believing the forged note I gave her about after school try-outs, so she thought I was at rehearsal. She would always be at work if there was ever a performance so I let that ride out the rest of the school year being sure to bring up fake details when we would sit down to talk to each other on weekends and her mid-weekday off.

Today I was not feeling up to hanging out in Tracey's club house. "No, Tracey, take me home please. Stevie made my favorite for dinner tonight and since I missed lunch, I want to get at it early."

"Baby Girl, I can take you to the drive-through. Come on! I owe you. Don't be mad."

"I'm not *mad!* I never got to work on my project yesterday, so I need to get started on it now."

"Fine."

He spun the car so abruptly my shoulder bumped into the window.

"Ow!"

"Sorry! I didn't want to miss the light."

As soon as we got to my house, I got out the car and refused a goodbye kiss. We had been angry at each other before, but I was not used to the way it felt this time. I peeked through my blinds in my room to watch him pull away. I could see he was dialing a number on his cell phone, but my phone never rang. A smile arrived on his face and he drove off.

BOOKER

KELPIE

B radley initially took the news of Olivia's engagement as a huge shock. He did not want his surprised reaction to come off as unsupportive. Bradley was truly happy that his daughter had finally found love. So, he let her know that he would do anything she needed to have the wedding of her dreams. After Olivia spoke with her father, she had completed every call she needed to announce her engagement to Lawrence. Well, almost every call. There remained one last person in her life she needed to tell and that happened to be Kelpie. To make that call would be a chore. Olivia decided to wait until after dinner with Lawrence and the kids before reaching out to Kelpie.

Telling your brother, you are getting married should be a joyous thing. A usual brother would want to approve. A usual brother would want to check the guy out and be sure this guy was good enough for his sister. As usual brother wouldn't want any man to marry his sister that wasn't going to treat her right. He'd want a man for his sister that would not abuse her, not cheat on her, and not abandon her. Kelpie wasn't a usual brother. He wasn't a brother that had protected his sister. Nonetheless, Olivia wanted him to know, in person, she was going to marry Lawrence. She invited him to meet her for coffee, and he agreed. Later that month, Livia sat in a coffee shop and waited in the back. There was a table secluded from the front entrance and down the hall from the bathrooms. It was normally the table that the baristas used during their breaks but was not closed off to the customers. There were so many things that Livia wanted to say but she did not know how to put her thoughts together.

She arrived twenty minutes earlier than the agreed upon time. Olivia used the extra time to meditate and pray over the meeting before he arrived. She brought her Bible and a journal. The Bible wasn't there for an impromptu Bible study or for her to berate him with scripture. For her, it was not meant to attack anyone, but more of a protective shield.

Opening her journal, she began to write out a prayer,

"Dear Heavenly Father. I don't know what to say to You. I have not trusted You for many years and somehow, I have always known You were there. My question Lord is why are You doing this to me? Why did You let this happen to me? Not just with Kelpie but with that girl that one time and with those guys that treated me so badly. What did I do Lord to deserve to be treated like a rag doll? Did I make you angry Lord? Did I not pray enough? My ~~husband~~ soon to be husband says You have a plan and I believe him but was there another way? Could You have used me for another purpose for another reason? Will this pain ever leave me God? Will I have to carry this for the rest of my life? Please help me talk to my brother today Lord. I love him and I forgive him, God. But every time I see his face, I see the hurt he has caused me and his utter disregard for my pain. Sometimes I see the great times we had and the good qualities about him but it's not long before the old visions start flashing before my eyes. Help me to love the way You love and to forgive the way You forgive. Give me the words to say and the way to say them. In Jesus' name I pray."

As she closed the journal and looked up, there he was at the counter ordering his drink and looking around to see if he could spot her. It was difficult to keep the droplets of tears from gliding down her face when he came over to the table. After her prayer she became extremely emotional, knowing that her memories haunted her and that certain things would never go away. She blotted her face and took deep breaths. Kelpie caught sight of her hand waving him over.

Olivia didn't stand when he got to their table. He put his hand on her shoulder, kissed the top of her head, then took his seat and began to speak. The conversation wasn't too long.

Kelpie started off by telling her that he forgave her for the way she acted towards his girlfriend the last time he came to her house. He had since broken up with the woman because she was too materialistic. No woman has lasted very long in his life, so this information did not surprise Olivia at all.

For a moment he shared some new pictures of Kelan and Kelvan that he had captured off the internet from a post that the twin's mom shared of a birthday party.

"Look how tall Van got now!" Kelpie mentioned with excitement.

Quickly moving on to avoid displaying her sadness over how much of the twins' lives she had missed, Livia shared with Kelpie that their mom and dad would be in town and the occasion was for her wedding with Lawrence.

"Well, glad one of us was able to get them in town! It's like they just abandoned us. Anyway, I thought you already were married to that old guy. He is older than me, isn't he? Well, I thought y'all been married so it's all good with me."

He was really just blabbing. Livia just listened to him talk for a while. Her pending thoughts wanted to know if he could bring Kelan and Kelvan to the wedding. She really wanted what little family she had to be there. She gave him the wedding details and hoped he would show up with his sons rather than a flashy date on his arm.

It was hard for her to tell Kelpie that he was the reason she had not gotten married to Lawrence all this time. It was hard for her to tell Kelpie she did not feel clean, or worthy, or valuable, after what he did to her.

She prevented herself from telling Kelpie that she suffered constant nightmares. She couldn't even tell Kelpie that she didn't hate him but that she just wanted to know why he abused her for so long. Kelpie would never tell her why he did the things he did, because in his mind it was a thing of the past. Anyone that she ever shared her story with swept it under a rug and nailed the corners down.

Kelpie's phone buzzed a few times. He looked down in annoyance and typed a few things in response and then got up out of his seat. He went around to his sister's side of the table for an awkward congratulatory hug, before heading out. Kelpie was barely five steps away before Livia lowered her head to the table and wept.

One of the coffee shop employees came to check on her. She thanked him, regained her composure, then gathered her things to head home. Right when she stuck the keys in the ignition of her car, her phone chirped. She dug the phone out of her purse thinking it was Kelpie. It was Bradley.

"Hey, Doll. Pops is in town! I made arrangements to come, as soon as you told me you were getting married. I really want to be here for you and to do anything you need me to do that helps. I'm staying in my old place. I'll be here from now until the wedding day, but do you have time to stop by today?"

"I'll be right over."

Livia started up her car to get it warm then dialed Lawrence.

"Hey, Guac. Honey, I was gonna call to tell you how things went with Kelpie, but my dad just called."

"Mr. Stone called? Well you already told him about the wedding. Is he changing his mind about coming? Is everything alright?"

"Honey, no, none of that. He's here. I'm going to go see him right now. He wants me to come by his old place."

"Wow, he's here? Do you need me to come with you? Will you be ok? Does Kelpie know?"

"No, I'm ok. I don't think Kelpie knows he's here. He didn't mention it if he does. Brad said he'd be here, like stay, until the wedding. He offered to help."

"Like he's going to pay for the wedding? Honey, you know I can do that for you. Whatever you want, I got you. However big you want it, it's yours."

"I know that. Really, I'm fine. I just don't know what he's going to say. I just wanted you to know I might be late coming home tonight. It takes me an hour and fifteen minutes to get there and I haven't left the coffee shop yet. If it's too late I may just stay over."

"Liv, let me and the kids come meet you out there. They will have to meet their grandfather sooner or later. It would be nice to meet him before the wedding. They've never even gotten a chance to speak to him. Hell, I've never gotten to speak with him outside of sending messages through you."

"We have time before the wedding. I'll make sure you guys meet him before the wedding. Let me do this by myself first. And um, well uh, he kinda doesn't know...he doesn't actually know about the kids."

Livia could not see Lawrence's face, but she could tell by the long pause and the sadness in his voice that this news crushed him tremendously.

"What? What are you saying, Olivia? What do you mean he doesn't know *about* the kids? He doesn't know about their personalities or he doesn't know they exist? All these years, Olivia!? Does he even know about me? Before you mentioned the wedding, I mean. Does he know? Are you ashamed of us?"

"Never! No! Please understand, I never meant to hurt you. I know this sounds selfish, but I never wanted him to come back because of them, or you. I wanted him to come back for me.

Just to be a dad. My dad! The only times Stevie has come back to town is for Maya and Salem's births and now she is only coming for the wedding. She never comes, or calls, on a regular day, when I need her, for me, just to be around as my mom. They have never been there for me the way I needed them to be; to care about me, for my needs as their daughter. Look, I know this is not fair to you or the kids. I want to make it up to you. I hope you can find it in your heart to forgive me. But he's back for me, kind of, and that's what I needed to see from him. I gotta go, Baby. Let me do this."

There was silence on both ends of the phone for a full six minutes. Both Lawrence and Olivia periodically were checking the phone to see if the seconds were still counting. Oliva completed the silence with an, "I love you, Guac." She ended the call and headed off to see her father.

The truth was she had kept in touch with her father through the years. He'd send a post card from time to time when he'd reach a different city, country, or continent. She often wondered if he and Stevie were secretly off, living a lover's life of their own together.

Stevie was so married to her work which is why Bradley took off in the first place, so the thought left Livia as soon as it arrived. Livia plugged her phone into the car and selected the Tamela Mann album. Mrs. Mann had a way of helping Oliva cope and push through hard times. She sang to herself the whole ride to Bradley's.

The sun was drooping in the sky by the time she pulled up. Bradley owned quite a few acres of land. He originally had commercial plans for it but without him being there to manage things, his vision never took flight. A property manager was paid to keep it maintained and it did get rented out periodically, but no renter ever seemed to stay long. Bradley wouldn't allow too many changes and didn't ever come across a deal he approved of to occupy his land, so it mostly stayed vacant. The home had a driveway a quarter mile long. The living space was very homey but smelled stale and lifeless without anyone being there for so long.

Bradley was sitting inside drinking a mug of earl grey tea and milling around the house looking at old family photos he had hung on the walls. He kept all of his personal items in the storage shed and had his property manager take down the staging and set up the place with his personal style anytime he was in town to stay, which wasn't often at all.

At the end of the gravel driveway was a small pond that divided the main house from the barn house. She never knew why he kept the barn house since he didn't ever have animals. She recalls going there a few times as a child and playing in the pond and losing the necklace Bradley gave her in that pond. She also remembered lying to him about losing the necklace.

Staring out the passenger side window admiring the land and the beautiful trees, it took three taps of Bradley's coffee mug on her driver window before she turned around. There he was. Dad. Bradley stood there very tall with caramel smooth skin. He looked about fifteen years younger than his birth certificate could verify.

He was bald with a close shaven salt and pepper beard. His skin was naturally tight and supple. Freckles speckled the outer corners of his eyes and there was no question as to what Stevie saw in him. He dressed very neatly; long sleeved tee, sleeves scrunched to his elbows, and a pair of straight legged slacks, no cuff. With his free hand he tried her door. It opened and he reached for her hand to help her out of the car.

He placed his mug atop the car and swept her up in his arms.

He planted his nose in her neck and shoulder and swung her around making her feel like she was twelve again. It was as if time had never passed between now, and the last time they saw each other. Bradley shared many stories of his journeys around the world and explained his array of knickknacks he collected along the way.

By this time, they had shared about two and half glasses of wine, which made Livia feel like divulging some of her own truths, forgetting Bradley asked *her* there to talk. Settling down on the large sofa, Bradley decided to launch into his reason for coming back to town.

"Doll, I just wanted you to know that I am here for you. I really love you and your brother. It has been painful being away from you all these years. I want to spend time with you and this new guy in your life; your fiancé. You know I just want the best for you. I came to make sure you are making the right choice. I didn't always make the right choices when it came to family planning. Things didn't go with your mother the way I intended. I have no regrets when it comes to you and your brother. I just wish I would have done things differently. You know?"

"Well Brad...Dad!" the wine was affecting her more than she had realized, and her volume was a bit high and then she fixed it, "Dad, I have to share something with you..."

"Well, me too Doll. That's really why I came back."

"No. This is serious. Look. Lawrence is not some new guy. I've been seeing him since college and"—

"Oh! Wait, since college? And he's just now proposing? Hmmm. You've been out of school what, six or seven years? So, why haven't I heard of him before now? You used to always tell me about your boyfriends. And I'd always tell you to drop them."

"Right. That's just it. I'm trying to tell you something here."

"I know. I know, Doll. And that is exactly why I came. I don't want you to not get married, but I just want to be here for you. Sometimes guys mean well and can hurt a woman's feelings and I just don't want you to get hurt. Have you been living with this guy all this time? Did you threaten to leave or something? Is he forcing you to stay? See this is why I am here. I won't have some man forcing my baby doll in a life sentence."

"No, no. You don't get it. You have the wrong idea about him, Dad. Lawrence and I have um, have uh, we uh, we have three...children."

"Whoa. What did you say? You have *what*?"

"I'm trying to tell you, Lawrence and I, we have three children together."

Bradly asked softer now, and more concerning, "Are they yours Ollie? Is he saddling you with some other woman's responsibility? There's no way you could have three children. I talk to you all the time. I mean, you know, we talk enough. Over the years. Why didn't you tell me? There's no way you have children. Look at you. Well, you're so tiny."

"Daddy, they *are* mine," Livia smiled. "Claire is the oldest, I got pregnant with her in college. Maya is right behind her and Salem is the baby." She took out her phone to show him the picture on her lock screen. He wiped his face hard to remove any

any tears that might be evident.

"Oh, Doll, you could have told me. I wouldn't have judged you. I would have come. I would have been here for you."

"That's why. That right there is why. You would have been here for *them*. Why couldn't you have come back just for me? I didn't want you to come back for grandchildren. Aren't I enough for you? Was I not enough for you to come back for me?"

Her words sunk in like cannonballs into an ocean.

He tried his best to give the most affirming response, "You have always been more than enough, Olivia. I hope this man that you are about to marry knows that too! You still haven't told me why he took so long. Why hasn't he asked you to marry him before now? Did you have to prove something to him – that you could be a lover and raise his children?"

"No. Honestly...it's you. It's you and Mom and Kelpie."

"We can't stop you. We didn't even know!"

"It's the dysfunction! You left. Kelpie left. Mom left. I want Lawrence to feel free to leave when he wants to go. I don't know why he wants someone as broken as me. He *has* asked me to marry him. He has *been* asking since my Junior year in college. And not just because of Claire either. He just loves me. He really loves me."

"So, what's the problem?"

"Sometimes I don't love me. And I sometimes I get severely depressed."

"Doll? Talk to Dad. Tell me. What's going on?"

"Sometimes I just don't want to go on. And I'm working on that. I am. I'm learning to trust God more, and it's good for me, but I still have a lot of questions."

"Hey, I am so sorry. Daddy is sorry I was not around, and I am sorry I cannot change the past for you. Lord knows I would if in my power. But I am here now, and I will help with whatever you need. I promise not to take off until you are ok."

Bradley held his daughter on the sofa for a long moment and then sat her straight up.

"I came back because I have something to tell *you*. This doesn't change anything about how I feel about you or your mom or your brother. But now that you are getting married…I was holding this information until you got married because I wanted to tell you before you started your own family. Now I know I am too late for that. But it definitely has nothing to do with you not being enough, ok?"

"Dad. What is it? Are you sick or something? Is this about mom?"

"Everyone is healthy. And really, I don't know why I waited this long. It's just that hearing the news that you were about to start your own family, I wanted you to have all the facts. And now I am still having to process that you have a full family, and I realize I should have come back sooner."

"What does it change? Why tell me now?"

"Like I said, I felt that you wouldn't be ready or be able to fully understand until you were ready to start a family of your own. I wanted you to reach that level of maturity on your own before I tainted your faith in marriage and family, but Doll, you seem to have it all under control."

He looked at her for a moment and then continued.

"So...," he let out a deep sigh, "I was not the guy that had it all together when I met your mom. Stevie was a beautiful woman and I could not take my eyes off of her. I saw her at the movie theatre. I was with my buddies, and"—

"Ok, Dad, I know this story. I have heard it a million times. She was waiting for a blind date, or something like that, to meet her for a movie and he never showed. But she stayed any way because she was too embarrassed to leave. But you noticed her waiting, and you noticed her go in the theatre alone, and watched her more than you watched the movie. And when you saw her leave alone, you ran to catch the door for her, and it was history."

"Ok, smart ass. You are still a smart ass," he laughed, "Well Missy, the part you're unaware of is – at that time, I was staying on the couch at my buddy's house. He recently married his wife and I needed help...I needed help raising my son."

"Dad? Your son!? Are you saying I have another brother that I didn't know about?! Naw. No. Nope. I don't believe this. Mom never said anything about this! Oh my god. Are you serious? If you have another son, then what happened to him then? Did his mother take him away from you or what? Or? Wait. No. No. Did something *happen* to him?"

"Doll. Just let me finish. I need to tell you this. It's critical you hear me right now more than ever. I was young and girl-crazy and when I got his mother pregnant, I told her I would marry her and make it right. I expressed my love for her and made a commitment not to ever leave her. And I did marry her."

"Dad. I don't think I can handle this. What are you saying?! You were married when you met my mom? Are you saying I have an estranged brother? Does he have children and a family? Do you have other children I should know about too?"

"I just have you and your brother, Kelpie. His mom, Jackie, and I had a small place. She felt cramped having the baby there, and hearing him cry all the time, she needed a break. I offered to take him for a ride, but she didn't want our baby being outside so young. So instead, she took a drive by herself, while I stayed home with our son." Bradley began to get choked up, and his words got clogged in the back of his mouth, "She was driving and, and, and, she was so tired from, from, from lack of sleep that she nod-nod-nodded off at the wh-wheel. She was driving down a windy road and ran right over the embankment. And um, she uh, she instantly lost her life."

Livia had no idea what to say so she just hugged her dad tightly. He received it but broke away from the hug, took both of her hands in his, and looked her in the face.

"Please let me get this out. There is more I have to tell you. I was left with my son. I had to quit work to take care of him full time which is why I was staying at my buddy Charlie's house. His wife, Sheila, helped a little bit but they were pregnant with their first child and she had responsibilities of her own. I wanted them to take my son but couldn't bring myself to do that. And your mom. Your mom was so beautiful. She still is. I owe her my life. I would do anything for your mother. After the movies that day, I instantly fell in love with her. Not because I was missing my wife, Jackie. Your mom was nothing like Jackie. Your mom was just so very kind and loving."

He got up from the couch to pour himself a glass of brandy from the bar to get himself through the next part of the story. Livia reached in her purse to check her phone. She shot a quick text to Lawrence (I know it's already late. Just so much I have to tell you. Kiss the kids and I will see you tomorrow.) She grazed the Bible at the bottom of her purse as she let go of the phone and gripped it tightly as if for strength to continue listening to the story. Bradley had poured two glasses and when Livia looked back up, he was holding it out for her. She accepted the glass, took one big gulp, and then handed the rest back to Bradley. He finished her drink then sat down with his.

"Like I said your mom was so amazing and loving. I had to see her every day. After two weeks I wanted her to marry me, but I had to tell her about my son. I invited her over for dinner and when she arrived, she automatically assumed the baby belonged to my friend and his wife. She never even judged me for sleeping on their couch. After dinner we were all sitting in the living room and when Sheila couldn't get the baby to stop fussing, I took him. Your mom remarked at how good I was with him and asked if she could hold him. At that point I couldn't keep it from her any longer because I knew I wanted to spend the rest of my life with her. So, I introduced her to him by saying,

'Stevonia, this is Kelpatrick. We call him Kelpie and he is my son'."

"Daddy?? No. No. No?! How could you do that to Mom?!" By that time, Olivia was on her feet, pacing the room, wishing she had finished her whole glass of brandy. She sat down then stood up again, then ran to the bathroom to get sick. She rinsed her mouth then came back.

"Daddy I don't think I want to hear the rest of this. This is way too much for one day."

"Olivia. Have a seat please. I have to finish saying everything. I need to. It's important. You have to know this before you get married. I wanted to tell you before you had children. I am sorry I was away for so long. But I just gotta tell you this."

She sat back down on the couch next to him after pouring another glass of brandy, this time she kept it all for herself.

Placing the glass down on the table, she put her elbows on her knees and ran her fingers through her hair. With her face pointed at the ground she mumbled one word.

"Continue."

"Well, okay, so Olivia I never wanted to hurt you and that's why it has been so frightening for me to have this conversation with you. When I got the call about your wedding, I called your mom to get permission to explain to you what I have been keeping hidden for all these years. I was prepared to hear some news too since she told me you might have some things to get off your chest as well. I'm guessing she meant about Lawrence and your kids. I thought all this time all I had was Kelpie's twins,

Kelan and Kelvan. Now there are your three beautiful little ones that I have never known.

—Anyway, back to the story. Your mother was very understanding and maybe she felt sorry for me losing my wife, Jackie, and being alone with an infant. She agreed to marry me a month or so after that dinner.

My grandfather that passed away around that time had left me this property. But I didn't want to bring your mother and Kelpie out here to live because she was finishing her nursing program, and this was too far from the university. That is when I started renting it out and we stayed with Charlie and Sheila for a while longer.

I stayed home with Kelpie and continued raising him. After the rental income was steady, we moved into our own place. Your mom finished school and landed a great job. She worked all the time, Olivia. And all I can say is that we fell out of love with each other. She was always working, and she didn't have time for me and Kelpie. But I stayed because I could never repay her for what she did for me while Kelpie was an infant.

I needed her and she was there for me, but when I got an opportunity to make some money overseas, I jumped at the idea. I didn't feel like a man staying at home with the kid. I needed to get out and bring home the bacon. I know that sounds pig headed, but it's the truth.

She agreed with me leaving to go to Madrid, since the job was only supposed to be for a month, and it promised to have been a lot of money for us. When the month was up, your mom wrote letters begging for me to come home. But I just kept sending fat checks in return.

I didn't want to stop making good money. So, I ended up being gone for almost two years instead of one month! And when I came back, she had you. You were only four months old. But I never said a word. I chose not to question her about you for one second. I embraced all of you and have loved you as my daughter ever since! You will always be my Doll."

Livia grabbed Bradley by the sweater and cried into his chest until she fell asleep. He laid her head on a sofa pillow and took a big blanket from the closet to cover her.

Sitting in the big chair in the corner, all he could do for an hour was watch her sleep until he saw a light beaming from her purse on the table. He walked over to turn the phone off, so it didn't disturb her sleep but when he picked up the phone there was a family picture of the five of them and the name read, "GUAC."

He picked up.

Later that morning when the sun came up it was shining through the living room window, right on Livia's face waking her up before she was ready. She acknowledged she was awake but didn't open her eyes until she heard her phone make a loud buzzing noise on the coffee table. She checked her phone. There were twelve text messages listed on her lock screen –

Message from Guac: Babe! I just talked to Bradley. He told me everything.
TIME STAMP 3:12AM

Message from Guac: Babe are you okay? Why didn't you call me?
TIME STAMP 6:00AM

Message from Guac: I hope Bradley is not looking at your phone still. He picked up when I tried to call you to check on you.
TIME STAMP 6:03AM

Message from Palmer: Hey, Girl! Call me right when you get up. Need to confirm some dates with you. Love you. Miss you.
TIME STAMP 7:14AM

Message from Guac: Olivia, your dad invited us to come out there, so we are coming first thing when the kids get up.
TIME STAMP 7:16AM

Message from Guac: Honey are you ok?! I'm getting worried about you. You still asleep? We're leaving the house.
TIME STAMP 9:30AM

Message from Guac: Had to stop. Salem had an accident in his clothes.
TIME STAMP 10:22AM

Message from Guac: Thank God you always keep extra clothes for him in the car or I'd be messed up.
TIME STAMP 10:26AM

Message from Guac: Salem is set. Be there in 20min.
TIME STAMP 10:48AM

Message from Unknown Number: Hi. My name is Hope. My mom, Mandy, said you design formal dresses?
TIME STAMP 11:04AM

Message from Auto Generated: Dental Solutions. This is a reminder of your dentist appointment Tuesday at 9:00AM. Please text C to confirm or text X to cancel.
TIME STAMP 11:09AM

Message from Guac: Comeeng down the drivwey Mommy. This is Claire. Daddy tole me to tex you. Why dinnet you tell us abowt Granpas howse?
TIME STAMP NOW

Livia sprang up from the couch, yelling down the hallway.

"DAD! What did you tell Lawrence?!?!?"

Olivia was in panic mode thinking about everything her dad just told her and how she and Lawrence would handle everything. At the same time, the last passage she wrote in her book flashed in her mind. There were secrets from her past she hadn't revealed to Lawrence, her therapist, or anyone. She never told anyone about her hot tub story, just as Bradley never shared his story before that night.

Chapter 9
So Where's The Hot Tub?

MORE AND MORE since I've been in high school, Stevie has been loosening the reins on me. It means she is not nagging me all the time. Sometimes I think it's because she would rather let go than sit down and have a real conversation facing real issues. She hasn't ever had the birds and the bees talk with me. But I have already learned all about the birds and the bees. Based off of my experience they should not even call it the "Birds and the Bees Talk," they should rename it "vultures and rattlesnakes."

It doesn't matter to me anymore that she never asked me how things were going with Tre. Tre is long gone. I take that back. He actually still calls me like at least once per week. I have moved past wanting a relationship with him though. I decided to let Sarah win. I guess he is rightfully hers since she dated him first. I thought I was in love with him. I did love him, and I still do but now I know the difference between being in love with someone and loving someone. So totally different.

When Tre drove away from my house the day we had that argument at school, I needed to know if he was driving to go see Sarah. It took me twenty minutes of trying to study and I couldn't get Tre and Sarah out of my mind, so I asked my neighbor to drive me to his place. My neighbor was usually bored anyway. She would just sit around watching TV.

My neighbor went along with my antics and took me to Tre's house. We hopped in her car and sped down the freeway. When we drove down Tre's street, I told her to tap the brakes. Even though I'm not certain he would recognize her car, I didn't want him to think I was some crazy stalker.

Someone once told me, *"When you're looking for something, you'll find it."* I was disgusted by what I found. I cracked the passenger door open, leaned out, and puked on the street. Witnessing Sarah's car parked in front of his house made me sick. I could imagine all of the things he was doing to her in his bed. Too stiff to use my own legs I convinced my neighbor to do what friends do and get out to peek inside his window. She came running back, got into the car, and sped off, not speaking for almost half the way back. I did not want to say what I was thinking, so I just stared at her big eyed until she spilled the beans. She gradually delivered the details: The music was playing loudly in his clubhouse. His window was cracked but the curtains were closed.

I am still not one-hundred-percent sure she wasn't spotted, but through the split in the curtain she described what she saw as two butt-naked bodies doing things you'd only see on Cinemax. The next moments in the car were spent in silence. I had no idea how to respond to her findings. When we arrived back at our house there were no words exchanged. I didn't thank her for the ride. She didn't tell me it would be ok. And I was not able to lift my head high enough to even check if she was giving me the *"I'm here for you girl"* face.

I ended my relationship that day. He called me that night to apologize for our argument at school. I accepted his apology, but I still didn't believe he was in the nurse's office. When I told him what *I* had done and asked him about Sarah's car being in his driveway, he denied the whole thing. I yelled through the phone for him to never call me again, then hung up in his face.

It's been three months since that day. I forgave Tre, but no longer wanted to be his girlfriend after that incident with Sarah. He told me Sarah wasn't even pregnant. She just wanted Tracey back so badly that she wouldn't stop trying. I believe she is truly in love with him, so when I do interact with Tre, it's strictly platonic. I wondered one day while we were on the phone if she knew he was calling me, so I asked him.

"Does Sarah know we still talk?"

THE MONSTER IN MY ROOM

"Yeah, I tell her everything about you. She asked me what I liked so much about you, so I told her EVERYTHING I like about your body."

"You are wrong for that. She doesn't need to know that."

"Yeah, she do. She wants to see for herself. She's into that."

"What? No! *I'm* not into that. You know I don't mess with you like that no more."

Come to find out he wasn't lying. Sarah called me three weeks later asking me to come over to her house to hang out with the two of them. I wasn't exactly sure what they had in mind, but it wasn't for me. I told her to lose my number.

Now that I was a senior and had my own car and my job at the fabric store, I helped Stevie with paying for household stuff. To be more accurate I helped myself pay for household stuff since Stevie was rarely there. I bought groceries with her money but cooked most of my own meals. Recently, on a shopping trip, the new cashier at the grocery store caught my eye.

I was very lonely after my breakup with Tre and determined that all guys couldn't all be vultures and rattlesnakes. This guy was super cute. We always chatted while he rang my groceries. He was living on his own and had his own car and own apartment. He also told me he graduated last year and that he couldn't afford college, so this job was helping him save up for his tuition.

Yeah, I bought that. I didn't believe he'd have any reason to lie to me. I was just a local grocery store customer. I knew he was into me by a few subtle hints. For instance, when he would see me in his line he would reach around and put his

"This aisle closed" sign behind my purchases so that he could walk me to my car, even if I only had three items. And then it happened after several weeks of flirting – he slipped his phone number in my grocery bag.

At first, I wasn't going to even call him. I just thought about how weird it would be if things didn't work out. I'd have to avoid his line and maybe I couldn't even shop at that store anymore. What if it did go well and I'd have to tell Stevie I'm seeing a guy that bags groceries. She would never let me hear the end of that. "Marry up!" she always said. Okay, well you know I called him, right?!

He really had a lot to say over the phone and it felt good to have someone to pass the time with. It was refreshing to have a guy not talk about my looks or my body or what he wanted to do to me. We talked about books and school and art and music. He made me laugh large belly laughs until I cried with his impressions and jokes. After a few weeks he began to ask about my family. I don't know why he had to ruin such a good thing we had going. I told him enough to pacify his inquiry and quickly moved on.

He found out that I was alone at home most of the time and he expressed that he wanted to be with me in person and he wanted to see my laugh. This was the first time he had ever mentioned my looks or my face or anything about the two of us together. I wasn't sure how to respond so I didn't. He carried on the conversation and it was more than a week before he brought it up again.

Somehow, we got on the topic of swimming. It was like we started off with school sports and talents and what he had done during his high school years. Me mentioning wanting to have tried out for the swim team turned out to be the perfect hook to get me over to his place. He offered to train me in his pool at his apartment complex since he was some kind of excellent swimmer or something. Right away when I griped about it being too cold for an unheated pool, he brought up the fact that there was also hot tub to help us get warm.

I had always wanted to get in a hot tub. I tried to hide my excitement so as not to seem super eager. Nevertheless, I was very interested. He was extremely attractive, and I am the one who brought up swimming, so I didn't challenge his motives. "What the heck?" I thought. Within twenty-five minutes he was at my door. Within five we were on the freeway and soon in his apartment. It was dimly lit but I took into account that it was nighttime and there was no daylight coming through the windows. He had the table set up with some glasses and some drinks. I walked in behind him holding my bath towel and had my swimsuit on under my sweats.

So, I sat with him in the dining room and he introduced me to a game called Quarters. I was not really a competitive person, but I was like a natural at this game. He poured me a tall glass of Italian soda and said each time I can bounce a quarter in the empty glass he would take a sip of his soda and vice versa. So the rules of the game were established. He had just learned the game from his cousin and wanted me to see how fun it was. "And then the hot tub?" I asked and he nodded in agreement.

After twenty minutes of playing the game and three refills of my glass, I figured we had not been drinking Italian soda but that we had been drinking some type of overly sweetened alcoholic drink or that perhaps he had spiked it. I mentioned getting bored with the game. He got up from his side of the table, walked around to the back of my chair, hooked me under the arm pits and walked me to his bedroom. My eyes were blinking slowly and when my eyes came in focus, I was face down on the bed and staring into a pillow. I felt exhausted and could barely lift my head from the pillow but was able to angle my face down towards his dresser where I could see him mixing up more of the "Italian soda." He walked over to the bed and tilted my chin to make me drink it. An adrenaline rush helped me to snatch my face away because my words were slow to come out of my mouth. My head immediately fell heavy on the bed sheets.

Next blink he was over me, telling me how pretty I was and how beautiful my body was and how much he enjoyed my company and the attention I was giving him. I heard him say something about when I first walked in the grocery store and let him walk me to my car. Next he was kissing me and groping me and, at first, I kissed back. Suddenly his hand was down my pants. I grumbled, "No, no, no," a few times then elevated to yelling, "NOOOOO!" but was muffled by my face being smashed into the mattress. My arms had no power to fight back. The legs I used to be able to move were lifeless. I blacked out.

✳✳✳

Oliva snapped out of her memory of the hot tub story, still in panic mode about what she'd say to Lawrence when he walked into Bradley's house. Bradley came walking down the hallway with a cold face towel that smelled like mint and cucumber. Livia put it to her face and breathed in. She peeked out over the top of the towel and raised an eyebrow at her dad. He tipped up his coffee mug and placed his other hand at the top of her back, gently rubbed, then gave a few pats and pulled her in for a side hug. After wiping her face, she looked around for where to put the towel. He took it and guided her towards the front door. Her family had arrived. Giggling and footsteps could be heard, and the silhouettes of her family could be seen through the glass panel next to the door.

When she opened the door, Salem jumped into her arms from hanging on Lawrence's neck. The girls hugged their mom around the waist. Lawrence only had room to lean in for a kiss. The couple looked into each other's eyes for a beat and grew smiles to hold the tears back. Bradley ushered everyone in and pointed the kids to the dining room. Once Lawrence crossed the threshold, Bradley and Lawrence both reached out for a handshake. Bradley embraced Lawrence and everyone sat at the table for brunch while Livia introduced her kids to Granddad.

It was love at first sight all over again for Bradley. He fell in love with his grandchildren as instantly as he did with their grandmother and Olivia. Bradley was extremely impressed with Lawrence. The two talked for hours while Livia showed the children around the property. The kids ran around finding multiple hideaways and attractions. Livia kept Salem close because of her fear of him getting too close to the pond. With the girls off having a grand time, she crouched over the pond with Salem while he splashed his fingers in the water making his reflection appear and disappear.

He laughed every single time. He screamed when his grandfather's reflection appeared the very next time. Livia heard him walking up, but Salem didn't. They all had a good laugh. Livia thought Bradley was going for a hug but instead he was placing a necklace around her neck. It still fit.

"I found it while cleaning out the pond years ago. I waited forever for you to tell me the truth that you lost it and you never did. You'd always say, 'Daddy it's in my pocket so I don't lose it' or *'Daddy I didn't want it to break while I was playing.'* So, I've just been waiting for the perfect time to give it back."

"Ahhh, Daddy. Thank you!"

"I can get a longer chain for you if you want. Or you can pass it down to one of the girls or something."

"This is mine! I am keeping it forever," Olivia beamed with a childlike joy.

She gave him a big smile and the two of them held Salem by the hands and let him swing back and forth while Lawrence gave the girls Piggyback rides.

"Honey! Be careful not to overdo it!" She turned to Bradley, "He had a pretty bad health scare not too long ago. I get concerned."

They spent the weekend on the property and the kids were reluctant to leave Granddad. They could let go of the ranch but letting go of him was harder. It was a matter of moments before his duffle bag was packed.

He and Livia followed Lawrence and the kids back home where he stayed a few days. Having him around the house allowed Livia more time to herself while Lawrence was at work. He delighted in taking the kids to their various obligations and Livia took advantage of the time by being able to write.

Bradley routinely traveled between both homes. The drive back and forth was taxing but there was no hesitation when it came to Livia calling him into the city to be around.

Amazed by the new light in Livia, Lawrence wanted to do something extra special for her. The last two times they had gone on any type of vacation was for each of their friend's weddings. Although Lawrence never regretted going to France for Sabrina's wedding instead of Hawaii for the family vacation, he did not forget. He still wanted a hot island getaway. Most people planned an elaborate honeymoon after their nuptials to consummate or maybe to bond with their new spouse. But for these two, that connection had been made already.

Grandma Sugar and Bradley had gotten along well, and Lawrence felt comfortable leaving the kids with the both of them for a while to make things happen with this surprise vacation for his soon-to-be wife. The kids were made aware that mom and dad would be gone for ten days. Grandma Sugar and Granddad had their schedules lined up, emergency numbers handy and tons of excitement ahead for the kids so there would not be too much time to miss Mommy and Daddy Pop.

Lawrence ended up telling Livia a little bit about the trip so that she would have time to prepare herself to leave the kids for ten whole days. It also was a precaution because Grandma Sugar and Salem were not the best at keeping secrets. He also had to remember that Livia had clients and that she would probably need to make arrangements for the time that she would be away.

That evening, Lawrence and the girls put up decorations that they made. They drew pictures of palm trees and made small palm trees out of green paper. Salem mostly scribbled, but his decorations were included as well. Lawrence ordered dinner from her favorite Caribbean restaurant. All of her favorite appetizers, favorite entrée, and dessert had arrived. Coming from her workroom, she inquired,

"What is all this, you guys? It's not my birthday. What is this?"

"Babe. Sit down. You deserve this more than anyone I know. You work so hard and you carry so much on your shoulders. The kids and I appreciate you so very much and this is my way of telling you that I am surprising you with a pre-wedding honeymoon."

The kids had begun eating and Livia sat there in shock and awe. Lawrence started to put food on a plate for her. Say something, Babe."

"Guac. Thank you! I'm just like, I have so much going on and so much to do."

"Yes, I realize that and so we are not leaving for two weeks and even longer if you need. I can figure out a way to push back the reservations."

"Well no, Honey, that would cost probably too much at this late of notice. I am sure I can figure it out, I'm just so"—

"Surprised? I know. It was meant to be a surprise. You stress so much that I am hoping to get you to relax before the wedding takes over your life. I know you are not about to be thinking of me, once you and Sabrina get together. And you know after the wedding is a very busy time of year."

"Yes. Let's eat and talk more after dinner. Thank you, Honey! Thanks kids! You guys, this is so awesome. Mommy loves it!"

After everyone had gotten full off of wings, rib tips, coconut prawns over rice, vegetable curry, and gumbo, they tried to have a bite of sweet potato pie.

Later after the kitchen was cleaned and the kids to bed, Livia had time to process her surprise getaway. They were cuddled in bed trying to find a movie to watch.

"Lawrence, I really do love this surprise. I am just trying to take it all in. I have a dress to finish and an upcoming consult and it's stressing me to think about this."

"Hey guess what? This is exactly why you need this trip and I need it too because I need you all to myself. We have not had that in so long. I need to reconnect with you. I even called your girl Palmer. She agreed to help you get some stuff done to make sure you don't leave with loose ends."

Starting to feel her nerves calm down, Livia was able to accept that she was flying off to the islands in two weeks.

"Where are we going anyway? You still didn't say. I have to schedule a sugaring and mani pedi. I should probably get my hair braided so I don't have to deal with it."

"Done. I already called Meeka and booked it. Don't act like you don't know your man got skills like that."

Livia couldn't hide her smile. Lawrence kissed her gently.

"Hey," he whispered. "There is something else I want to say, too. When I met you, I wanted you so bad and we had sex right away. I didn't really expect things to go that far that day. But Liv, it's like recently I have learned so much more about you that I didn't know when we first met.

I was fully aware of something special about you though. That's why I have wanted to marry you since your junior year in college. I didn't want anything but you. I wanted to know I'd be able to wake up to you every day for the rest of our lives. I've wanted you to be mine from the very beginning. Before Claire. Before Maya. Before Salem. I wanted you and everything that came with."

"I know that you are not just with me because of the children," Livia confirmed.

"What I am getting at is, now that you accepted my proposal, I want a do-over. I want to take time with you on a spiritual and emotional level. Please believe the house I reserved for our tropical getaway, is going to make you want to jump my bones! But I want to experience your mind. I want to make love to your mind over and over again. I want to court you. I really want our wedding night to feel like our first-time making love. I want to feel what it is like to wait for you. So...no sex until our wedding night."

"But Lawrence! That is like...," she looked down and started counting fingers.

"Seven weeks away. But don't worry about that. Soon you will be so busy with all of the final details and Sabrina will be here. I really feel like this will be good for us. Until our wedding night, I will be sleeping in the guest bedroom. Love you Honey. Get some sleep."

He left her standing in the middle of their room. She wasn't sure whether to be upset or in admiration. Olivia had stopped blaming herself for losing her innocence when she was young. For so long she had felt guilt and shame as well as sorrow. It bothered her that she could never give her husband the one gift that a wife and husband should be able to share on their wedding night. They had shared many passionate moments together and had three children to show for it.

Livia crawled into bed, but she didn't let herself count the weeks until she would experience Guac again. Laughing aloud, she remembered the episode of Martin where he and Gina bet to see who could last the longest without sex. The difference here was that Lawrence and Olivia were not trying to win a bet by tempting one another to make abstaining impossible. They both took this as an opportunity to gain a deeper relationship.

✱✱✱

The kids were happy to see Palmer around the house helping Olivia finish her interior design storyboards and proposals. Palmer and her husband just bred a litter of puppies and brought one over for them to test out. Over the last week and a half, Livia felt pretty caught up and ready to relax on her trip. She thanked Palmer for taking the extra time to be there and gave the little puppy one last hug before handing him off to Palmer. Still rubbing his back, she took a long stare, halfway contemplating buying him for Salem but then shook her head to get rid of that thought.

"Hey Hun, anytime. I was happy to help. You sure you don't want me to take the kids tonight?" Palmer offered. "Give you time to pack and maybe get into some pre vacation screwing in your own home without having to be quiet."

"Girl, you crazy! No, thank you," Olivia declined. "You've done so much already. I am pretty much packed. I don't have to bring too much clothing on account of where we're going." Both of them laughed.

"Oh, I totally get it! And with all that wild, island sex you will be having, you won't have time to wear clothes."

"Well. Funny you should say that, Palmer. Actually, I was meaning since it will be so hot, I'll be spending most of my time in bikinis and sun dresses. Also..." Under her breath, "Lawrence decided...and I agreed... to stay abstinent until our wedding night."

"Oh my god, Hun! Are you joking? That's like..."

"SHHHHH. I am trying not to count the weeks, Palmer. Thank you! I think it will be good for us. You remember I slept with him on the first night, so will these...however many months really be that bad?"

"Yeah, but you are going to exotica and not going to put it on your man? How can you be in such a romantic place for so long and not have something happen? Impossible."

"Well I don't know actually, but I am trusting God to keep me on my best behavior. Our relationship is built on more than sex you know?"

"Totes, but—"

Livia cut Palmer off, "But nothing. It is so much more than sex and we never got the time to get to know who we are without that piece. Would you leave your husband if his *dick* stopped working?"

"Hun. Don't ask! Freaky is in my DNA. Blondes may be beautiful but –"

"–But redheads have more fun. I know. I know. You always say that. Shut up Freckle Face. I love you. Now, let me go. Thanks for coming over."

"No prob, Hun. Hey, when's the last time you talked to Momma Stevie?" Palmer asked, still standing in the doorway.

"I called to tell her when Lawrence proposed to me. She said she'll come in for the wedding. So, we'll see. Have you talked to her?"

"No. Not for a minute. It'll be good to see her."

Palmer grinned and took one last hug smashing the puppy in the middle.

With Lawrence giving Livia a deadline on finishing her book she hoped she could get a few lines down before leaving for the trip. She also wanted to take a nap,

"No Olivia. Nap on vacation. Stay focused," she reminded herself.

✳✳✳

I woke up still in his bed. It felt like I'd been out for hours. The bedside clock said 3:14am. When I came to, Mr. Grocery

Bags was snoring in my ear with his arms and legs wrapped around my body. I pulled my pants up as I wriggled my way out of his tangle. He was stripped down to his boxers. Barely able to remember what happened, I found my way to the bathroom and checked to see if I was bleeding or sore. Both were true. After washing my hands and face in the sink, I looked up in the mirror, confused by what to think of myself. My bathing suit bra showed through the top of my shirt.

I clasped my hand to my chest in some effort to claim modesty. Frantically pulling on my shoes and jacket, I hit the front door. Jumping back and hoping he didn't wake up before I could escape, I stopped because someone was banging on his door like the police.

"I know you got that hoe in there! OPEN UP. OPEN UP!" a female voice shouted.

I looked in the peephole to see what she looked like and jumped again as her fist came banging at the door some more.

Mr. Grocery Bags did not budge so I sat on the floor, in the hallway, holding my knees until I guessed the girl gave up and walked away. On my next try to leave his house I was stopped again.

I hadn't any idea where I was or how to get home and there was no way I was going to wander outside in the pitch black. If his girlfriend, or whomever, was coming back I didn't want to run into her.

Shaking off my tears, I kept tugging at his arms until he woke up.

"You have to take me home! My mom is gonna be pissed."

Groggy, and moving at snail speed, he dressed in jeans and a t-shirt, slipped his keys in his pocket and walked out the door. I went right behind him and prayed he was good enough to drive. It was silent the whole way.

When we pulled up in front of my house, he asked when I wanted to come over again and attempted to kiss me.

Hands shaking and about to wet myself, I said I'd call him and pushed open the car door.

Sneaking into my room, trying not to wake Stevie, the thought popped into mind that I needed a person. A person that I could go to for anything I needed. That person neglected to show up.

Instead of a shoulder to cry on I rested my face in my hands and sat on the bed. I stood back up when I heard a crunching noise under me. A note from Stevie was on my bed.

"Look little lady, you are 18 now and I have tried to give you space. I just don't like you spending the night at Tre's house. It could lead to things you're not ready for. College starts in the fall and you have potential to do good.

Love,

   Momma"

I ran down the hall to talk to Momma, but she was knocked out. I turned around gently shutting her door behind me. In my own room I fell face first into my pillow to cry. There was no way I could tell Stevie what happened with Mr. Grocery Bags. She would hate me. She would call me a whore and kick me out for sure. I didn't even want to think about how I would get through college on my own. Growing up,

Stevie always talked about wanting me to do better than her. Not one time did I ask what that meant. I knew she had married young. I was in the clear for that since I had not one suitable character to fill that position. I was kid-free unlike my neighbor friend. I had never gotten pregnant. I crossed my fingers, hoping I hadn't ruined that by going over to Mr. Grocery Bags' house.

Stevie was right. At eighteen years old I was a woman and I needed to start acting like one. That started with finding a new grocery store right away. The new grocery store was an extra seven-minute drive away. The good thing is that I would be off to college soon and only inconvenienced for a few more months.

As a senior in high school I hadn't been nothing more than a book worm. I stayed faithful to my job at the fabric store and other than that, I was in the books. I studied hard and wanted to finish strong my senior year. When the time got closer to graduation, Stevie wanted my ideas for my graduation party. I really wasn't thinking too hard about all of those things. My head was geared toward starting a new life in college. I was excited to go to a place where no one knew me or my past. I had the opportunity to be fresh.

When it came to my graduation ceremony, I had no intention of going. The morning of, I faked having food poisoning so I wouldn't have to attend. By later that evening I managed to feel "better" in order to attend the graduation dinner that Stevie put together. Why on earth Kelpie was invited, I couldn't understand. It was weird to see him, but good to get a chance to meet his twin baby boys. I was occupied with his twins while Kelpie mingled with Stevie's coworkers. He could charm any girl, so it was no surprise he'd gotten someone pregnant. I wondered if the twins' mom felt nervous to meet us since she let Kelpie out, alone, with the babies.

Despite Kelpie's attendance, the dinner actually turned out to be a good time. It was mostly friends and coworkers of my mom. The neighbors even stopped through to wish me well, bring a gift, and share news that they were moving out of the house next door.

After everyone filled their bellies and downed a few alcoholic beverages, the music got louder, and everything livened up another notch. All of the dancing and laughing made me forget a lot of the sadness I was experiencing from relationship woes.

While Stevie was occupied with the twins, Kelpie had taken off to go hang out with some of my mom's younger colleagues. He didn't answer his phone when Stevie tried to reach him to come back for the twins. That meant I was stuck with the twins by myself. As always, Stevie had to work. Although she exchanged shifts with a friend to be able to attend my evening party, she still had to get a good night's sleep and be to work early the next morning.

By 8:00am, Stevie was long gone to start her shift at work. I was asleep in my bed and the twins snuggled up on a makeshift basinet I had conjured up for them on my bedroom floor. I tossed all my dirty laundry in the wash, lined the basket with my pillow and some blankets from their diaper bag.

I hadn't let myself fall into a deep sleep in case the twins needed me, so I was able to hear footsteps coming toward the front door. I got out of my bed to see who it was. I assumed it was Kelpie, hoped it wasn't Mr. Grocery Bags, but didn't expect it to be a woman. I glanced at the clock. It was nine-ish.

I tip-toed around the basket and got to the front door. Before she could knock, I opened it. The woman looked at me as though she knew me and started to take a step over the threshold. I placed my fingertips on her chest and demanded answers.

"Excuse me. May I help you? Do I know you? What do you want here?"

"Kelpie didn't tell you I was coming?" she said suspiciously.

"That doesn't answer any of my questions, but I haven't heard from Kelpie since he left last night. May I ask who you are?"

"Sorry. I'm, Tia, the twins' mom. I came to pick up my babies, so may I please come in and do that!?"

"Oh, *you're* Tia," I recalled her name from a previous conversation with Stevie. "You can wait here a second," I informed her and pointed to the sofa.

As soon as I let her in, the babies started to cry. I had no idea what to feed the little guys, so I figured I was doing fine as long as they stayed asleep. I walked in my room and picked them up. They were snuggling tightly.

"They don't want to let go." I said.

"They probably want my milk. I bet they could smell me. That's probably what woke them up. That and my voice. Here. I'll take them, thank you."

While she sat breast feeding, I got their bag together, which wasn't much. I set it by the door. I began going around the house picking up stuff from the party.

"Well, I guess Kelpie was telling the truth. Looks like there *was* a party here last night."

"Look, you're my nephews' mom and that is it. I am not your friend. I don't know you and I don't discuss my brother's business with nobody. If you want information, you best call him and find out whatever it is you want to know."

I took one of the babies from her and put him in his baby car seat. I kissed him on the forehead. I felt like I missed him already. Here it is a day ago I had no idea about the two little ones and all of a sudden, I'm someone's auntie. I was pretty sure I would never see them again, so I didn't make a point of getting too attached. I didn't even bid farewell to the other one since his mom had strapped him in his seat.

I shut the back passenger-side door without acknowledging Tia, waved a "Bye bye" to the little princes and marched back in the house. It was hard not to clean up just a little bit more. I straightened up as much as was appropriate and then gave the floor a good vacuuming. Passing through the kitchen, I saw a few extra dishes that could be loaded before starting the dishwasher. Turning toward my bedroom door I happened to notice Stevie had left a load of laundry in the hall. Assuming she wanted me to take care of it, I went to put it in the wash and found my dirty clothes already in the machine. Ugh. I was too tired to start it last night so now I had two loads to do, mine and Stevie's.

I desperately wanted to go back to sleep but could not ignore the clothes that needed folding since the dryer was also full. I was beginning to not like being a grown woman so much but knowing Stevie was not coming to college with me meant I had to start taking more initiative. Not that I hadn't done a lot on my own with Stevie being gone to work, but something about graduating high school made growing up seem more real. I folded only a few things before the comfy bed took me over. I had barely closed my eyes and here were her footsteps again! Taking a quick scan of my bedroom, I could see no trace of baby stuff. On my way to the front door I looked around for anything she could have left behind, and nothing caught my sight. I swung open the door.

"Look, Tia!" I paused and was briefly caught off guard. "Tracey!? What are you doing here?" He leaned in and kissed me on the lips during my sentence. I halfway kissed back.

TEMPTATION ISLAND

Leaving the kids behind with Granddad and Grandma Sugar had Livia feeling slightly emotional. The nonstop flight was seven hours. Olivia packed a few books, not only for the flight but since sex was out of the question, she needed something to occupy her time on the island. Her hair was braided up into a top bun which made it difficult for wearing her new, sound-blocking, headphones. So, she traded Lawrence for his ear buds. He was concerned about getting a crease in the top of his hair but far too excited about the trip to make a fuss over it.

Livia slept almost the entire flight. She ordered one drink and was out like a light. Lawrence watched her sleep for a while and took several photos of her drooling and mouth agape before he rummaged her bag for snacks. He started watching *The Godfather* on his laptop while his future bride slept on his shoulder.

Once the plane landed and all their things were gathered, the two of them were prepared to have a relaxing ten-day escape. Walking through the outdoor-concept airport, Livia experienced the sensation of warm air on her skin. She was even able to catch a small breeze under her sun dress as her feet flip flopped down the corridor. Lawrence was bobbing his head to the musicians as they played a catchy beat.

The aroma of ocean breeze and tropical flowers tickled their noses. Waiting on the checked luggage to arrive, Lawrence and Livia shared a moment. They gazed into each other's eyes without saying a word.

Day One:

Using the lockbox code, Livia retrieved the key to the rental house. After letting herself in, she dropped the bags in the entry way and took a tour. Lawrence was not far behind. They packed only one oversized suitcase with enough outfits and shoes to get them through the week. There were so many windows it was hard distinguishing the outside from the inside. It was an open concept home with the living space being the first stop. Off toward the back end of the house was the kitchen, dining room, and living room that led out to the back patio. Down the hall to the right were the first bedroom and a bathroom across from it. The downstairs bedroom led out to a hot tub and pool.

Upstairs was a loft area which was the master bedroom space. On the opposite of the bedroom was an open shower with five shower heads. Livia was imagining all the ways she could use that shower and had to flood her thoughts with the likes of her reading material. Lawrence came up the stairs behind her. He wrapped his arms under hers and kissed the back of her head.

"Ugh. This bun braid is gonna' get on my nerves, Girl," he teased. "Does it come down?"

"No, it doesn't come down. You know that. It's only for a week and you are not planning to be too close to me anyway so I figured it wouldn't be a big deal."

"Hey now. Who said anything about not being close? I want to be very close to you. But since you did mention that, I wanted to tell you that this will be your room up here. I am taking the downstairs one."

"What?! Guac, this is going too far. You mean, I cannot even sleep next to you out here? This doesn't seem like fun to me."

"Trust me. You will thank me later. Plus, when will you ever get a bed to yourself again?"

Lawrence had an entire agenda for the whole ten days. He planned to pamper and spoil Livia to the fullest. The property he rented included kitchen staff that was hired to cook meals. Livia was starting to pout about the sleeping arrangements, but Lawrence encouraged her to take a relaxing shower and get dressed for dinner. He went down to his quarters and prepared himself as well. Already two weeks into the abstinence pact, Lawrence was not having an easy time abstaining. Livia's beauty and outfit selection combined, made for a tempting recipe.

His intent was not to punish either of them. He really wanted to convey to his fiancé that their relationship meant more than sex. He was ashamed that he didn't take the time to court Livia originally. Not that he could have done so in an appropriate manor, anyway, having been a college basketball coach when he met Livia in her freshman year of college. He also thought about if her family would have even accepted Livia dating a man ten years her senior as a freshman in college. Mostly, Lawrence just wanted to show Olivia he had no intentions of ever walking out on her.

Lawrence started off impressing Olivia on the first night. He had just enough time to set it up while she unpacked. Waiting at the bottom of the stairs was a trail of rose petals she followed, leading her to the patio. The patio was illuminated by tea lights. She covered her mouth with both hands. Lawrence helped her to be seated and they shared a gourmet dinner while the sun set. The kitchen staff cleared the table and brought more wine to the couple seated at poolside. Both dipped their legs in the water and toasted to the beginning of a wonderful vacation. Lawrence talked to Livia about her hopes and dreams when she was a young woman entering college and what she imagined her future to be like back then.

She talked about all the places in the world she wanted to visit and how she thought she was destined to become a basketball wife and how looking back now she sees how foolish that all was. Even if Cole had been the one for her, he eventually ended up being a physical therapist after tearing his ACL senior year.

So, she still wouldn't have been a basketball wife. Lawrence talked about his heart for the players as a college basketball coach and his dream to get one of his boys drafted to the NBA. Then he revealed his passion for always having wanted to reach black boys well before college to provide an educational foundation. His dream was that young black boys would not rely on sports as their only path to success. He reflected on being most proud of his last ten years as The Academy's President and Co-Founder. She talked about Lawrence being the missing key to what she was looking for in life. That if she had not left her keys in the gym that night, they might not be sitting on the edge of the pool that very moment, vacationing away from their three lovely children.

Slowly her eyes became heavy and she drifted to sleep on his arm. While he watched her sleep, he was coming up with several other ways, he would have tried to make sure she noticed him had it not been for her losing her keys that night. Concluding his reflection, he gently nudged her awake so he could help her get upstairs to bed.

He covered her with the blanket, softly kissed her lips and whispered in her ear, "I love you, Olivia." Next he knelt down beside her bed and prayed over their coming week. When he got up to head back downstairs, she opened her eyes. In a groggy voice she mumbled, "Hey you. I love you too. Stay a while longer." He grabbed her hand, kissed it, and told her he wished he could. Then at the top of the steps he turned around to give a few last words for the evening. Hanging over the top of the railing he warned, "Also, no self-exploration allowed either! That would be cheating, Babe."

Livia yanked the blanket over her head and turned over to face the balcony doors. Lawrence laughed louder than he intended to as he walked down to his room. Livia tossed and turned, unable to fall back to sleep.

Day Two:

Lawrence went upstairs and quietly knocked on the headboard over Livia's bed. "Wake up Babe." She lifted the pillow from covering her face. "It's vacation. Can't I at least sleep in?" Livia had stayed up late to write since she needed something to take her mind off of Lawrence. She didn't know if she would have down time to write but fortunately, or unfortunately, to her surprise, with Lawrence sticking to the *no sex* rule, she would have more time to write then she had imagined.

Lawrence smiled a big cheesy grin, "I want you to take a walk with me. I have a different bed for you to lie on." She sat straight up. "But you said...."

"It's not in my room...Just come on." He led her through the back patio through the beautiful plants, flowers and bushes and out to the beach. There was a little hut set up with two massage beds under it and two massage therapists waiting to give them each a relaxation massage. Livia squeezed his hand and pinched her own arm. After planting a kiss on her cheek, he said, "By the time your massage is over, breakfast will be ready by the pool. After that, we can get in the pool, or take a nap."

The massage was perfect. The ocean sounds were serene. But ever since Lawrence asked Livia to take a trip down memory lane, she couldn't help but to imagine her potential future with the suitors she'd encountered before meeting Lawrence. Livia's teenage escapades spoke behind her closed eyelids:

✳ ✳ ✳

Tre had totally surprised me by showing up on my doorstep the day after my high school graduation party. I admittedly missed him and gave in fully to the kissing which led to my bedroom. We fooled around in my bed for a couple minutes and then I opened my eyes. His eyes were still closed, and his hands were all over me. I glance down to the floor and spotted Stevie's note, "Wait. Wait, Tre, wait, wait, wait." He looked at me and was confused. "What Baby? I don't want to wait anymore. I don't want Sarah, anymore. I want you. I'm here with you. I told Sarah I'm done with her. I love *you*! Plus, every time I think about you, my dick gets hard. I mean I *really* wanna be with you. Let me show you."

It was difficult to reject him because I really liked Tracey. I wanted him to be completely in love with me. But seeing Stevie's letter made me come to my senses. I couldn't continue disrespecting myself. I knew I deserved to be treated with more dignity.

"Look Tracey. I can't do this with you."

"What are you a nun now? You can't say 'no' after teasing me like that."

"No, I'm not a nun! And I'm not trying to tease you. It's just that, you know I'm going away to college. You knew my graduation was yesterday and you didn't even call! That's messed up. Look, I won't lie. I have strong feelings for you, but this just isn't—let me go off to school and get started with my life. After I finish a year and you still want me then, we can talk."

"A year Olivia?! What do you take me for? I ain't no punk. That's real messed up. I'm outta here," he got up from my bed and stormed out like a toddler.

I had to chase after him to finish talking, "Is it like that, Tracey? I'm not saying we can't talk during that time. Let's just take a break from all the sexual stuff and be friends for a minute."

"Bye Olivia."

I was heartbroken after closing the door behind Tracey. That was the last time I ever saw him.

Chapter 10
Which Way Do We Go?

THE SUMMER WENT by so fast that I hardly had time to reflect on it. Working at the fabric store was easy money, but I put in a lot of hours. They were sure sad to see me go. I tried to set it up so they would let me work there when I come back during school breaks. That is pending I come back during school breaks. There really isn't much to come back to. My idea of going off to college was that I would find new friends and a hobby to keep me busy.

My college sendoff wasn't very eventful other than welcoming Stevie's new neighbors and asking them to watch the house while she was gone. She delivered a "welcome" casserole to the freckle-faced-redhead and her husband. Stevie told me their names were Palmer and Cody. A young couple with no kids, just dogs. I didn't know they would later end up becoming two of my best friends. The neighbors accepted the casserole and waved us off, Stevie and me, as we pushed off for the 15hr drive down the West Coast.

Stevie refused to let me drive my own car while she was in it, which designated me DJ the entire way down. I bumped some Destiny's Child, Sade, Tina Marie (for Momma), Usher, Jagged Edge, Maria Carey and Brandy. I sang each and every song which made it pretty difficult for any heart to hearts to emerge. The most we talked about, at first, was the stupid long line at the In N Out drive-through and who was gonna eat the last of the Wheat Thins. When the seventh hour passed, I took a bold step and opened up to Stevie about my disapproval of Kelpie's presence at my graduation party. I let her know that allowing him to move in with Cousin Perry when he was seventeen, was the best thing she could have done for me mentally. Not having him around, minimized my flashbacks of his abuse. I got a lot of things off my chest I'd been wanting to unload on Stevie for years. The draining outpour of emotions put me to sleep. I woke up right as we were pulling into my dorm parking lot.

I chose not to physically notice the roll of condoms and pamphlet to Planned Parenthood Stevie tucked in the front of my backpack. She helped me unload my car and get checked into my dorm room which had a pretty cool courtyard entrance. The dorm itself was a small studio style room with two beds, two closets, a mini fridge and a bathroom. Stevie and I ate dinner at a local diner, and finally she let me drive my own car to drop her off at the airport for a short flight home. "You're gonna do fine here. See ya kiddo," is all she said and kissed me on the top of my head.

When I got back to my dorm room, Carrington Hall South Square, there was evidence my roommate had checked in as well, but she was out at the moment. It was crazy because I had only been gone for two hours and Genila had destroyed the room like we were weeks into the school year. Panties and bras were on the television stand. Dresser drawers were overflowing with unfolded tee-shirts sticking out. Wet towels had been sprawled over the bathroom. Shoes of all colors and styles stacked in a pile on the closet floor. I just accepted the fact that I'd be the clean one around here.

The sound of keys followed by Genila busting through the door, startled me. I yelped and I pivoted to face the open doorway. "Hi Jen-eye-lah or...sorry never saw a name like yours before. How do you say it?"

"Oh, hey Girl! It's Juh-nee-luh like Jamila with a G and a N. My mom was on crack when she named me," she explained.

I laughed out loud, waiting for Genila to say she was joking.

Genila confirmed, "No really. She was. I believe she wanted to name me Jamila but couldn't spell it. Whatever! Thank God she dropped me on my uncle's doorstep before she ruined my life. And thank God, he was rich as hell! The good life. You feel me?"

I froze, searching for the words to say while she paused to search her purse for something.

Genila continued, "Whatever, Girl. I just came back for my purse. Me and my friend Sabrina are going to a Rush party if you wanna come, but you need to change. I have plenty of dresses that would fit you. I buy smalls instead of larges so it can make me look skinnier like you. Oh, and so you know, everybody calls me Gene. I get tired of explaining my name."

"Thanks Gene. I'm gonna chill here for tonight because I just got here and..."

Before I could finish my sentence, Gene was already outside with her head peeking through a crack in the door, "Okay bye!" The door shut tightly and the clickity clack of heels could be heard trotting away. I stood there a minute shaking my head and wondering what kind of year this would be. After setting up my boom box, I put on Jill Scott. She and

Lauryn Hill helped me focus on getting my side of the room set up just right. I taped a few posters up, nailed a tapestry behind the bed my great aunt gave me before she passed away, put a picture of me and Stevie on my desk and placed my neatly folded clothes in the dresser. The stuff that needed hanging got hung in the closet and I used my desk drawer to keep the snacks we didn't finish on the drive down.

I had a cute fuzzy rug to lay on the floor that matched the bedding I brought. I decided to hit the shower first and get my pajamas on so that once the bed was made, I could find a movie to watch. I felt refreshed after hopping out of the shower and realized I still needed to take the broken-down cardboard boxes and empty wrappers of all the new college dorm accessories I opened. First, I hooked up my TV and the cable connection. I was glad Gene didn't bring a TV, too. That would have been awkward trying to figure out whose TV to use and what to do with the extra one.

I put on animal slippers and a hoodie to travel to the dumpsters. It wasn't cold out but since I had just gotten out of the shower, and my hair was not completely dry, I covered up. Of course, the dumpsters were too high for me. I tried a few times to lift the lid. It wasn't heavy but I wasn't able to get it open wide enough for my trash to fit inside. I was shoving everything in the side of the dumpster by the wall.

An authoritative voice came directly to my ear. "Excuse me hooded girl! You can't leave that there." I was completely embarrassed. First day on campus and I get caught misusing the dumpsters. I stood to the side with a guilty look on my face. I had no idea what the repercussion would be.

It was dark outside now but even in poor outdoor lighting I could see this guy was handsome. He was towering over me as most people do and had the sweetest smile. "They call me Cole. I play basketball here. Sophomore. Just handing out flyers to the Meet N Greet happing tomorrow. You should definitely be there, Baby."

Blushing inwardly, but still offended, I quickly corrected him. "I'm not your Baby! My name is Olivia. That's what you can call me." My eyebrows pushed up against each other so hard I was almost getting a headache, but I had to make sure he knew I was serious. He never stopped smiling. I pushed my lips together just as tight as my eyebrows were and crossed my hands over my chest, so he knew I was a girl that stood up for herself. At the same time, I tried not to notice his amazing calf muscles with the night light bouncing off of them and focused hard not to let his smile melt me.

He cut the tension with his voice again and a shy laugh, "My bad, Shorty. Excuse me. Olivia. I call everybody Baby. Even my boys. It's just a thing I say. I'm not trying to holla at you, but if I was, you would know."

I snatched the flyer and walked off quickly. "Thank you! Bye!" I called back over my shoulder, then closed my door.

"Yeah, Girl. You better get back inside before somebody snatch you up out here. Imma put your trash in the dumpster for you! We try to keep things looking neat and clean out here," he yelled loudly, since I had already closed and locked my door.

I did not make the best first impressions with anyone on campus right away, but things did get better as the time went on. The next morning is when Gene returned, as I was brushing my teeth to be exact. She didn't mumble a word, or even shut our door. Gene just climbed into bed, hair looking tore up and skirt twisted to the side. She got in bed – shoes, makeup and all. I walked across the room to shut the door. "NOT SO LOUD!" she said.

Good thing all I had to do was slip on my clothes and head out. "I SAID NOT SO LOUD!" Gene yelled out the window as I walked away after shutting the door gently behind me.

Saturday was my day to get all of my school stuff in order. There was a two-hour line to pick up my lunchroom food card and school ID. They take the photo on-site and print it while you wait. Then, I waited for another half-hour to check on the waitlist for Calculus 101. They had an online waitlist, but my adviser told me if you show up and put your name on the physical waitlist, you had a better chance getting enrolled in the classes you needed. I waited all that time just to find out that I was already enrolled. Three people had changed their schedules online and that had automatically bumped me up to be registered for the class. That was time wasted.

The worst part of the day was the three hours it took to find and pay for all of my textbooks. Stevie tried to tell me to order ahead of time so I could just go straight to the "pick up line" but I just forgot to do that. Completely starved, after waiting in endless lines and driving around campus from location to location, I was excited to find a good parking space near the cafeteria.

It was lonely at dinner. So, I entertained myself by people watching. There were a lot more locals that went to the school than out-of-state students so cliques that formed in high school had transferred to college level mean girls and jock boys. After observing the live show for more than twenty minutes, I was uninterested and glanced up at the large clock on the wall over one of the entrances. It was five past seven and the Meet N Greet had already started so I packed up and headed out the door.

Trying to determine where I was going by looking at the flyer had me walking with my head down. From behind me a voice called out, "Hey, Cardboard!"

I thought there was no way someone from my middle school years could have enrolled in the same school as me. I used to get teased badly for being skinny and the term "flat as cardboard" got shortened to cardboard. I swung my head around to find out that it was the guy from the dumpster.

Once again, I gave Cole "the look" with my arms folded. And once again he gave me the most addicting smile. A smile I could absolutely get used to having around but I had to play it cool. "Well, I knew you would get all pissed if I said *Hey Baby,* and I couldn't remember your real name."

I promptly crumpled the flyer in my hand, dropped it on the ground at his feet and split towards my dorm room. "Olivia! Wait. Dang girl. I was just fucking wit chu. You don't play I see. I see." Catching up to my pace, I let him grab my arm to turn me back around. He held out his right hand for me to shake it and said, "Hi Olivia. Nice to meet you. My name is Cole. Would it be okay if I escort you to the Meet N Greet?" There he went again with that seductive smile and so I smiled in return but didn't say anything. I just held my arm and hand out as if for him to lead the way.

We entered the meeting room adjacent from Harrington Hall and the space was filled with people. Cookies and lemonade stations had students lined up and booths for campus clubs framed the perimeter. The notion of attempting another line brought me to nausea. Cole walked me up to a group of his friends and said, "Hey fellas, this my girl Olivia."

"Cole!" I scolded him.

"Okay, okay. I was just playin," he quickly clarified. He introduced me properly and then I meandered around a few of the booths. No line standing, just perusing. The other attendees weren't as friendly as Cole. The refreshment table looked as lonely as me, so I snagged a few cookies to take to my dorm. Cole approached me at the table, asking about my plans after the Meet N Greet. I shook my head, stowing away another cookie in my mouth with shoulders to ears, and stared at him wide eyed. A few of his friends were going to this late-night ice cream shoppe and he had an extra seat in his car. I agreed to go but instead I told him I would follow them in my car so I could leave on my own terms.

Although we were all a bunch of college kids, I went back to the room and asked Gene if she wouldn't mind going with me so I would feel safer. At first Gene scrunched up her face at the sound of ice cream but when she heard who was going to be there she quickly freshened up and asked if we could pick up her friend, Sabrina, on the way. The three of us followed at the back of the caravan. When we arrived, it was the coolest place for ice cream I had ever been to.

Hype music was playing. The lights were dim, and the seating reminded me of a sitcom called Happy Days. My ice cream was yummy, the mood was right, and I had no plans on leaving early. Previously I mentioned, I am a people watcher, so I experienced the party from my seat. I was sitting at my booth savoring my ice cream when Cole came sliding in next to me.

"So, what's up with you? You're different," Cole asked in a flirty tone.

I sighed, "Here we go. Cole you're cute and funny but I know how jocks are. You are the kind of guy that has two or three girlfriends and is always on the lookout to replace one of them with a new hottie. I'm not the one."

"You got me all figured out, you think? I ain't like that...no more," he paused. Another spoonful went into my mouth as I gazed out beyond the view of him. He shifted slightly. Patiently, I waited for him to reverse slide out to hang with the next willing female in queue. Instead he continued, "So long story short, I had this girl for a while, and she ended up going to school where my sister was going back east, and they fell in love or some shit. Done deal. My sister broke her heart and she got violent. So, my sister transferred here, to our school, to finish her senior year so she wouldn't have to trip about it.

I'm tired of competing for girls with my sister. But you. You're not her type at all. And I think you're cute. I'm not trying to be your man. I just wanna get to know you a little. How you feel about that?"

Here I am trying not to put on my judgmental face about what he just shared and at the same time show that I am intrigued that he wants to find out more about who I am. I raised my eyebrows while devouring the last big bite of mint chocolate chip cream and asked, "So, whaddya wanna know?"

The massage therapist snapped Livia out of her memory of Cole by asking if she'd enjoyed her ocean-side massage. The therapists collected their materials and wished the couple an enjoyable stay. Livia and Lawrence hung out by the pool after their relaxation massage and hearty breakfast. They were just chit chatting about the breathtaking view, how talented the massage therapists were, and about their favorite breakfast dish. Livia had just finished talking about how well the bacon was prepared. She couldn't pin down the flavor since the bacon had a savory flavor like hickory smoke to compliment the sweetness.

Lawrence told her he was still listening as he stepped inside to grab something. The bacon admiration stopped, and Liv's eyelids got heavy as she let the sun toast her skin with her oversized sunglasses shading half her face. As the drops of pool water hit her exposed belly, a facial expression formed that Liv was known well for. Her brows squeezed together, and her lips smashed tightly, Liv pulled up her glasses with one hand and shielded her eyes with the other. Lawrence was standing over her, straddled with his fists palms down. "Pick one," he said.

"Babe, you're dripping cold water on me."

"Just pick. And then I'll move."

She tapped his left hand. He flipped it palm side up and opened his grip. It was a gumball machine sized pair of goggles. "What does this mean, Babe? I don't get it. What was in the other hand?"

He brought one leg to meet the other and took a seat on the lounge chair next to hers, "They're goggles." He opened the other hand and it was a tiny horse. "You had the choice of snorkeling in the reef or horseback riding along the beach."

"Wait. That's how we're deciding? What if I wanted horseback riding? Am I out of luck?"

"Nope. We're doing both. Just wanted to tease you. They will be here to pick us up in 25 minutes to head to the reef, so get dressed. And pack a small bag for your horseback riding clothes and something for dinner afterwards. We won't have time to come back to change."

Livia smirked and got up from her seat, taking her towel along. She packed easy stuff to change in and out of, so getting a small bag together was a breeze. Her hair was already done in the braided bun so after a rinse in the shower, she slid into a zip-front, one piece, bathing suit and draped on a cover-up. The zip-front was swimsuit number two out of the four she packed. Meeting him at the bottom of the stairs the couple had a few minutes to hold each other and kiss before their ride pulled up.

"Too many more kisses like that, Guac, and I will be forced to break your rule."

After a full day of snorkeling and riding along the beach, they rightfully devoured the seafood bake that was sprawled out on the table. They chowed down on crab legs, crawfish, shrimp, corn and baby red potatoes. The meal was reminiscent of the Creole spread Lawrence had set up for her to explain that she was going on a trip.

Together they tossed back a few drinks and moved freely on the dance floor. Back at the house they snuggled in front of the living room fireplace. Livia permitted her eyes to close for the night as she was cozy in his arms. Lawrence had a hard time with the bun hitting him in the jaw, but he tried to ignore it.

DAY 3:

Lawrence and Olivia were still laying together on the living room floor, "You broke your own rule, Honey."

Lawrence reached under the blanket and felt that his pants were still on. He didn't remember having had enough drinks to forget his rule. "What do you mean?!" he said.

"I mean, we are overnighters. We technically slept together."

"Yeah, okay. But not for real. And we have to try not to do that again. It was such a long day and I was afraid if I woke you to go upstairs it would ruin the ending to a perfect day. I do want to ask you something though and I hope it won't spoil our time here."

"What Baby? You can ask me anything," Livia said with a carefree attitude.

"Uh. Okay. I know it took a long time and you really like it, but will you please take those braids off? You just don't feel like...you. We're on an island. This is the perfect place to let your hair out."

"Are you serious? You know it's not so easy to take these braids *off*. Technically, it's "take them *down*." I don't understand. You booked my hair appointment. It's not so easy to get my curls to behave. You have no idea. Plus, I don't have product here! I don't have, I don't have..."

"Your blow dryer and comb?" Lawrence helped to finish her thought.

"Yeah that, and where around here would I get that? I can't believe you're doing this right now. Now I will be self-conscious all week, thinking about this. This is so stupid." Almost in tears, Liv headed towards the stairs.

Lawrence cleared his throat, "Hey Liv? So, I, um, packed your hair stuff in my personal bag. I didn't know I would upset you like that. Leave the braids on if you want. You look good."

She stomped up the stairs and blasted her Pandora on the in-house speaker system. She put on her Lauryn Hill Station and sung every song at the top of her lungs. After listening to her sing four songs he figured she might be doing this for a while, so he put on his joggers and took off for a run along the beach. During his run, he discovered a small little hidden cove with a waterfall on the inside. He felt really bad for saying anything about Liv's hair. He had no idea she would feel so strongly about braids.

This was only Day Three and Lawrence's plan to bring them closer together had done the opposite, causing a temporary rift. He discovered a sturdy rock to rest upon and he prayed to God concerning the duration of the trip and petitioned for peace, clarity and a way out of the mess he caused. He was out there exploring for a couple of hours, before getting hungry.

Walking back up to the house he heard her calling out to him, so he picked up the pace a bit. When he walked in, she was standing in the middle of the living room with just her robe on and her curls hanging down and dripping wet. After a short embrace, Livia playfully retorted, "I don't need a hug Guac. I need my product. My comb. And my blow dryer. Now." He grabbed her by the shoulders, held her out in front of himself, mouthed the words "I'm sorry," then searched through his bag to get her stuff.

Liv looked at everything and back at Lawrence, "How did you get this on the plane?" Answering herself, "Oh, this must have been in the suitcase." Realizing which curl-cream he packed, she grumbled, "So this is the almost empty one so I can get two maybe three days out of this; tops. You know that means the last couple days I will be rocking a raggedy ponytail or two French braids."

Lawrence taking a shot at positivity, "I like the two braids. You're cute like that. Do it!" He thought to say – *It's just that bun that was not working out*. But he didn't want to risk it while he was ahead.

"I'm really sorry I offended you. You are beautiful to me in every shape and form. You were most beautiful to me after the birth of all three of our children, with your hair puffed out, face sweaty, and crying. I tell you this because I'm in love with your soul, not your shell."

"I get it, Baby. Apology accepted. Thank you for bringing my products," she smiled. "Now, we are not allowed to talk about hair the rest of the trip. That is my rule." He nodded his head in agreement and took her by the hand.

The kitchen staff made a few tasty salads for lunch and dinner, so they didn't have to go out for dinner later that night. He took her by the hand and led her back to the waterfall he found. It took them a little longer to get there the second time, since they were going at Olivia's pace instead of Lawrence's jogging pace. The waterfall was glistening four stories high and created a double rainbow as the sun was setting.

"You know we can't hang out too late. The path back is not lit, and it will be pitch dark soon. Plus, I know you're hungry so we can eat and chill for the rest of the night."

Lawrence needed to make some calls updating his reservations. Although Livia had turned it around and did what he asked, he took blame for it taking up almost a whole day. Next on the agenda was good but he needed it to be spectacular. After eating dinner Lawrence conked out. Between two trips to the waterfall and the heavy potato salad, he was bound to be sleepy.

Livia took the opportunity to go back upstairs and write. She loved the fragrance and crash of the ocean she could hear from her patio doors. It made for great background noise. Livia was eager to continue writing about Cole:

✳ ✳ ✳

I left the ice cream shoppe that night grinning about my conversation with Cole. The next morning, I blinked my eyes until they gained strength to stay open. My legs directed my feet to the floor allowing me to lift my body out of bed. I did a slow shuffle half-way to the bathroom when I caught glimpse of a note taped to the TV screen. I pulled it off although it could be read from a foot away. Gene peered from an opening of her blanket cave in bed to tell me Cole slipped her the note sometime last night.

The note was concise.

Call me at 555-2734. Ya boy Cole.

I planned on calling. I was impressed with his tactics. He wasn't the best mac daddy, but the attraction was there, no doubt. The plan to call came three days later. I had met all of my class professors, got a list of office hours and extra credit guidelines. I was only late to one class the entire week. The off-campus class was held in Professor Miles' home.

Seventeen people enrolled and that was the maximum capacity he would allow. No audits. Professor Miles taught a class called "Finding Your Way." We were expected to spend the entire quarter learning about whether or not college was the right path to take. I found the class off-putting since this is the sort of subject more suitable for high school. High school, as in the place you are before you've gotten accepted to college and before you took out student loans and bought books and moved away from your parents. Either way, it counted for three Sociology credits. I knew I would skate through the class.

Familiar with the campus, settled in with my roomie, and eager to take on adulting, I needed to get to know the area. Gene did know what, where, and how to get what I needed when I needed it, but she declined being my tour guide. Cole was a Sophomore and would surely know his way around. Needing Cole to serve as my tour guide would justify my call. I dialed his number nervous to hear his voice on the other end. After two rings I hung up. That was stupid. This means he has my number. I blurted, "Aaaaagh!" as a way of cursing myself for being an idiot. Buzz, buzz, buzz came from my phone. My clumsy thumbs sent the call to voicemail rather than answering it. Tiny cellular phones were the new hot thing. They were cool if not for the tiny buttons. I rarely hit the right one.

No voicemail from Cole. The phone buzzed again but this time a double buzz. A message came across the small screen, CALL BACK COLE. I attempted to write a message back, but I had a hard time with the T9 texting feature and doing the "ABC" method to text took forever. I just wanted to say, "Sorry, I meant to answer but the tiny buttons made me send you to voicemail." Three minutes had passed by. I was on the last three words of the text when my phone started to buzz again. This was another incoming call from Cole. I answered. We had a laugh about my cell phone illiteracies, and he confessed he was using the built-in auto reply. When we got down to the nature of the call, I could hear in his voice he was disappointed I wasn't calling to just hang out, but he didn't turn me down on the opportunity to show me around the city.

I followed him in my car to the top three dine-in places to eat. The best drive-through spots were on the tour, too. I still needed to know where the grocery store, bank, and beauty supply locations were. During our lunch break, he invited his sister, Vanessa, to join. He trusted us to be friends. Since I wasn't her "type." Vanessa was part of the crew that always hung out together. Before she arrived, I asked why she didn't come to the Ice Cream Shoppe and Cole said she had other plans that night.

Vanessa was funny and as friendly as Cole. She was tall like him too. She rocked two long French braids that hit the middle of her back. She dressed in baggy jeans and an over-sized plaid button up shirt. Timberland boots finished off the look and to soften it, Vanessa wore flawless makeup. She was stunning once you looked past the rough exterior. She had baby smooth skin, perfectly lined lips painted dark burgundy, freshly arched eyebrows and super long lashes that framed her dark brown eyes.

Cole needed to bail on us for a basketball meeting, to get the practice schedule for the season. So, that left Vanessa to finish the tour. Vanessa had been dropped off to the lunch spot making her my passenger seat escort for the other stops I wanted to make. The trip was mostly to get a feel of which way to go when I was in need, except I had to pick up a large bottle of conditioner sold at the Beauty Depot. My dry hair guzzled conditioner and not having conditioner would lead to a hair disaster I wanted to avoid.

She lived on campus, too, in one of the apartments. The campus apartments were strictly for seniors and their roommates. If you were not a senior or didn't have a senior to room with, you could forget about trying to get placed in one of those units. They had full accommodations including a full kitchen, full bath, and separate bedroom from the living space. The caveat is they were all single bedroom units. No two-bedroom units, so all bedrooms were still two beds to a room.

She invited me inside her apartment, and I was curious to see the layout since all I knew about the apartments were from word of mouth. Once inside they were precisely like people described them. The other side of the bedroom was bare and Vanessa told me it was because her roommate dropped out two weeks before school started but didn't notify the housing department, giving Vanessa the apartment to herself for at least one semester until a transferring or late start student needed a place to live.

I found the remote and clicked her TV on while sitting on her bed. I didn't take long for me to realize that Vanessa was friendlier than Gene. Soon, I would be on a mission to see about transferring rooms. After grabbing me a water bottle from the fridge, Vanessa asked if I minded her hopping in the shower. The person that dropped her off to me and Cole was where she had spent the night. The plan was to come home last if the designated driver stayed sober. I laughed at the way Vanessa told the story. She changed her voice to represent each person that was talking in the story and she was overtly expressive with her hands.

I flipped through the channels and found Class Act was on and had just started. When it got to the part with Kid in the school parking lot, Vanessa was calling me. With all that hair, I would never let myself run out of conditioner. The fact that we got along so well, and I was really into her brother, I chose not to get pissed at her using my brand-new bottle of conditioner. I had long hair but hers was way longer than mine.

"You can come in here, Girl. I don't care if you look. We got the same thing. Just bring it in the shower please. I don't want to get my floor wet."

The bathroom didn't have an actual door, just a doorway. No shower curtain, just glass shower doors.

"Here!" I elevated my voice to be heard over the water, since there was no response the first time I said it. Her hair flowed down her back stopping at the curve of her spine, a few inches above her butt. She turned full frontal to me to take the bottle of conditioner. I spun my neck in the opposite direction holding out the conditioner toward the shower door. She didn't take it. When I looked back, she was sliding her hand up her breasts and through her hair, using the other hand to wipe the water from her eyes.

"Vanessa!" I gave her a puzzled stare trying to search her face to reveal if she was flirting or really didn't know I was standing there. She took it with a "Thank you" and smile. That smile was another thing she and her brother, Cole, had in common. Mad that I'd missed my favorite part of the movie already, I gave up on watching it to see who was knocking at the front door. Cole filled the light of the doorway with each hand rested inside the doorjamb when I opened it. He pulled me into his arms, which I welcomed. It felt natural to be embraced by him. I complained about him making me miss my movie. Almost immediately, I confessed he wasn't the culprit, but his sister had done something I wanted to make him privy to.

"Well, she was in the shower and..."

"Hey, Baby Bro. How was the meeting?" Vanessa had entered the living room dressed in an oversized Brown University t-shirt and men's basketball shorts, one hand drying her hair with a towel. "Olivia thanks for the conditioner. You know how to braid?"

✱✱✱

Lawrence and Olivia were on two different sleep patterns during their romantic getaway, which she blamed on not being able to sleep in the same bed as him. But Lawrence gathered it was from her staying up late at night to type.

Lawrence jogged upstairs to witness a sleeping beauty curled around her laptop. She was lucky not to have kicked it onto the floor with her involuntary sleep movements. He left her there but secured the laptop back in its case. Taking a quieter trip down the stairs to leave Olivia undisturbed, Lawrence used his solo moment to have a date with The Lord in prayer. Ever confident that his plan would bring them closer and stronger as a unit, the prayer was weighted in requests for strength to carry the plan through to the last day of the trip.

Although Livia was impressed with each gesture put on by her fiancé, she was becoming overwhelmed. Following the Day 4 paragliding, came a plea to slow down on the extreme dates. It was gratifying for Liv to lie out on the beach for three hours. Most of all, she was looking forward to the peace and serenity the island had to offer.

Lawrence defaulted to Olivia for following day's agenda and listened to what activities she wanted to participate in. He thoroughly enjoyed every moment they spent together. It dawned on Lawrence to take a vacation from his vacation. He was comforted in knowing it only required minimal effort to make Livia happy. Not that she seemed unhappy other times, but most of their relationship had consisted of parenting. The two were great parents and took pride in all of the mommy and daddy duties. The romantic, sexually frustrating for Olivia, but romantic, getaway was to remind them their love was established before the children.

During the final evening, luggage packed, Lawrence stood at the overhang of Olivia's loft. Her eyes and grin permitted him to speak his mind. His voice opened in a low rumble like the purr of an engine. His sexy attributes were never lost on her. For their last night, Lawrence wanted to sleep with Livia. Finally adhering to the rules, at will, she began to refuse. Lawrence came from behind the overhang, revealing a blanket and pillow held in hand. They both busted out laughing when Olivia realized he intended to sleep on the floor. The only amount of touch they succumbed to was holding hands.

The room was silent and dark as Olivia stared at the ceiling. Gripping Lawrence's hand with more intention her breathing became deeper and more audible.

"It finally ended."

"What? The nightmare?"

"Yeah."

"Are you ok?"

"I am. It's been a while, but the nightmare came back last night. It was the same, like before. I open my eyes and I'm in the bedroom sleeping next to you. It's dark but I can tell the walls look wet. Dripping with mud. My foot slips off the bed and I scream from the feel. It's cold, gooey...it's the swamp beneath my feet. The hands from the swamp grab my leg and start pulling my body while I grab the sheets, the pillow, you. And you're knocked out, so you don't budge. I scream your name so loud and we both wake up in real life. Except this time, we don't wake up. You don't wake up and the swamp takes me down beneath the surface. I'm suffocating and trying to scream but instead I swallow weeds and mud. I can't kick. I can't move. I'm screaming at myself on the inside saying, 'NO! NO! NO! I don't want this! Please Stop!' And then I swear it felt so real and I don't know if it's all in my mind, but my arm is sore right now. The one you're holding. My arm kept getting yanked and yanked and I was out of the swamp sitting in the grass. When I opened my eyes, I had my arms wrapped around my knees. I was young, like seven or so. I looked around. The grass was bright green. Flowers in the field were purple and pink and orange. It was sunny out and warm too. Between my knees and chest was the teddy bear my grandma gave to me. I stood up and smiled so big and swung my teddy bear in circles until the sun became too bright for me to see. I put my hands to my face to rub my eyes. When I opened them again, I was lying in bed, here, on this trip with you."

Hours later, one leg partially out of bed and a hand resting on her man's chest, she squinted at the intruding sun rays. Morning meant paradise had come to an end. However, the feeling of missing the babies turned home into the new paradise. Although it took the same hours traveling back, as it did to get to the island, the time zoomed by. Once their feet touched Washington soil, the realities of wedding planning set in. Uber pulled up to the Livingston driveway. They expected the house to be quiet since Bradley texted forty-five minutes ago that Grandma Sugar went home. It was after 11:00pm and the kids would be deep into dreamland by this hour. Yet the main lights of the house were still on and laughter could be heard from the doorstep. Livia wasn't aware she needed to give Bradley the "No company while we're gone" speech. She aggressively unlocked the door and barged in, Lawrence's hands on her shoulders. He was prepared to hold her back from going off on the mystery woman Bradley was entertaining in the living room.

When Bradley glanced toward the door, the woman retracted her bare foot from his lap. After seeing her face Lawrence let go of the shoulders.

Livia volumized with childlike excitement, completely forgetting the kids were asleep, "Mommyyyyyyyy!!"

With Stevie back in town and the vacation ending meant the wedding was close. Olivia was elated to have finished her book on the flight back home. Her first thought was to thank Dr. Luke. She planned to deliver a copy of her book to his counseling office. Olivia felt like she finally "survived the monster in her room" which was a phrase Dr. Luke used to refer to her depression and anxiety.

Too embarrassed to refuse, I braided Vanessa's hair that time. To ensure it wouldn't become a regular thing, I intentionally tangled her hair and finished the braids bumpy and uneven. I topped off the act with pride in myself for the amazing work I did, encouraging Cole to compliment me. Because Cole and I happened to be super convincing she stood up from the dining chair, smiling, leaning over to squeeze me by the shoulders.

From the bathroom I heard Vanessa cuss, "What the..." When she came back in the living room, she had a scarf on her head, describing to us how the scarf would help lay the braids down. I know she was covering up the eye sore I put on top of her scalp. On the inside, I trapped guilt. Don't judge me. I had to do something to turn her off since Cole was obviously wrong about me not being her type.

A full month had passed by the time I told Cole the truth about Vanessa's braids. We were love birds by then so nothing much I did was upsetting to him. His sister's spot was still the main hangout and she was no longer a threat to our relationship. Cole was sweet. Being with a new guy was an adventure. We dated openly versus sneaking around behind Stevie's back, like I did with Tre. However, Cole's athletic prowess gave me doubt he'd stay true. Bronson Palmblen scarred me heavily.

I was supportive of Cole in his skill on the court. I pushed him to practice harder at perfecting his shot. Between studies, practices, and games, the euphoric stage was wearing off. Studying together, coming to his practices and showing up at games failed to bring us closer. I even landed a late spot on the cheer squad during mid-season tryouts. Gene had the inside scoop telling me a girl got kicked off the team for getting pregnant.

Cole and his teammates typically trumped me in post-game partying. Not that I got excluded but most of the teammates were single. Having to watch the guys run through different chicks each night curdled my stomach. The girls that gave it up were more than willing, no foul play from these guys as far as I know. They were just a bunch of party girls. Cole would say most of those girls were just hoping to bang the next Ray Allen.

But what kept me committed to the practices and games more than Cole was his cutie coach. Coach Livingston blew Ray Allen out of the water, maybe not in stats but most certainly in sex appeal. Each time I came to the gym, he looked at me. The look came off completely differently than how he'd scowl at a student interrupting practice or a tardy player. He genuinely looked at me in a special way. He wanted me. I guessed he was a young coach because my "creeper" alert didn't buzz.

Coach Livingston kept a quiet disposition when it came to me. The dreams I had about him gave me immense guilt. I just wanted to hold his hand or at least shake it; nothing lusty or naughty. But I had a boyfriend to do that with and the coach, though young for his job, was probably still too old for me. My mind on the coach caused me to totally miss the moment Cole lost interest in our relationship.

At a playoff game, our whole team was performing poorly and fouled the other team for the fifth time in a row. Coach Livingston shifted his back to the court, head in hand. After wiping imaginary disgust off his face, we caught eyes. We cheerleaders stood right behind the players' bench, arms lifted, pom poms shaking with team spirit in the "miss it" stance. Immediately I bit the corner of my lip. To this day, I'm unsure if it was towards the coach or in discouragement for the rebound Cole missed.

The failed attempt landed Cole on the court floor, hugging his knee. My eyes transferred from Coach Liv's eyes to over his shoulder, making him face the court to see the damage. Landing like that could have put a player out for the next two games but rather than rest, Cole undoubtedly chose to kick it at the after party. Boys!

In the final minutes of the game, we gained control of the ball, only to lose it, and then gain it back for our Tigers to make the game-winning shot. Unfortunately, I had given the game to the opposing team, the Wildhogs, which put me in shock more so than excitement for our win.

Proud of our team for the comeback gave me the desire to celebrate, but I ditched the party to get an assignment done instead. My own shot clock was running out. After my "goodbye" and "congratulatory" kisses to Cole I slipped out the side door closest to the dorms. The opponents tucked their tails and sulked back to their side of town, long gone before our guys made it out the locker room. I closed down the gym in the sense that I always waited for Cole to shower and change before making my exit. I always preferred to shower in my own bathroom. While waiting, I looked back with embarrassment, to steal a sight of Coach Livingston but he'd left already, too.

All of us Tigers were growling with school pride over the close-call victory. We planned to take the championship this year, by the skin of our teeth or bust. I waved or pumped a fist depending on what car was passing me to exit the parking lot. Within five minutes of me leaving the gym, it was near silent outside. Walking through the dorm courtyard, something felt odd. I was empty handed! No keys! My duffle bag with keys and wallet stayed tucked under the bleachers all the way back in the gym.

I dashed back to the gym praying to catch any stragglers. Almost back to the gym entrance, beaming headlights met my path. Relief rushed over me. It was Coach Livingston. I asked him to let me back in to get my stuff and he said the custodian left for the night. Also, that he didn't have his keys to the gym. Trying to suppress my feelings of stupidity and forgetfulness, I couldn't ignore feelings of attraction. His voice rumbled as he spoke, and my ears quivered. I accepted his offer to give me a ride back to my dorm.

He drove me the short distance down the street to my dorm and kept watch while I climbed through my bathroom window. Safely inside, I opened the door to send him off, but it was too late. He stood in my doorway. We were closer than we had ever been. I can't decide if him asking to use my bathroom and then wanting coffee immediately after was cheesy or smooth. He stayed for more than just coffee. Gene rarely slept in our room, so I didn't worry about her barging in. If Cole popped up, there would be no explanation to justify his findings. Imagining camera and crew from the show I always watch, "Cheaters", busting down my door helped me decide to take Lawrence up on his offer to come to his beach house for the weekend.

That's right, Lawrence was his name. How sexy is that!? Honestly though, I already gave him a nickname. Everything about him is so smooth and thick at the same time, like guacamole. Affectionately I named him Guac. After the dirty dancing we did, Guac is the first thing that came to mind.

I spent the most amazing weekend at Lawrence's beach front condo. I finished my assignment on his computer and enjoyed getting to know him more. The night before he brought me back to campus, we sat on the sand sharing bits of our lives with each other. I told him a few small details about my past I never felt comfortable telling anyone before. Everything about him was easy. We moved on to lighter topics as the sun melted over the ocean. Two thirds into my spiel on why Day-Day was funnier than Smokey from the first *Friday*, Lawrence had fallen asleep. I coaxed him into it by stroking his hair and face, talking low, and taking thoughtful pause between points.

Pulling up to campus two days later on Sunday afternoon, brought reality to my attention. Knowing basketball season had some life on it, we agreed to keep secret our rendezvous until after the championship game. During my time at Lawrence's I looked up the number to the dorms online and asked the RD to leave a note for Gene about me staying with Stevie's relatives for a few days. My phone was in my gym bag. I raked through Cole's eleven voice messages from forty-five missed calls. Cole rejected any excuse I came up with about where I stayed all weekend. An even deeper rift was wedged. We went three weeks and two days without communication. He was livid. Word spread around campus that I was to blame for losing the Championship game. That Cole was so hurt over me, that he blew the game.

In the midst of it all, a deep level of intimacy developed between Lawrence and me. Lawrence and I snuck off to spend time together ever chance we got. Breaking it off with Cole was like deciding not to have the whipped cream topping on my caramel frap.

Do you want whip Olivia? No whip please. Okay, thank you, have a great day.

Not so "piece-of-cake" was Coach Liv's decision to resign from coaching at my school. If the school found proof of our hidden love he'd have been fired. The notion devastated me. I moved off campus for more privacy but continued to cheer on the squad; warding off unlikely coincidence. Come senior year I became ineligible for the cheer squad because I was pregnant with my first born, Claire.

That was a pivotal time in my life where depression grabbed me by the neck. It was embarrassing going to class. I could part any crowd like the Red Sea. No one would sit by me in class, choose me to be their partner, or for group assignments. And my professors were no better. They suggested I turn in solo projects. This is not as cool as it sounds. Turning in a solo project meant I had to do four times the work and all while pregnant.

I will never forget how Sabrina was there for me when it felt like I was abandoned. You could say we were there for each other. Sabrina was feeling abandoned, too. She was still grieving her seven-year relationship. Her long-distance boyfriend, Kyle, had broken up with her our junior year, after being together since the eighth grade. It took her half of junior year and well into our senior year to get over Kyle Drew. Maybe even longer than that. We were also both business majors and had spent a lot of time in classes and study groups together when we weren't hanging out with Gene.

Lawrence rented out his beach front condo so that we could live closer to campus. But he still chose to work and put in a lot of hours as a high school basketball coach and gym teacher at a private school. That particular high school was an hour and fifteen minutes away. So, Sabrina never left my side. She kept me smiling, reminded me to elevate my feet, ate dinner with me, felt Claire move and most of all she kept me sane.

She and Lawrence were pretty close too. He knew she was providing something for me that he couldn't at the time, and her presence did not intimidate him. Never once did I ask why she was so kind and loved me so much. I was just grateful to have her in my life. All I ever asked her was, "Where have you been all my life?!"

Sabrina was my family, along with Lawrence and Claire. I found phenomenal love in the most unconventional ways. Lawrence wanted to get married after the second pink stripe appeared on the pee-stick. I declined the proposal. It was his second time proposing. He first asked at the end of my junior year after finals, but I wasn't sure I believed in marriage. Instead, I declared my endless dedication to love him.

My senior year of college was anxiety ridden. During my final trimester, of pregnancy that is, I was grateful my school accepted a few online courses. I obtained my BA with Claire in tow. Once I was finished with school, we were able to accept the business opportunity Lawrence was offered up North. He and a grad school classmate of his, co-founded an all-boys school for grades Kindergarten through twelfth grade. Moving home meant having both of Claire's grandmas in close proximity which is awesome. The toughest part was leaving Sabrina.

After the decision was finalized, my only request was to have Lawrence find us a house on the lake. The first night in our new home, I asked Lawrence to get Claire changed into her new pajamas. He kissed Claire's bare toes five times, making her laugh, before he noticed the words on her onesie. He looked up at me for approval and beaming with joy, I was already nodding in affirmation. Bright pink letters on her onesie read: BIG SISTER.

The End.

✱✱✱

Olivia accomplished her promise to Lawrence and finished her book before the wedding. Coming back from her own pre-moon, voyage, to see her mom in the middle of her living room, was even more of a thrill! They rocked each other back and forth and concluded with a nonverbal apology on both ends. It is common that love conquers most disagreements. Many years advanced without Olivia being completely truthful about the abandonment she felt from Stevie similar to how Bradley left during Olivia's adolescence.

One of the deciding factors of Olivia moving back home after college was to be close to Stevie. Which was unfortunately bad timing for Stevie's new job opportunity to be a traveling nurse. Stevie's departure gave way to Livia's bond with Stevie's neighbor, Palmer. Palmer became like a second daughter to Stevie after Olivia left for college. The few times Livia came back home to visit, it was often the three of them hanging out – Stevie, Palmer, and Livia. Stevie's decision to become a traveling nurse less than a year after Livia's college graduation caused distance between the two in more ways than just the map.

Olivia now understood the reason Bradley left. Stevie coming to terms with Olivia knowing the truth, opened a door for reconciliation between her parents. But before that could be fully hashed out, there was a general consensus to first, get some rest.

"Oh, Momma. Does Palmer know you're back in town? If she kept that from me – I'm gonna strangle her!" Olivia teased.

"No, Baby. I wanted you to be the first to know. I'll be here for at least the next four weeks. I love you so much! I am so happy to see you. And your babies are growing up, so precious. But for now, get some sleep. We have the whole day, tomorrow. Just you and me. Huh? I'm looking forward to it," Stevie kissed Livia on the cheek.

Lawrence and Olivia set up sleeping arrangements for the slumber party. Olivia gave Lawrence their bed since he spent one night of their vacation, sleeping on the floor. Lawrence set up Bradley on the pullout in the family room downstairs. Stevie got the guestroom. The air mattress was set up for Livia in the living room.

BOOKER

306

IT'S ALL WHITE

After unloading the final chapter of the book, Olivia was free to advance in life to a level not accessible to her in the past. The fifty-pound kettle bell of guilt had been removed from her chest, dumped into a book, and wrapped forever in buckram. Olivia's secret childhood trauma and mental struggles were now her truth, and opened up space to let Lawrence in. She was able to allow room for a spiritual awakening.

WEDDING DAY

Three weeks later, the big day was finally happening. Olivia and her glam squad of girlfriends stayed overnight at her dad's. Sabrina, Palmer and Gene were in charge of getting Olivia beautified. Freshly showered and wrapped in her fluffy white robe embroidered with *The Bride* on the back, Olivia found a seat in the dining room. Palmer put out an unusual spread of food and other treats. All peeled to expose their white interior and sliced for presentation were white peaches, pears, golden delicious apples, cucumber, bananas, and coconut arranged on platters next to the one-part cream cheese and one-part mallow fluff fruit and veggie dip. Hardboiled egg whites with the yolks removed, cauliflower crowns, jicama, white mushrooms with ranch dip, white bean dip with rice crackers, bagels with cream cheese and a few bottles of Lugana White Wine were all on Olivia's list, and Palmer did her best to oblige.

Olivia's requests were to have all décor and even the food on the reception menu to be as white as possible. Her wedding was the opportunity to represent the purity once stripped from her but now regained in as many ways imaginable. Her squad - maid of honor, matron of honor, and bridesmaid all had French tipped nails. Olivia's nails were painted solid white and shaped into pointed tips with a few choice nails encrusted with bling.

They all laughed and told old stories, played For the Culture app, snapped a bunch of selfies, and then transformed into a dolled up bridal party. Gene smoothed down the final touches of the hair. Sabrina used a finishing mist to set Olivia's makeup before they posed for their first professional photo. The photographer had been shooting a few candid shots while they were getting ready. She told the girls they looked heavenly and that is exactly what Olivia wanted to hear. Each of them wore white. All of the guests were asked to wear white to the wedding as well.

Bradley allowed the wedding planner to transform his barn into a heavenly display of flowers and lights. The floor of the barn was coated in white silk flower petals. Ecru fabric covered benches that framed the aisle way leading up to the wooden arches painted in an alabaster coating. Ivory floral arrangements wrapped in frosted ribbon bordered the outskirts of the room. Appropriately placed strings of lights glimmered throughout the space. The décor was complete with a floral chandelier.

Outside, a white Hummer entered the driveway with Lawrence, Xavier and Jordan. Grandma Sugar, Stevie and the kids drove up with Bradley Stone. Pastor and his wife came ahead of the main guests as well. Xavier's wife Mimi, Palmer's husband Cody, and Sabrina's husband Drake would show up shortly along with the other guests. The guest list was not long. A few family members, neighbors, colleagues, and some people from the church made up the crowd. Thirty-seven people total.

Each guest found their seat. The pastor, in his First-Sunday robe, took his place in front, standing next to Lawrence. Lawrence sported a full white tailored tux and bow tie. Xavier and Jordan escorted Gene and Palmer down the aisle. Sabrina came down solo in her gown with a white rose bouquet held in front. She was followed by Bradley who escorted Maya and Claire. The girls were blowing bubbles instead of dropping rose petals. Salem, the ring bearer, was escorted by Stevie and Grandma Sugar. Finally, the time came for Lawrence's bride to meet him at the altar in her white dress.

The song changed and all the guests rose to their feet. At the end of each bench were baskets of rose petals. As she advanced down the aisle to her forever love, the guests tossed flower petals at her feet. The dress draped her, hanging off-shoulder, and continued to swoop and gather all the way to the end of the four-foot train. It was a dress Cinderella herself would want to borrow. At the final step, Olivia handed the bouquet to Sabrina and allowed Bradley to lift her veil before giving her away to be wed. Bradley kissed her on each cheek and then pinched her nose making the entire room laugh.

Lawrence joined hands with his bride as they exchanged vows of love, trust, understanding and support. A sweet and sensual kiss locked their vows and the pastor announced them as Mr. and Mrs. Lawrence J. Livingston.

Handfuls of confetti erupted from the pews, showering Lawrence and Olivia joined arm in arm during the recession of the bridal party. The newlyweds snuck off into hiding to have a few moments alone. The bar opened, and the planning crew rearranged the barn for dinner.

The food for the reception was exquisite. A delicious seafood inspired option of crab and white corn chowder, lobster macaroni and cheese, and shrimp alfredo was served in bread bowls. The cake-cutting was classic, and the dance party didn't want to stop. Lawrence and Olivia kept true to the challenge and still hadn't been intimate, since the two weeks preceding their pre-moon, tropical getaway.

The hotel was only booked for two nights. They planned to use up every second of every minute doing things married people do. Before the big send off, Olivia presented Bradley and Stevie each with a decorative box. Dozens of kisses and cuddles got shared between the married couple and their guests. Lawrence opened the passenger door of the Hummer, swooped his bride into his arms and lifted her into the truck before jumping in on his side. The engine roared and the wheels spun into the night under a tunnel of lit sparklers.

Bradley and Stevie watched the last of the taillights pull out of the driveway. They stood face to face, staring at all they'd missed over the years. Not being able to resist any longer, they met lip to lip in a passionate exchange of desire.

Back inside, on the coffee table, rested two gift boxes from Olivia.

"What do you think it is Bradley?" Stevie queried.

"I have no idea. She didn't mention anything to me about this. Let's open them."

They lifted the cover of the boxes and inside were identical gifts. Olivia's finished novel entitled, I A M F O R G I V E N.

On the inside flap it read:

"Pain should not be bottled, trapped, locked away or hidden in the basement. For pain left alone will fester and mutate and begin to devour and destroy everything that encapsulates it. Pain may be fed with bread and water to keep it tame, but that is only a momentary adjustment. Now it is time to release pain. Chains are broken. The prison guards put down their rifles to let pain out into the open field to run and be enveloped by nature. It is time to let pain go. For pain is not welcome here, because the blood of restoration has been pled."

Epilogue

Two months after the wedding, Olivia was sitting in Dr. Luke's office once more. Dr. Luke and Olivia sat in silence as was usual for her sessions and why Dr. Luke used the writing assignment to spur Olivia's progress in healing. They took turns starring at each other and then back at the clock. Dr. Luke sat with a relaxed posture, one leg crossed over the other, dressed in thick corduroys, brightly colored socks, and walking shoes. He shifted his shoulder length dreadlocks, adjusted his glasses, and took a break from making eye contact with Olivia and the clock in order to write down a thought on his yellow notepad. He focused back on Olivia who was sitting on the edge of her seat, elbows resting on her knees and hands folded. She was still looking at the clock in anticipation. Dr. Luke cleared his throat to ease the tension in the room.

"He's five minutes late. We'll give it another five or ten, and go ahead with just the two of us," Dr. Luke decided.

"Ah, yeah. Well, he was a no-show at the wedding, so... I wouldn't be surprised if he skips out on this invitation too," Olivia responded. Glad that Olivia actually opened her mouth to speak, Dr. Luke took the opportunity to engage in an ice breaker.

"I'm impressed with your book. I've given the writing assignment hundreds of times, and never has it resulted in a full-blown memoir!" Dr. Luke praised.

Before Olivia could reply, there was a knock. Dr. Luke got out of his chair to open his office door.

"Well, hello Sir. You must be Kelpie."

BOOKER

Acknowledgements

I am so grateful to have Christ in my life. I have not always had a cheerful relationship with God in understanding why certain things happen. Over the years I have looked for purpose and ways to overcome the monsters in my room. Monsters can be, for some, the offender or the incident that caused harm in their lives. For the purpose of this novel, I am speaking to those that are dealing with residual effects of trauma, be it abuse, loss, discrimination, or self-doubt, and the list continues. Depression, loneliness, anxiety, and self-destruction are some of the monsters I am referring to.

I am thankful for all of those who have been, in any way, a part of making this novel available in the hands of those that need to know they are not alone. Thank you for listening to me. Thank you for giving me honest feedback. Thank you for showing up when I needed you most. Thank you for not leaving my side. Thank you for keeping me on track and encouraging me to finish what I started - *(This novel is ten years in the making.)* Thank you for letting me know that people need to read these words. I am thankful for your continued support, time, talents, and treasures given to me out of the kindness of your heart and your drive to help me build awareness around mental health in all of its shapes and sizes.

The Monster in my Room
Discussion Questions

Olivia is faced with many destructive male relationships. How and why do you think Lawrence was able to overcome this and not give up on Olivia?

What do you think about the way Olivia coped with her trauma before meeting Dr. Luke?

How differently do you think Olivia's life would have been without the support of Sabrina?

How do you view Stevie's choice to care for Kelpie?

How do you view Bradley's choice to care for Olivia?

Olivia had a strong reaction to Kelpie's girlfriend being in her daughters' room. What do you think about Olivia's choice to keep her children sheltered from friends and outsiders will do to their ability to trust others as they grow up?

In what way has your parents' experience with marriage or your childhood experiences shaped your view of marriage?

Olivia picks an interesting title for her memoir. In an instance where it may seem like she was betrayed by so many people in her life, why do you think it was important for Olivia to claim forgiveness for herself? Or do you believe she is challenging those who have offended her to forgive themselves?

Do you believe Olivia has any loose ends worth pursuing?

Who would you say hurt Olivia the most?

BOOKER